DRIVING BLIND

DRIVING BLIND

A NOVEL BY

STEVEN BENSTEAD

TURNSTONE PRESS

to Jack & Joan

We go back longer than we all would like to remember.

Og roots are at 102 Queenston.

[signature]

09/12/98

Turnstone Press
607–100 Arthur Street
Artspace Building
Winnipeg, Manitoba
R3B 1H3 Canada
www.TurnstonePress.com

Turnstone Press gratefully acknowledges the assistance of the Canada Council for the Arts, the Manitoba Arts Council and the Government of Canada through the Book Publishing Industry Development Program for our publishing activities.

Le Conseil des Arts | The Canada Council
du Canada | for the arts
depuis 1957 | since 1957

Cover photograph: Debra Mosher

Design: Manuela Dias

This book was printed and bound in Canada by Printcrafters for Turnstone Press.

Canadian Cataloguing in Publication Data

Benstead, Steven, 1951–

Driving blind

ISBN 0-88801-224-1

I. Title.

PS8553.E563 D75 1998   C813'.54   C98-920196-1
PR9199.3.B379 D75 1998

for Charlotte

TABLE OF CONTENTS

LEO

ONE

Her real name was Leona—Leona Hamilton—but all her friends called her Leo.

She watched Eddie Valentine stroll towards her. They had been sitting in the bar for two hours, and this was the first time he'd been to the can all night. She'd been twice already, and thought she might have to go again.

Eddie had a pug's face—flat—and a square head. Dressed in one of his floppy black suits, he walked with a rocking side-to-side gait and an air of easy confidence. He dropped like a heavy beanbag into his chair and settled. "Let's grab some beers and go for a ride," he said.

"Like to where, Eddie?" Leo had a broad face with large, clear, brown eyes that sometimes wandered from the person she was talking to.

He sat up, if only to get her to look at him. "I wanna show you this place I got."

"What place?"

"It's an old gas station."

"A gas station." The smile that was tugging at the corners of her mouth tugged harder. "What are you gonna do with a gas station?"

He looked around the room as if she was just about the stupidest person in the whole wide world. "I'm gonna rent cars out of it is what I'm gonna do."

She put her fingers in her hair and lifted it away from the

side of her head. "This isn't gonna be like that pizza joint you were gonna open, is it? Or that chain of fancy shoe-shine parlours you were gonna get in on the ground floor on, or the used car lot?"

He leaned forward. "Your problem, Leo, is you don't understand business."

"And what's your problem, Eddie?"

"My problem?"

"Yeah."

"Besides you?"

She lifted her hair again and let it slide through her fingers. "Yeah."

He sighed. "Money. You know, cash flow. I need an investor."

"Like a silent partner."

"Yeah."

She took a sip of her beer. It was warm and flat. "But in the meantime." She raised her eyebrows.

"In the meantime? I work the order desk at Abel Auto Parts. But you gotta look beyond that, Leo."

"Is it a big place?"

"It's an empty gas station. Right now. But it could be a gold mine."

"So let's go if you wanna go."

On the way out they stopped at the vendor and Eddie bought a six-pack.

"Carry it, will you?" he said casually, as if it was no big deal, and as if it was no big deal, she did.

Eddie's car was a rust-eaten two-door Dodge Colt. As she climbed in she put the beer on the floor behind the driver's seat. He started the engine then reached behind and pulled out two bottles. He opened them and handed her one. She took a swallow and put the bottle to her cheek.

"Hot night," she said and noticed not a headache exactly, but a kind of pressure behind her eyes.

"Too hot." He pressed the bottle to his lips and tilted his head back. He stayed like that, bottle pointing straight up like the stern of a sinking ship, until the last of the beer disappeared in a pulse of bubbles and foam.

He tossed the bottle onto the back seat. "Maybe we can do the gas station later."

"But I thought that's where we were going."

He pulled away from the curb, fast.

"I got a better idea."

"What?"

He didn't answer.

She shrugged and turned her eyes to the road. They were rolling along at about fifty k.

Two blocks later she said, "Eddie."

He said, "Yeah?"

"Red light, Eddie."

"So?"

"Don't do this to me, Eddie. Not again, Eddie."

"What's a little red light?"

"It means you're s'pose to stop."

"Why?"

"'Cause like maybe a semi or something really big might be coming."

"I don't think so."

"Shit. Eddie."

"D'you wanna stop?"

She placed herself squarely in her seat and forced herself to stare straight ahead. "No."

When they hit the intersection, they were doing seventy. Leo's heart was pounding. The soles of her feet were jammed against the dashboard, her right hand was clutching her beer bottle, and her left was gripping the edge of the bucket seat. As they crossed the white line, she expected something—a car, a truck, a pedestrian, or a dog even—to suddenly appear in front of them. It would just be there, without warning, filling up the whole world, and so near you wouldn't have time to do anything but close your eyes.

A block later, Eddie was easing back on the gas. Leo finished her beer and reached for another. She took a sip. She said,

"Shit, Eddie." Then she started to laugh. "Shit." She hit him in the shoulder as hard as she could. He was grinning from ear to ear. "Shit, Eddie." She hit him again and then again, but his grin only grew wider, and her laughter, which had started out as something between a sob and a cough, rose to a sputtering wail.

Then she said, "I gotta pee."

"Later."

"No, really."

"Later. I wanna know"—he shrugged—"you feel like doing a little huntin'?"

"Is this your better idea?"

"Why not?"

"I thought we were gonna go see your gas station."

"After, maybe."

They hit the CP underpass heading north and continued up Main Street. Some of the poorest neighbourhoods in the city stretched off to their left.

"You got the gun?" she said.

The *gun* was a compressed air-pellet rifle. He nodded. "It's in the trunk."

"Okay," she said as if making up her mind. "Okay." She wanted to laugh. It was so stupid. Part of the thrill was knowing you might get caught, and that if you did get caught you might find yourself being dragged out of the car and having a dozen guys put the boots to your head. Tempting this fate was Eddie's idea of having a good time.

They turned off Main Street onto Burrows and parked. Eddie took the rifle out of the trunk while Leo climbed over the gearshift into the driver's seat.

What they were looking for was the right combination of parked cars and gloom. A burnt-out street light would have been welcome, but burnt-out street lights were hard to find, even here. After cruising for fifteen minutes, Eddie said, "Down there." He was pointing at the shadowy mouth of a back lane coming up on their right. She felt her stomach turn over. Back lanes were where you got caught, but they were also the best places to go huntin', and she'd known when they came out here that they would probably end up in one sooner or later.

The first window they took out belonged to the back of a Ford Pinto. The wide, flat hatchback made a perfect target. The pop of the rifle was followed by a dull crack. She glanced to her right over Eddie's shoulder and along the line of the barrel. The glass had not shattered, it had been turned into an opaque sheet of thousands of tiny pieces held together by a fine film of plastic. She leaned forward and closed her eyes against the sudden rush of pleasure.

Eddie levered the rifle and turned to her. His face was close, his breath hot on her cheek. "We got the bastards, Leo," he whispered. "We got 'em."

She turned her eyes forward, straining to see past the headlights and into the murkiness beyond.

Pop, out went another piece of glass, this time the side window of a mid-seventies Chevy.

In the quiet stillness of the night, the noise seemed incredibly loud. She couldn't figure out why the whole neighbourhood hadn't come out to see what all the racket was about. She glanced between the cars and fences, watching for a back door to open or porch light to come on. It was like walking through a cage of sleeping tigers. The fear was there, solid and real, locked into her muscles, but she was managing it, controlling it. That was part of the kick.

She could sense Eddie in the seat beside her moving almost without emotion like a finely tuned machine. They rolled past a Dodge Dart. Pop—crack. The window did not break so much as shatter and then fall in, section by section, leaving a ragged, broken-toothed grin where the windshield used to be.

They had slipped into a comfortable rhythm with the car moving at just the right speed for Eddie to lever the pump, take aim, and squeeze the trigger. Unless she glanced to the right, however, it was all sound to her and Eddie's dark outline as he worked the rifle and then poked it out the window.

He was taking aim when she said, "I gotta pee, Eddie."

"What?"

"I really gotta pee."

"Now?"

She was biting her lip. "I'm gonna bust." With a tiny squeak from the brakes, she brought the car to a halt. In a second, she was out of the car. She went into the nearest back-yard and ducked behind a fence. There was an apple tree in the middle of the yard. On her return, she pulled the bottom of her tee-shirt out and used it to carry a bunch of the apples back to the car. Eddie was in the driver's seat. She let the apples fall onto the floor of the passenger side. They were green and small.

"What's this?"

"Apples." She pushed them to one side with her foot and climbed in.

"Cheesus," Eddie said.

She laughed and pulled the door shut. As they started to move forward, she picked an apple off the floor, polished it on her jeans, and handed it to him.

He bit into it and instantly spat it out.

"What's wrong?"

"Sour."

She took the rest of the apple from him and bit into it herself—"Oh yuk, is it ever"—and tossed it out the window. Laughing, she kneeled on her seat and draped herself over him, crushing one breast against his shoulder and then the other.

He pushed her away. "Cut it out." She came back at him. "Cut it out, Leo." He had put the clutch in and he was staring at something up ahead.

"What?" She turned to see what he was looking at. A set of headlights had appeared at the far end of the lane. He stopped the car. Leo sat back down. She looked at Eddie and then at the headlights and then back at Eddie.

"Wha'd'we do?" She was surprised at how calm she sounded.

"Get out of here."

He put the Colt in reverse. The engine whined. He was peering through the back window, zig-zagging them towards where they had started.

"It's a truck, Eddie, a half-ton or something." She could see the row of amber cab lights behind the headlights now. "And it's picking up speed."

She felt their momentum falling away. "Don't slow down, Eddie. Eddie?"

He was staring out the back window. They had almost come to a stop. He jerked his thumb over his shoulder. "Take a look."

She turned her head. "Shit." A new set of headlights was coming towards them from behind.

They had never been caught before, had never come close to being caught. Images of the two of them being dragged out of the car and of her having her arms held and being made to watch a bunch of guys beat the shit out of Eddie reeled across the back of her mind, but they were lost in the rush and tumble of trying to figure out what to do.

Then he said, "I want you to make a run for it. Okay? Get far away, flag down a cab, and go home."

"I don't have any money." She was staring straight ahead at the lights of the truck coming towards them.

"Don't you have a purse or something?"

"Yeah, but I still don't have any money. A dollar maybe."

He looked pissed off. He put a hand in his pocket and pulled out a balled-up twenty. "Go."

"I'm not gonna leave you."

"I'll call you tomorrow."

"Eddie."

"Look, I can handle this, but only if I'm by myself."

She stared at him.

"Go."

She reached into the back for the rifle.

"Leave it," he said.

"Then they'll know for sure."

"It doesn't matter."

She hesitated.

"Leave it."

Keeping her head down, she made for a chest-high picket fence between two garages. She threw her purse over the top and then clambered after it. Once on the other side she saw that there was nothing between the houses. She had a clear run to the street. But she turned and peered between the pickets. Eddie was climbing out of the car.

She didn't decide to stay exactly, she just decided not to go, at least for a little while. She wanted to see what was going to happen. She crept along the fence to the corner of the garage and crouched. At least, she thought, she'd be there to pick him up off the ground and drive him to the hospital.

The truck stopped about twenty feet in front of him, the car about twenty feet in back. Two guys got out of the truck and two more out of the car. Behind the glare of the head-lights, she could see that half of the car's windshield was missing. Eddie stood there waiting for them with his hands in his pockets. He said, "Looks like we got a bit of a traffic jam here. I know the lane's kind of narrow, but I figure if one of us squeezes to the right we can maybe sort of inch by."

One of the guys from the car had come up behind him. He had long black hair and was wearing a buttonless plaid shirt over a black tee-shirt. He was white. The guy with him stayed back, leaning against the front of the hood, arms folded. He was Native. The two guys walking forward from the truck were both Native. The tall one wore cowboy boots. The short one was sort of roly-poly. He was wearing a loose Hawaiian shirt. He had a round, almost smiling face that reminded her of Don Ho.

The white guy said, "Where'd the chick go, man?"

"What chick?"

He grabbed Eddie by the front of his shirt, twisted it in his fist, and pulled him to within a few inches of his face. "Don't piss around with me, man. This ain't no joke. D'you see my car? D'you see it? The fuckin' windscreen's been smashed to fuckin' hell—by you, man, by you and your fuckin' little bitch of a girlfriend. Now where the fuck is she?"

Eddie didn't looked so relaxed anymore. But the nervous panic that seemed to come over him was only half real. The other half was smokescreen. "Leave her out of it. Okay? She didn't have nothing to do with it. She was just along for the ride. Okay? It's me you want. Okay?"

"So you admit it?"

Eddie turned to the Don Ho guy who had spoken. All of a sudden he didn't look like Don Ho at all. In fact, Leo didn't even really know what Don Ho looked like. And Don Ho was supposed to be a nice, friendly guy. This guy, although he was smiling, didn't seem friendly at all. He was too smart to be friendly.

"Yeah," he said. "I admit it. I took the apples. I'm sorry. Look, I'll pay you for them if you want."

The guy in the plaid shirt let out a single high-pitched laugh and then kicked in the side panel of Eddie's car between the door and the back wheel.

Don Ho said, "You got a nasty dent there, mister. Looks like it's been there a long time. You can see the rust."

Plaid Shirt shoved Eddie. "Apples? Apples? We're not talking about fuckin' apples, you asshole. We're talking about maybe twenty cars with their windows smashed out." He jerked his thumb over his shoulder. "And one of 'em's mine."

Eddie drew a deep breath. Then speaking to all four of them at once, he said, "Guys, I took the apples. Okay? But I promise you, we were gonna eat 'em, and Sally—my girlfriend?—she said what was left over she was gonna take to her mom to make a pie out of. I know they're still a little green and all and kind of hard and somebody could toss 'em pretty good, but we didn't use 'em to smash out those windows you're talking about. Twenty cars? I'm telling you, we wanted them for eatin'." He turned to Don Ho. "You can understand that, can't you?"

Plaid Shirt started swinging. Good thing for Eddie, the guy who had been leaning against the front of Plaid Shirt's car had come over so he could hear what was going on. He put his arms around his friend's chest and held him back. "Take it easy, Cecil."

Now Don Ho was all business. "The cops are on their way. We'll just sit tight and wait."

"The cops?" Even peering between the fence pickets, Leo could see the look of disbelief on Eddie's face. "The cops?" Leo thought of the open case of beer in the car, the empties on the floor, and the rifle. "Shit." He started to move towards Don Ho with his hands up as if he was going to take a swing at him, but the guy in the cowboy boots swung his arm into Eddie's chest and Eddie was slammed back against the side of the Colt where he remained for the next minute trying to suck air back into his lungs.

Don Ho smiled. "Yeah, the cops. Neighbourhood Watch and all that. My old lady's idea."

It was one thing to get beaten up in a North End back lane. It was something else to get hauled down to the cop shop and have a bunch of charges laid against you. And be finger-printed. Leo couldn't think of a whole lot of things worse than having your fingerprints taken. Eddie might be a schmuck from time to time, and he might have some pretty crazy ideas about who he was and what he wanted to be, but there was something about him being fingerprinted that she didn't like.

Clutching her purse to her side, she moved along the fence and down the wall of the garage to the far end. There was no gate, just a couple of garbage cans at the end of a cracked side-walk. She followed the sidewalk to its edge and, squatting down, peered over the lids of the garbage cans. She saw them for the first time at a distance: five men standing in an arena cut out of the night by the headlights of Don Ho's truck and Plaid Shirt's car. There was little to choose between the men. They all came from the same flesh, they had all been born into the same life of lousy jobs and no money. And that's probably why Eddie hated them. If you took off his floppy black suit and drained out of his head all the crazy ideas he had about building pizza parlour empires or car rental conglomerates, he was one of them, and for Eddie that thought was unthinkable.

He was facing her direction. She could see his eyes con-stantly moving, and she couldn't help smiling at the fact that he was still looking for a way out, that he had not given up. The eyes of the other four were concentrated on him, their bodies ready to jump if he should try to take even a single step in any direction.

She had to work quickly. The cops would be here soon. They would roll up with red lights flashing and a "Well, well, well" look on their faces, and it would all be over. Eddie in the back seat of a squad car, handcuffed maybe, and on his way downtown—to be fingerprinted and locked up with a lot of other guys just like him, though he'd probably be the only one wearing a floppy black suit.

All three vehicles were still running. She could hear them: the ticking valves on the half-ton, the sputtering of the Colt's muffler, and the whining of a loose belt on Plaid Shirt's Chevy.

It took her only three or four steps to move from the garage to the back of Don Ho's truck. There she froze with her back pressed against the tailgate. She listened to the silence between the idling engines and almost believed she could hear the five men breathing. No one said "Hey!" and there was no sound of feet running towards her.

But something had changed. The silence had grown suddenly deeper. The tension that filled the space between Don Ho's truck and Plaid Shirt's Chevy began to stir far below the surface. She realized what it was when she heard Eddie's voice. He had seen her.

"It's a hot one, eh? Never seen it so hot for so long. Have you?"

She peered over the top of the tailgate. Don Ho and Cowboy Boots had their backs to her. Don Ho lowered his head and pushed his face forward as if he was trying to figure out what was going on.

Plaid Shirt laughed. "The fuckin' guy's got his ass in a sling and he's talking about the fuckin' weather."

Crouching again, she eased herself around the corner of the truck and began to move slowly along its side. She figured she was probably hidden at least a little in the glare of the half-ton's headlights, but she also figured the lights from the two cars facing it must wash out a lot of that glare. However, Plaid Shirt, who was facing her and might have seen her easily if he had looked, was too busy being beside himself over Eddie's stupidity, and his friend was too busy watching Plaid Shirt.

Don Ho was starting to get nervous. "Shut up, Cecil."

"It's just this guy . . ."

"Shut up."

Eddie began to shift from one foot to the other.

"Stop that," Don Ho said.

Eddie said, "Stop what?" She could hear the smile in his voice.

"That."

"What?"

When she lifted the handle on the truck door, it went *click* and the door popped open about an inch. The others heard the click too, but for a moment they didn't seem to know what it was.

By the time they did, Leo had scrambled into the cab, thrown the transmission into reverse, and was backing the truck off to the side of the lane. From the corner of her eye, she saw Eddie jump into the Colt. There was a general cry of "Hey" and "What the . . ." but it was too late already.

She stopped the truck and leapt out. The Colt shot forward, and then slowed. Eddie pushed open the passenger door. She took two steps and was inside, pulling the door closed behind her as Eddie banged the transmission through all four gears.

They were still accelerating when they reached the end of the lane. He braked hard, pulled back into second, and they shot out onto the street making a tight left turn. Just then Leo saw the flashing red lights of a cop car coming up behind them. She almost had a coronary. But then the flashing lights turned up the lane, and she knew they had made it. The cops wouldn't let Don Ho and his buddies leave until they had sorted out who were the good guys and who were the bad guys. By then it would be too late.

They finished the beer on their way back to Eddie's place. Five minutes after they walked into his apartment, she had her arms and legs wrapped around him. She moaned between breaths that were coming faster and faster. Then Eddie grunted, and it was all over. He rolled off her and went to sleep.

She lay there for a while staring up at the ceiling. Then she went into the kitchen, opened the fridge door, and enjoyed the cool air for a moment.

She reached for a beer, then decided not to.

She didn't feel so good. The pressure behind her eyes had ballooned into a real headache. She got dressed and started for home. There wasn't much point in staying. Eddie would've sprawled himself all over the bed as soon as she got up, and he would be all grumpy in the morning, wouldn't talk to her. He had stopped talking to her after the first few times she'd stayed over. It was like he didn't want to know anymore.

It didn't bother her walking home. She wasn't worried. She was feeling too lousy to be worried. She was concentrating—on not throwing up. God, she hated that, being sick behind a tree or someplace.

But this, as Eddie would have told her, is what having fun is all about.

TWO

Four hours later Leo was standing in the shower. It was five o'clock in the morning. Today was Wednesday, her early shift. She had to be at work by six. So why had she let Eddie drag her off to the North End to blow out car windows? That was the question. She felt lousy, and it wasn't only because she hadn't had enough sleep or because her head hurt.

She kept thinking of those guys standing there trying to explain everything to the cops. Before it had always just been the cars, they had never seen the faces of the people. When she told Eddie last night that she felt sorry for them, he had laughed and said, "The cops probably arrested the dumb fuckers."

She washed down a couple of aspirins with her coffee, got dressed, stuffed her swimsuit into a Safeway bag, found her sunglasses under an old *People* magazine, pulled on her jean jacket, picked up her purse, and went outside to wait for the bus.

She worked in a twenty-four-hour doughnut shop. It was called "the 'Nut." That wasn't its real name, but that's what everybody who went there called it. She walked in at one minute to six. Betty, the day manager, was already there. She took one look at Leo and said, "Rough night?"

"Tell me about it." Leo ducked into the office to dump her stuff. A moment later she came out wearing her little hat and tying the strings of her apron.

One of the regulars was sitting at the counter. "Hi, Frank." She gave him her best good-morning smile and he grinned back. "You want a fritter with your coffee?" She grabbed a mug off the drying rack and filled it.

"You got it."

"So how's business?"

"The pits."

She put the mug down in front of him. "It always is."

"It's a lousy business."

"You can't smoke at the counter, Frank."

"I'm getting ready. Okay? I'll take it over there. Betty, I go through this every day with her. Tell her for me."

"You tell her."

"I've told her a hundred times already."

Leo took an apple fritter from the case and put it on a plate. "Smoking's not good for you, Frank."

"What are you, my mother? Just bring me my stuff, Leo. Come on. I got a living to make here. The dispatcher's probably dropped me to the bottom of the call sheet three times already."

"Here you go, Frank."

"One day, Leo . . ."

"Yeah?" She put her hands on her hips.

"Hey, Betty, she's one tough little broad, huh?"

Betty smiled across the top of the cash register. "Yeah, she's one tough little broad all right."

"Enjoy, Frank." Leo patted his bald head. She was beginning to feel better already. "Enjoy."

She started another pot of coffee, then wiped the counter, picking up empty mugs as she went. She was thinking if she'd been smart she would've stayed at Eddie's last night. His place was only two minutes away. It was why, she sometimes thought, he had started going out with her. Not because he came into the 'Nut all the time but because it wasn't far for him to go to pick her up after work.

It wasn't as if he was a regular customer who'd all of a sudden asked her out. Actually she hadn't been at the 'Nut that long, and he didn't even know she worked there until after.

She'd met Eddie last November—at the Pandora way over on the other side of town, in Transcona.

She used to go drinking with this guy, Chip. They'd go from bar to bar. He was a dealer, in pills mostly, nothing really hard. It wasn't much of a social life but it was better than staying home. And he was nice enough. She liked him. Only thing is he'd landed himself in money trouble with some drug guys. From then on, he started acting nervous all the time, which wasn't like him.

For about a week every bar they went into he'd be looking around all the time. Even when he figured the coast was clear he kept glancing at the door.

This one night, Chip had done a couple of deals. He could've done more if they'd stayed, but he told her to drink up. They should get going. She went to finish her beer when she saw Chip's face go white. He jumped up and started pushing his way across the room. It was pure panic. He ran over people, bumped into tables. He knocked over a waiter with a tray full of beer.

She turned and saw two guys, both of them kind of skinny, greasy hair. Chip was heading towards a corridor that led to the vendor, but he hadn't exactly made himself invisible.

He reached the corridor first but only by a few steps. One guy went after him. The other guy stopped at the entrance. He looked around with a kind of mind-your-own-business look, then he turned and took off after his buddy and Chip.

There was a door at the far end past the vendor that opened onto the parking lot. That's where Chip was heading. She didn't know if he would make it or not, but she didn't figure on waiting around to find out.

As she started towards the front door, though, she half thought there might be more skinny guys with greasy hair waiting outside, but if there were she didn't see them.

She started walking—anywhere, as fast as she could.

But she hadn't gone more than a block before she heard Chip screaming on the other side of the building. She froze.

Part of her thought she should try and help him. The rest of her just wanted to run away.

Somebody grabbed her arm. "Come on."

She stiffened and saw a guy in a floppy black suit step in front of her. "Who're you?"

"Later. Come on."

"Where?"

"I'm parked on the street. You don't want to be around here right now." He had a coat tucked under his arm. He let go of her and slipped into it.

"They're gonna kill him."

"No."

"Can't you hear?"

"Break his legs maybe."

"His legs?"

"Look, don't even think about trying to help your friend." He pointed with his head towards the parking lot. "You'd just end up like him, or worse."

"I have to."

"No." He took her arm.

She was totally wired. They went back to his place and screwed their brains out. It was great, it really was. She figured it was exactly what she needed. She slept better than she had in weeks. In the morning Eddie said he would drive her to work. She said it was okay, she'd walk. When she told him where she worked it was as if he realized they both came from the same place, sort of. Not soulmates exactly. But, you know.

"You can see it from your front door."

"The 'Nut?"

"Yeah." She felt all soft and gooey which she figured was because she'd spent the night with this guy Eddie and here he was not only talking to her but actually offering to drive her to work. So they weren't Antony and Cleopatra, but what the heck. When a girl gets to be twenty-four years old, she starts wondering about how many rocks she's willing to look under.

At five after two she walked out of the air-conditioned coolness of the 'Nut and into the packed heat of early June. She had changed into her swimsuit in the washroom and was carrying her clothes in her Safeway bag. Her swimsuit was a little ratty, but she figured it would hold together for another year, especially with Eddie not taking her to the beach. Not even on the Victoria Day long weekend did he take her. He was always too busy driving all over the city with the classifieds on his lap looking for cars to deal on. His game was to make an offer on a car and then try to sell it to somebody else before he had to come up with the cash. He actually made a few bucks this way, enough at least to buy her a nice pair of gloves for Christmas. Her present to him was a box of business cards. She'd had them made up, special. They said:

Eddie Valentine
Businessman

and had his address and phone number and everything on them. She would never forget the look on his face when he unwrapped them Christmas morning. All through January he gave them away to people he said were his clients.

"Clients? Is that what you call them?"

"Yeah." He stared her down.

It was almost worth going with him to look for cars just to see his face as he handed them out.

When there was snow on the ground she didn't care much where they went. Staying in town looking for cars was okay. They would stop for coffee and a burger or maybe a beer, stuff like that. It was okay. In fact, he'd been checking out cars in Transcona and had stopped for a beer the night he followed her out of the Pandora.

But after the snow melted and every weekend they were still looking for cars, it started to get her down. She wanted to go to the lake. She wanted to go to Grand Beach like everybody else and soak up the sun. It was killing her watching all that gorgeous weather go to waste. Summer had started early and it had stayed. By the end of April it was hot. So she had started walking down to the neighbourhood park on Wednesdays after her early shift. The park wasn't far and the last three Wednesdays she'd spent most of the afternoon there reading magazines and otherwise lying in the sun. She usually stayed until she figured Eddie'd be home from work. Then she went over to his place, and they'd usually do something.

She stopped at the Mac's to buy a Big Drink, but they didn't have the new *Cosmo*, and she already had the *Elle* that was on the shelf, only she had left it at home. "Sold out," the guy at the till said. She had her jean jacket hanging off her shoulders. She pulled the front together so the guy wouldn't look. "Try Stookner's."

"Where?"

"Stookner's." He waggled his finger. "Around the corner. The bookstore."

She went. They had lots.

"It's Leo, isn't it?"

"Yeah. Oh, hi." She didn't look up until she was almost at the counter. But when she did she recognized the woman behind it right away. She came in every morning a few minutes before ten and bought three coffees to go: one black, one with milk, and one with cream and sugar. She was tall, maybe half a foot taller than Leo, with short dark hair and a long face that was full of hollows and shadows, especially around the eyes and under the cheekbones. She had a way of suddenly smiling, though, that made the shadows disappear. She leaned forward now, leading with her eyes which were a clear, almost ghostly green and full of what looked like tiny darting silver fish.

"How much is it?" Leo was digging around in her purse. She couldn't find her money. "I thought I had a five-dollar bill," she said.

"Take your time."

"I was sure I had a five-dollar bill."

"I can hold it for you."

"This is embarrassing."

"Don't worry."

"I was just going up to the park for a while anyways."

"I'll hold it till the end of the day." She wrote "Leo" on a slip of paper, tucked it into the magazine, and put it under the counter. "Okay?"

Leo was backing up towards the door. She felt silly. "I don't want to be a bother."

"It's no bother."

The first thing she did when she got to the park was look for her five bucks. She went through her purse, she went through all her pockets. But it wasn't there. She didn't remember spending it but then again she couldn't remember exactly when she'd seen it last either. She'd told Eddie she didn't have any money the night before but that's what she always told him. Then again, maybe she'd given Eddie the five bucks by mistake when she gave him his twenty back.

But it was no good worrying about it. If she'd lost it, she'd lost it, and that's all there was to it.

She spread her towel and sat down to put Coppertone on the places she could reach. She was doing her shins when she saw the woman from the bookstore walking across the park towards her. The woman gave a little wave, then smiled and broke into a kind of romp.

She stopped at Leo's feet. She was wearing a long rainbow-coloured skirt. It shifted gently as a breeze came up off the river.

"Hi," Leo said.

"I brought your magazine." The woman gathered her skirt and kneeled down on the edge of Leo's towel.

Leo didn't know what to say. "Can I bring you the money tomorrow?"

"No rush."

They looked at each other.

Leo said, "D'you have to get back right away?"

"No. Not right away."

Leo held out the bottle of Coppertone. "Will you do my back?"

The woman's fingers were long and cool. "My name's Sheila," she said.

She was older than Leo, but not old old, just older.

"What d'you do there?"

"Where?"

"At the bookstore."

"I own it."

"Oh."

Sheila laughed.

"So you're the Stookner in 'Stookner's'?"

"Along with my husband."

"Does he work there too?"

"No." Sheila became silent as she applied the lotion. Then she said, "You have beautiful skin, Leo."

"Yeah?"

"And hair. It's like mahogany. I mean the colour—all soft and shiny. And so thick."

"Really?"

The next morning when Sheila came in to pick up her three coffees to go, she asked Leo if she could stop by the store later. There was something in the way she asked the question that made Leo think it wasn't about the five dollars she owed for the magazine.

THREE

"I got a job, Eddie." Leo sank into the couch, stuck her feet straight out, and tapped her toes together.

He was reading the paper. "You already got a job."

"Yeah sure, but this is extra. It's only once in a while. At the bookstore. You know. Just around the corner?"

"The bookstore?" He lowered his paper. "Doin' what?"

"They have these special events. Like when somebody's written a new book? Sometimes they have a party—at the store."

"And what are you s'pose to do?"

"Help out."

"How?"

"I don't know. Doing whatever needs doing, I guess. We have to make a display for the book and make room for the food and the wine and the coffee. And it all has to be cleaned up afterwards. Like the glasses have to be washed and dried, and everything has to be put back."

"When'd you apply for this?"

"I didn't. Sheila just asked me."

"Sheila?"

"She's the owner."

"Of the bookstore."

"Yeah. She says I'm used to the public and that I know how to treat people. I'll be like a hostess."

"She just walked up to you and said d'you want a job?"

"I know her from the 'Nut. We got talking the other day and one thing led to another."

"And she offered you a job?"

"Yeah. She said she's been looking for somebody for a long time but hasn't been able to find the right person."

"And you're it?"

"I guess."

He shook his head.

"It's not something you can advertise for, Eddie. She needs somebody flexible, and since I work practically next door, she said she thought it might work out for the both of us."

"And you said yes?"

"Sure I did. I've been in for training once already. I know how to work the cash register. They've got computers. And everybody's so nice. I've never worked in a place like that before, Eddie. It opens your eyes."

He disappeared back behind his newspaper. "Did she drive you home at least?"

"When?"

"When you went in for this training. It must've been late by the time you got out of there."

"It wasn't late. But yeah, she drove me."

It was early Sunday afternoon. She had worked half a shift at the 'Nut and then walked over to Eddie's thinking they would be going to her mother's right away. But Eddie was reading the paper when she arrived and he didn't want to go until he was finished. The truth is, she was nervous about visiting her mother. More often than not mother and daughter got into some kind of fight that left Leo feeling lousy. But if they were going she wanted to go and get it over with. Besides, the only reason they were going really was because she had mentioned to Eddie that Mike was trying to sell his car.

Mike was her mother's boyfriend.

They were going too because of the books, but Eddie wouldn't have taken her for that.

When she had called her mother to find out if she still had her father's books boxed up in the closet, her mother had first asked her why on earth she wanted a bunch of dusty old books, and then had gone on to talk about a million other things including Mike's car. It was only at the very end that she said that yes the books were still there and that yes she could take them if she wanted.

Mike was sitting on the front steps when they pulled up. He and Leo's mother lived in a rented house in a triangle of houses between the Red River and CN's Fort Rouge Yards. He was tall and wiry but strong in a way a guy had to be to do the kind of work he'd done all his life. He'd been at Canada Packers for years, but ever since they closed he had been patching two, sometimes three, part-time jobs together. But the money wasn't the same and he couldn't afford to keep his car on the road any longer.

He came down the steps. "She's asleep," he said, nodding back towards the house, "your ma."

Leo felt all the old pain spring to her chest, and with it the anger. She tried to let it go but it simply sank back down inside again where it always sat, waiting.

"I'm Eddie."

The two men shook hands.

Mike flipped his cigarette onto the grass. "Come on round back, I'll show you the car."

"How much you asking?"

"Twenty-two."

"Hundred?"

"Sure."

They started walking.

"It's a little high."

"Or best offer." Mike stopped between the houses. "It's in good shape."

"It's still high, Mike."

"I'm not giving it away." Even from here she could see the pinched look on his face. He used to make good money. Now he didn't. That car was the last thing he had from the better times—that car and her mother.

He came back to her. "Your ma's got that box of books out of the closet for you. It's in the hall. Leave her sleeping though. She's gonna wake up mean."

"What happened?"

"She didn't think you was gonna come."

"It's only three o'clock in the afternoon for chrissakes."

"You know how she gets. I tried to tell her."

Eddie said, "Maybe twenty." He came back to where they were standing, hands in his pockets, belly out. He nodded slowly. "It depends."

"It's a good car," Mike told him, "and it's in good shape."

"Yeah, but it's the market too, eh? And the market's soft right now."

"Come on, I'll start 'er up for you. She runs smooth, Eddie. She purrs."

Her mother was in the living room, sprawled in the corner of the couch, her legs apart, her head back, her mouth open and her hands palms up in her lap.

Leo took the glass from the coffee table and rinsed it out in the kitchen sink. The rye smell drifted up to her. Silk Tassel. The almost-empty bottle was on the counter.

When Leo lived here her mother and Mike would usually start drinking around nine or ten at night and be arguing by eleven. Sometimes they'd argue till three or four in the morning endlessly about the same things over and over again. Sometimes it was money, sometimes it was who smoked more of the other's cigarettes, sometimes it was the name of an actor in some stupid movie—as if it mattered. It was as if all they had to give each other was pieces of this shared pain, as if they wouldn't have known who they were without it. And so out of a perfectly quiet moment in front of the TV one of them would start picking at the other. And that would be it. Half an hour later, all-out war. It was nuts. They might go through a whole pack of cigarettes each before it was over, and a bottle of rye or ten cups of coffee, or both.

Leo was sorting through the box of books.

"Is that them?" Mike had come up behind her. "What you wanted?"

"Yeah."

He held a cigarette in front of his face. "He's waiting for you."

"What he say about the car?"

"He's got some list he's gonna put it on."

"You might wanna put an ad in the paper, Mike."

He let the smoke out through his nose. "His list ain't so hot?"

"It is and it isn't. Just don't count on it." She pushed a pile of books towards the door and put the others back in the box.

"These the ones you want?" He didn't wait for her to answer. He clamped the cigarette between his lips and picked up the books she had set aside.

They were going down the front steps.

"She got cigarettes?"

"She can smoke mine."

"She doesn't like yours."

Mike stopped at the bottom. He couldn't take the cigarette out of his mouth fast enough. "Tell her that."

They started walking again.

"You still smoking Rothmans?" She squinted up at him.

"Sure."

"She still smoking Craven 'A'?"

He nodded.

Mike put the books on the back seat of Eddie's car. "See what you can do for me, Eddie," he said.

"The word goes out as we speak, m'man."

Mike waited on the curb smoking his cigarette and watched them drive away. She wanted to wave, but Mike wasn't a waving kind of guy. Mike was Mike, her mother's boyfriend. He was never any kind of stepfather to her. He'd never tried to be and if he had she would've probably told him to fuck off.

"Stop at the 7-Eleven, Eddie."

"What for?"

"Cigarettes."

"You don't smoke."

"Just stop, Eddie. Okay? They're not for me. Okay?"

"Oh."

It was going to rain. The question was when.

The hot, muggy days just kept piling up. It made people nervous. In the 'Nut customers said how the farmers needed the rain, the gardeners, everybody.

But the clouds seemed to collect over the city during the day, breaking up for a few hours in the early evening and then collecting all over again.

Whether it was going to rain or not wasn't the biggest thing on Leo's mind that week, however. She was getting ready for her first book launch. The store was going to be hosting a poet from Saskatchewan. Sheila said she thought they should have a pretty good crowd. The invitations had been mailed already. They didn't have the books yet but they were on their way.

"I want a relaxed, friendly gathering." Sheila had sat Leo down in the back room and was giving her an idea of how she wanted things to go and what she expected from her. "This is a celebration. I want people to enjoy themselves. I also want the author to feel good about the evening. So we, you and I, have to be organized. If we're running around like chickens with our heads cut off, it makes everybody uncomfortable. We've got to appear relaxed even if we're not. We have to be able to tell the author when she's going to read and where and for how long without putting pressure on her. But that's my job. You don't have to worry about that."

Leo was starting to feel overwhelmed. The more Sheila went on the more it sounded like they were planning some huge cathedral wedding instead of a small party in the bookstore.

But Leo was worried about one thing more than any other.

"It's serving the wine," she said. "I've never done it."

That stopped Sheila dead. "You haven't?" Her stern, lecturing face softened into a smile. She climbed out of her bookstore armour, and there she was, just Sheila, a soft body, in black cotton slacks and a white shirt. "All right. I'll teach you."

"When?"

"Right now."

There was a cardboard box underneath the receiving table. It was marked "launch stuff." Sheila crouched down and pulled it out. Inside were serviettes, paper cups, paper plates, coffee, sugar cubes, plastic forks, stirring sticks, and a corkscrew. "We always check this the day of the launch to make sure we have enough of everything." She slid out two more boxes. "These are the wineglasses." She reached in one more time and pulled out a round, silver tray. "It's not real silver"—she looked up at Leo as she handed it to her—"or it would tarnish."

Leo balanced it on her fingertips like a waiter.

"Don't get too fancy." Sheila smiled. "And don't try to take more than a few glasses at a time." She took six glasses out of the box and filled them from the tap in the bathroom. She set them down on the receiving counter. Leo put four on her tray and began to walk around. It took her a few minutes to figure out the best way to carry the tray because she wouldn't be just carrying it, she soon realized, she would have to be able to turn it and extend it. "Would you like a glass of wine?"

"Slowly," Sheila said. "Don't rush."

"Would you like a glass of wine?" she said, more slowly this time. She leaned forward with the tray and smiled.

"Perfect."

"Really?"

"And you'll have orange juice on your tray as well."

"Is there anything I should watch out for?"

"I don't think so."

"Like, what's the worst thing that can happen?"

"The worst thing?" Sheila said. "The worst thing is having a book launch without the book. It hasn't happened yet—cross my fingers—but there've been some close calls."

"Like what?"

"Anything can happen. You schedule too close to the release date and the printer runs into a problem"—she shrugged—"and there you are running down to the airport to pick the books up at three in the afternoon—on the day of the launch—because they've had to be airfreighted in."

"By plane?"

"But that won't happen this time. The publisher's bringing the book, so if we don't have it we can blame him. Everything'll be fine." She looked around. "Come on, help me put this stuff back and I'll give you a ride home."

Leo looked at her watch. "Eddie's s'pose to be picking me up."

"Here?"

"Is that okay?"

"Of course."

"He's off looking at a car. He buys and sells."

They put everything away, and Leo said, "Would it be all right if I did some shelving while I'm waiting? I don't mean for pay."

Sheila pulled out her keys. A lot of them had different coloured liners around the edge of the grips, but she selected a plain one and let the rest of the ring dangle from it. "Shelving is working, Leo. If you're here and you're working I want you to mark down your hours. This is a job and you get paid for it."

"Okay." But she felt shy.

"Look," Sheila continued, "there's always something to do around here. If you can spare more time, I can find things for you to do. Don't worry about that."

"Thank you."

"I should be thanking you." Sheila picked up her briefcase and slung a bookbag stuffed full of catalogues over her shoulder. "Homework." She smiled.

"I'll get the door."

Sheila's car was parked out back. It was a white Volkswagen Rabbit with a convertible roof. Leo stepped outside with her and waited while Sheila put all her stuff in the car. Before she climbed in, she stopped and looked up at the sky. "Are we ever going to get rain?"

"I don't know."

When Sheila's face came down Leo was waiting for her eyes. She didn't know why, but she wanted to see them, see into them. There was a strangeness about this woman which she couldn't put her finger on, a mystery that she couldn't figure out. They stood there looking at each other. For Leo it was like standing in front of a very intense light, more warm than bright, and full of energy. She looked bravely back, more bravely than she had ever looked back at anyone and with a deeper curiosity. Then she became aware of what she was doing and blushed. Sheila tilted her head to the side. Then she smiled and said good night.

She thought he would come into the store. But by eight o'clock he hadn't so she figured he wasn't coming. She had shelved most of the books and was thinking she might as well go home.

Then Lisa said, "There's that guy again."

Lisa was part-time but she worked regular shifts. She was doing her M.A. Leo pretended to know what she meant and left it at that.

"Which guy?" Leo turned. Somebody was peering in through the window. It wasn't dark yet and it was easier to see out than in. He had his nose pressed against the glass and his hands cupped around his eyes.

"Creep," Lisa said.

Joanne, who worked one night and Sunday afternoon, said, "Maybe we should call the police."

There were no customers in the store.

"Wait," Leo said.

The guy was looking at her. He knocked on the glass, jerked his thumb over his shoulder, and stepped back.

"It's Eddie," she said. She had not recognized him with his face squashed up against the window.

She went outside. "What are you doing out here?"

"Waiting for you."

"I thought you'd come in."

He had his hands in the pockets of his floppy black suit. He shrugged. "Naw."

"How'd it go?"

"How'd what go?"

"With the car."

"The guy was just looking. A waste of my time. Same ol' same ol'." He looked around, nodding to himself. "You still wanna go someplace?"

"Sure."

"Manny and those guys are at the Albert. I said we'd stop by."

Manny and those guys had put a couple of tables together.

Eddie had his arm around Leo's shoulder. "Hey, listen up. Hey, you guys. I'm trying to tell ya. Leo's got a new job. Tell 'em, Leo." Everybody looked at her. There were Rachel, Little Joe, Big Joe, Ken, Margaret, Sophie, Arthur, Neil, and a couple of others whose names she couldn't remember.

"Cut it out, Eddie."

"In a bookstore, no less."

"It's only part-time."

"A fucking bookstore. Go figure."

"Doin' what?" Rachel, who never smiled, sucked on her cigarette and then tapped it with her finger until the ash fell off. She breathed out a cloud of smoke. "Doin' what?"

It was after eight o'clock in the morning and still the street lights were on. Normally this time of day during this time of year it was so bright you could hardly see without sunglasses. Waiting for her bus, Leo watched the dark clouds roll slowly across the sky and wondered, like the guy on the radio said, when the weather was going to break.

She heard a *beep-beep*. She turned, and saw a white Rabbit had stopped right in front of her.

It was Sheila, waving for her to get in.

"Morning," Sheila said as they pulled away from the curb. She was full of a bubbly brightness and seemed very pleased with herself. "I thought I'd swing by and see if I could catch you."

"Thanks. What's up?"

"I brought some old wine bottles from home so you could practise pouring if you like." She shifted gears and the pitch of the engine dropped. "They're in the back there. Pouring a glass of wine sounds simple, but if you haven't done it before . . . "

Leo swung towards her. "No, that's great. Thank you."

"D'you know about turning the bottle?"

"No." Leo glanced at the buildings going by. "What is it?"

"As you finish pouring . . . you turn the bottle and lift. So it doesn't dribble."

"Really?"

"It's not a big deal, but you can practise it."

"Absolutely."

Leo went to the bookstore that night.

Sheila had told her there would probably be about twenty minutes when both of them working flat out would hardly be able to keep up. Sometimes you simply could not open wine bottles fast enough. You'd turn around with your tray and all the glasses would be gone. You'd do it again, and again all the glasses would be gone. And then again and maybe again. The point is, Sheila had said, it gets hectic. So being able to do things without having to think about them would make everything go more smoothly.

She found the empty bottles—there were three—and filled them with water. She set out some glasses on the receiving table and began to pour. She turned the bottle as Sheila had suggested, and it worked. No dribble. What was tricky, though, and what she hadn't counted on, was the shape of the glass. If you poured into the centre and too fast the water ran up the sides and spilled over the top. But all in all it wasn't that much different from pouring a cup of coffee. Once you got used to it.

It was after six by the time she arrived at the store. Sheila had left already. Leo would have been there earlier, only she had wandered over to Eddie's. Mike was starting to bug her about the car. But Eddie wasn't home. She waited on his steps for a while but he never showed.

She poured and re-poured for almost half an hour, loaded up the tray and walked around with it, even went out into the store and offered Lisa a water cocktail, which she graciously accepted.

She washed the glasses before she went home, but as she was drying the last one, it came apart in her hands. She felt the sharp edge go in. The cut wasn't deep but it bled a lot. She held her hand over the sink with a paper towel pressed against it. She had no idea Sheila was in the store until she heard her call out as she stepped into the back room.

"Leo? Are you still here? Lisa said . . . Leo?"

"I'm in here." She looked over her shoulder. "I cut myself."

Sheila squeezed into the tiny bathroom and carefully took Leo's hand in her own. "Let me see."

Leo pulled the paper towel away.

"What happened?" Sheila put Leo's hand under the tap and ran cold water over it until they both could see the cut.

"I broke a glass. I'm sorry."

"Don't be silly. Does it hurt?"

"A little."

Sheila opened the medicine cabinet and pulled out a box of Band-Aids. "I think you'll live." She took off the wrapper. "Ready?" Leo nodded and held up her hand. Sheila pressed the pad over the cut and then smoothed the sticky ends down.

"Are you going to kiss it better, Mummy?"

A little girl was standing outside the door. She was dressed in jeans and a pink tee-shirt.

Sheila turned. "Sweetheart."

"When we get a cut my mummy kisses it better."

Leo leaned forward and smiled. "Does she?"

"Yes. And it works too. Doesn't it, Mummy?"

"Will you kiss it better for me?" Leo held out her hand to the little girl.

Her face lit up in surprise as if nobody had ever given her the opportunity to heal like this. "Okay." She glanced at her mother to make sure it was all right and then gave Leo's hand a gentle peck.

"That feels better already," Leo said. "Thank you."

The girl twisted her hands and arms together. She was almost dancing with herself. "It's sure-fire, isn't it, Mummy? It's sure-fire for sure."

"This is Laurie," Sheila said. "And Laurie, this is my friend, Leo."

"Hi, Laurie. I'm so happy to meet you."

"Hi."

"We were on our way to get ice creams," Sheila said. "I just stopped in to cash a cheque. D'you want to come with us?"

"Mum, are we going, or what?" A tall girl had come around the corner and was standing at the other end of the room.

"Leo cut herself," Laurie said.

The tall girl shifted her weight onto one long leg and said, "Excuse me?"

"Leo, this is my eldest daughter, Samantha. Samantha, this is Leo."

She glanced at Leo—"Hi"—and then looked back at her mother. "We're s'pose to be going for ice cream. Remember?"

"Leo's coming with us."

"Great," she said, then rolled her eyes.

"Don't be rude."

"I'm not being rude."

They all squeezed out of the back room and into the store together.

"She's eleven," Sheila said quietly to Leo. "It's an awkward age."

The car was parked on the street, and they were walking through the store.

"Talk about being rude, Mother. I mean, you're talking about me literally behind my back."

"I like your earrings," Leo said.

Samantha touched one of the little seashells dangling from her ear. "Thanks. But they're clip-ons. Can't you tell?" She glared at Sheila. "My mother won't let me get my ears pierced. Can you believe it? In this day and age?"

"Not now, Samantha."

Laurie slid in between them. "I'm six years old," she said, "and I've graduated from grade one at St. Mary's Academy."

"Laurie," Samantha scolded.

"What?"

"You're such a snob."

"And I like blueberry ice cream and blueberry milkshakes and blueberry anything. Don't I, Mummy?"

"You sure do, honey."

They went to the Dutch Maid, and although they talked about ice cream all the way there, they ordered milkshakes when they sat down at the counter.

Later they moved to a table. Laurie was looking around with big eyes but she didn't see anything. She was tasting the milkshake. "Sure-fire," she said to herself when she stopped to take a breath, "sure-fire. For sure."

"How's your hand?" Samantha said.

"It's fine."

"Where'd you get the ring?" She pulled Leo's hand towards her. "It's a signet ring, isn't it?"

"It was my father's."

"Did he give it to you?"

"My mother. After he died."

She gave Leo her hand back. "Sorry."

"It was a long time ago."

"It's still a cool ring." She stirred her milkshake with the straw. "So, when did you get your ears pierced?"

"Samantha, I've told you and I've told you."

Samantha grinned. She nodded at her mother but she spoke to Leo. "She doesn't think I'm old enough for anything."

"That's enough."

Samantha shrunk into her chair.

"Fifteen," Leo said.

Samantha looked horrified. "Fifteen? For your ears? I mean, that's like forever. Some of my friends . . . Never mind. Oh brother."

They drove Leo home. It was Laurie who said they should make sure Leo got in safely. She had taken one look around and did not like what she saw. Leo knew it wasn't the greatest neighbourhood. She had never had any real trouble, but all the same she knew she could run into it at any time. But she didn't make the kind of money that left her with a lot of choices.

Apart from her bathroom, she had one room, and everything was in it: fridge, stove, bed, TV, chest of drawers, chair, and couch. Her building was three storeys high and she lived on the top floor at the back. All three of them saw her up the stairs.

"D'you wanna come in for a sec?" Leo tried to remember if she had made the bed that morning. Sometimes she did, sometimes she didn't.

"Yes," Laurie said with the hot-eyed look of an explorer.

Leo unlocked the door and stepped in. Yes, thank God, she'd made the bed. Everything else, she thought, could be excused, but the place actually didn't look too bad—neat, more or less.

Singing quietly to herself, Laurie started to walk along the edges of the room. Samantha leaned against the wall near the door.

"I like this," Sheila said, "how you've got them arranged," and picked out one of Leo's books.

Leo had set them up on top of the TV. "They were my dad's," she said.

There were maybe a dozen paperbacks and three or four hardcovers held up between two bookends. Sheila ran her finger along them. There was an Arthur Conan Doyle, some science fiction, a worn copy of *David Copperfield*, a novel by Norman Mailer, a couple of books each by Morley Callaghan and W.O. Mitchell, and two or three popular histories on World War II and a popular science book by Asimov. Three of the hardcovers were Reader's Digest Condensed Novels. The fourth one was an odd volume of Churchill's *History of the English-Speaking Peoples*.

"There's more," Leo said, "but I've got no place to put them."

"D'you mind if I ask . . . how he died?"

"He was a switchman on the trains. He slipped one day and fell under the wheels of a boxcar." She shrugged. "I was eight years old. I don't remember much about it."

"It must've been hard for you. And your mother."

"I guess." Silence. "I don't like to talk about it."

"It's good to remember."

"Is it?"

"Yes. Of course." Sheila rubbed her hands together. "Okay, girls, time to go. Laurie."

Samantha pushed herself away from the wall. "Mom? How old d'you have to be before you can have your own apartment?"

"Can we discuss this later?"

"How old were you, Leo?"

"Nineteen."

"Samantha."

"I'm only asking." She turned and gave a little wave over her shoulder. "Bye."

"Bye, Leo." Laurie stood in front of her with her face turned up waiting for a kiss. Leo gave her one on the cheek and Laurie ran out into the hall to join her sister.

Sheila turned around in the doorway. "They like you," she whispered.

Laurie's voice rose up from the stairwell in a fading singsong. Her mother said, "Watch your step." And then the big heavy outside door banged shut and it was quiet.

The book launch was two days later.

And then the rain came.

FOUR

Lisa ducked into the 'Nut carrying an umbrella. She had come to get the morning coffee, which was a good thing because if Sheila had picked it up Leo wasn't sure what she would've done.

The rain had started last night just as everybody had begun to leave the bookstore and Leo and Sheila were cleaning up.

She had walked out the back door and straight to the bus shelter. It was less than a hundred feet away and still she got soaked. The rain was coming down so hard it bounced straight up so that there was a constant spray of water almost to her knees.

Sheila had followed pleading to give Leo a ride. But Leo never turned around even once. She slipped into the bus shack, went to the other end, and folded her arms. Sheila had stood by the entrance—for how long Leo wasn't sure—but when her bus came a few minutes later, she was gone.

"So what's bugging you?" Eddie leaned back and let his arms hang at his sides. They were sitting at his kitchen table. She was bent over it. "You said you wanted to talk. This isn't talking, Leo. This is sitting here watching paint dry. I could be making phone calls. You want a beer?" He went to the fridge and got them both a beer. He sat down again. "Is this about Mike's car?"

She shook her head.

"What then?" He twisted the caps off the bottles and pushed one over.

It was the day after the book launch and the evening after a long day of Leo wondering if Sheila was going to come into the 'Nut, and if she did what Leo would do or say to her. She hadn't had to do or say anything though because Sheila hadn't come in. But it was only a matter of time before they saw each other sometime, somewhere.

"I don't know who else I can talk to about this, Eddie."

It was still raining, but not as hard as last night.

"I'm listening." He was sitting sideways, propped up on one elbow and staring off into space. "I'm listening."

After they'd locked the door Sheila had said that they deserved a drink. She had been holding back, she'd said, a bottle of wine. It had been started but there was enough left for a glass each, maybe two. Leo, who had started washing glasses earlier, so as to keep clean ones in circulation, went into the back to get a couple. Sheila followed her with the bottle of wine.

"It just seems so totally weird."

"What seems so totally weird?" Eddie took a pull on his beer. "What?"

Sheila had raised her glass. "Cheers."

"Cheers." Leo had taken the swivel chair. She sipped on her wine and turned the chair slowly from side to side. Sheila lifted herself up onto the receiving table. Her feet dangled.

They talked for a while. They finished the wine.

Sheila had climbed off the receiving table and had gone to stand in front of Leo. Leo had looked up at her. She had started to smile, then stopped. She didn't know how she knew that Sheila was going to kiss her. It was the way she stood maybe or the look on her face. Leo kept telling herself not to be so stupid. Why would she kiss you? She's not going to kiss you. And so she sat there, watching Sheila's face getting bigger and bigger.

"I don't think I can go back there."

"Where?" Eddie said. "I don't know what you're talking about, Leo."

"To the bookstore. My job."

"Why not?"

"I just can't."

"You didn't accidentally take some cash out of the till, did you?"

It was a soft kiss, a gentle kiss, almost not like a kiss at all. It was more like a tasting, as if there were a flavour on Leo's lips Sheila wanted to try.

She waited—for it to be over, for Sheila to sit down so that they could pick up where they had left off and pretend that nothing had happened.

But then she felt her tongue.

Leo turned her head to one side, and Sheila's face followed like a reflection chasing itself across the water, and there it floated for seconds that seemed like hours, floated while the world changed for Leo and changed for Sheila, forever.

"She tried to hit on me, Eddie."

"She what?" He sat up.

"She tried to hit on me. You know."

"Who?"

"Sheila."

The grin spread slowly across his face. He said, "No shit."

FIVE

He'd said he'd pick her up after work at six, sharp. It was important, he'd said, that they get away on time. It was business, he'd said.

It was always business.

He was parked on the lot at ten to six. She saw him waiting.

Then Lisa walked in. She asked Leo if she'd seen Sheila.

She hadn't.

In fact, she'd only talked to her once since the book launch. Sheila didn't pick up the coffee in the morning anymore. Lisa and the full-time person, Kenny, now took turns. Sheila apparently still paid for it, though. One morning Leo mentioned that Sheila hadn't been picking up the coffee and asked if she was okay. Kenny paused and said, "Between you and me, she seems a little down lately. And moody. She keeps telling us how bad business is, and if we don't shape up around here . . . I haven't seen her like this for a while."

The one time Leo had talked to Sheila had been on the phone. Sheila said she was sorry for calling her at home but wanted to know if she could work an evening. Lisa had to prepare for a seminar. Leo was taken by surprise and the silence that followed Sheila's question seemed to go on forever. "Leo?"

"I thought—I was going to come by and give you my key to the store."

Now it was Sheila's turn to be silent. Finally she said, "If it's because of me, because of what happened the other day."

Silence again. "Look, I'm sorry. It was a mistake. I took advantage. I just thought . . . you knew."

"How would I know?"

"No, of course not. But please—whatever you do—don't quit because of me. I'd never forgive myself. At least think it over. Maybe we could sit down and have a talk. Everybody likes you. Lisa likes you, Kenny likes you, even Joanne likes you, and Joanne doesn't like anybody."

The phone call had started awkwardly but it had ended with Leo feeling as if, walking for days to put as much distance between herself and Sheila as possible, she had turned around at the last minute and wondered was she making too much of a fuss over this. Her first burst of anger had mostly drained away. She remained disappointed maybe, and a little confused. She had been disturbed over what had happened. If Sheila had been a man, the sex thing would've been there, out in the open, declared. With Sheila it was like she had come walking in under a false flag. But she hadn't blamed Leo, hadn't yelled and screamed at her, hadn't fired her. In fact just the opposite.

She worked the evening with Kenny. When she arrived he handed her a paperback book. "Sheila said to give you this."

"What for?"

"To read, I guess."

"Is it any good?"

"*The Stone Angel*? Yeah, it's pretty good."

"I phoned her at home," Lisa said, "but the line's busy. I can't get through."

"What's the problem?"

"This." Lisa showed her a long woman's wallet that folded over on itself. "She left it at the store. It's got all her credit cards and everything. Money. I guess she'll figure it out, but I thought she might be worried."

"Let's see."

They opened it. Leo found Sheila's driver's licence. "Here's her address," Leo said. She studied it. "Eddie's got some stuff he's gotta do, but maybe we can drop it off after."

"That would be great if you could."

So by the time she got out of the 'Nut it was a couple of minutes past six.

Eddie said, "I told you, I gotta meet this guy."

"Can we drop this off?" She showed him the wallet as she climbed into the car.

"Later."

"Later's fine." She put the wallet in her purse beside what was becoming a battered copy of *The Stone Angel*. She was almost halfway through it. "So what's up?"

Eddie leaned towards her. "I got a guy," he whispered, then looked around as if somebody might be listening. "I got a guy— wants to put money up for the u-drive. An investor, Leo."

"Really?" She'd figured he had forgotten all about the u-drive.

"A money man who's happy to stand back and let some-one else run things."

"Your silent partner."

"Exactly."

"That's great, Eddie." And she meant it. Eddie could be a schmuck, but at least he had plans and ideas.

They had left the parking lot and were rolling to a stop just as the light turned.

"Green light, Eddie."

"I know, I can see."

She leaned over and put her right hand over both his eyes. "And now? Can you see now, Eddie?"

He was shifting into second. He paused for a moment, and then she felt his face stretching into a grin. He continued to pick up speed, shifted into third, and then into fourth.

They were on Osborne heading towards the downtown and doing about fifty k.

"Curb, Eddie, curb. On the right."

He steered away from it.

"Perfect."

"Fuck," he said. His cheeks felt like hard little peaches.

"Bus up ahead, Eddie. Parked. Four-ways on. We gotta change lanes. Give her gas. Slowly. We got lots of time. More gas, Eddie, more. Okay. Now ease over to the left. That's it. Straighten out." She giggled. "Guy gave you a dirty look, Eddie." She swung her head around.

"Fuck him."

"A suit, driving a Caddy."

"What year?"

"Red light, Eddie, coming up."

"Is it new or old—the Caddy?"

"It's big."

"New?"

"Yeah."

"Black?"

"What?"

"The Caddy."

"White."

"A Caddy oughta be black."

"Red light, Eddie."

"Now?"

"Soon. Start easing up. Clutch in. Start with the brake. That's it. You're doing fine."

"Piece a cake."

"Harder, a little harder on the brake, Eddie, a little harder."

"Piece a cake."

"The brake, Eddie, the brake. Stop, Eddie. Eddie, stop the car. There's people crossing."

She pulled her hand away but it didn't matter. He had already jammed on the brakes. The tires screamed and she was slammed against the dashboard.

People were looking at them.

"Why'n't you stop when I said stop?"

He was still grinning. "Just wanted to make sure you wasn't shitting me." He put his arm around her. "Stop me somewhere in the middle of the road, make me look like some kind of dumb asshole."

"I don't have to stop you in the middle of the road to make you look like some kind of dumb asshole, Eddie."

They drove slowly down the side street, passing a lot of places that looked exactly like the place they finally turned in to. "Here it is," Eddie said. The long, single-storey building was constructed of cinder blocks, painted white.

He parked near five or six other cars and headed towards a door. Leo followed. There was a plastic sign in the window: "The East-West Printing Company."

"Who is this guy?"

"Larry Dorfman."

"You know him?"

"What's to know? He's a businessman. He does business."

A buzzer sounded as they stepped into the small office. A moment later a door in the far wall opened and a tall, skinny guy came out from the back. He had greasy black hair and was rubbing his hands on a rag. "We're closed," he said.

Leo had worked in a place once that had a little offset, and she recognized the *clank-oosh*, *clank-oosh* of a printing press coming from the room behind where the guy was standing.

Eddie put his fingers on his chest. "Name's Eddie, Eddie Valentine. S'pose to see Larry. I'm expected." Eddie stuck out his chin, pushed back his shoulders, and did up the centre button on the jacket of his floppy black suit.

"You here for the game? 'Cause they's started it already, eh."

"I'm here to see Mr. Dorfman."

"Who'd you say you was?" He turned his head sideways and squinted. "And who's the broad?"

"Listen, Ace, just tell the man Eddie's here. Okay?"

The guy's mouth twitched. "The name—it's Otto."

"Great. I'm happy for you. Now tell Mr. Dorfman I'm here. Okay . . . Ace?"

Five minutes later Otto returned and made a follow-me motion. "Mr. Dorfman like forgot to tell me you was coming. But it's okay."

Sometimes Eddie got this happy, sort of smug look on his face when he figured he was going to get laid, and he had that happy, sort of smug look on his face now. "No sweat, man," he said. "Mistakes get made. I understand. You can't just let anybody in." Over his shoulder he said, "Wait here, Leo. This is business."

She felt like saying "So why did you bring me here for?" but didn't.

Instead, she counted to three, then stepped around the counter and up to the door. Eddie had not closed it behind him and it wasn't on a spring, so after he followed Otto through, it stayed open about a quarter of the way.

She watched them cross the print-shop floor. She could see a couple of printing presses, but only one was working, and somebody else, not Otto, was working it.

Otto knocked on a door leading to an office maybe, or storeroom. The door opened a few inches, Otto said something, and then the door closed. A moment later it opened again. The room behind it was full of smoke. Leo edged to one side to get a better angle and caught a glimpse of a table with a whole bunch of men sitting around it. They were holding cards, and in the centre of the table there was what looked like a big pile of money.

The hairy little guy who stepped out of the room had to be Larry Dorfman. The rings on his fingers glittered as he pulled the cigar out of his mouth.

Too late, she saw Otto striding towards her.

She stepped back into the office.

"You didn't see nothin' here," he said from the doorway. "Understand? You didn't see nothin'."

She sat down on a vinyl chair.

"Some broads, they got big mouths, gotta yap yap yap yap yap."

She picked up an old copy of *Maclean's*.

"So don't try nothin' funny."

He went back through the door and this time he locked it.

A few minutes passed—not a lot of time for the deal of the century. She was paging through the *Maclean's* and half listening to the *clank-oosh* of the printing press.

All of a sudden something thumped against the door. About the same time she heard Eddie on the other side of it. "You're crazy, Dorfman. Who d'you think you're talking to here? Huh?" The knob rattled but it wouldn't turn. "Just who the hell d'you think you're talking to?" The knob rattled again. "What's with this door?" He kicked it. "Is this thing locked?" He kicked it again. "What the hell is going on here?"

A calm, older voice said, "Open the door for Mr. Valentine, Otto."

"Fuck you, Dorfman." The door started to swing open. "And fuck you too, Ace." Eddie slammed his way into the office.

He crossed the floor and then turned around. "You coming?" he said to Leo, "or are you just gonna sit there all night?"

She climbed into the car with him. She didn't think it was a good time to start asking questions.

He started the engine and then surprised her by saying, "So where's this Sheila live?"

She'd almost forgotten.

"The wallet," he said, "the wallet. Or d'you wanna eat first?"

"Maybe we should get out of here first." She was looking at the place they'd just come out of.

Otto had appeared at the door. Only now he wasn't holding a dirty rag, he was holding a piece of pipe which he kept thumping into the palm of his left hand.

Eddie backed the car up across the parking lot. He gave Otto the finger. "Give that to your boss, you little cocksucker." Eddie's car didn't have enough power to make the tires squeal, but he drove it hard, and they almost hit the far curb as they turned onto the street. "The fuckin' guy tries to take me for a ride, Leo. Me."

"What happened?"

"He's a loan shark. Tried to take me."

"You didn't sign anything." She looked at him. "Did you?"

"No, no, no."

"So what's the problem?"

"I got no investor, I got no silent partner, I got no money. I got shit."

"I'm sorry, Eddie."

"T'hell with it anyways. . . . Where is this place we're going?"

Leo opened Sheila's wallet and read him the address.

"Oh yeah. I know where that is."

They turned off the Norwood Bridge and drove along Lyndale Drive as it followed one of the long curves of the Red River.

"What's the number again?" She told him. "It must be up a ways. You are looking, I hope."

"I'm looking." Five minutes later she said, "There it is, on the corner."

Eddie stopped the car out front. "Wow," he said. "Nice place."

Leo leaned forward to get a better look. It was a nice place: two-storey, split-level with a long balcony and big wide windows everywhere. From the front door the river wasn't more than fifty yards away, and the only thing between it and the house was the road that she and Eddie were parked on.

"I won't be a sec." Leo took the wallet and walked around to the back of the house. She got ready to be friendly without being too friendly. She wanted things to go back to being normal without being sure what normal was. She had already begun to wonder what kind of life Sheila must be living. Married with two kids, but with another side to her that didn't fit with that or a house like this. Not in Leo's mind anyways. What kinds of mental tricks did Sheila have to play, or did she have everything under control? Maybe, maybe not. She remembered Sheila's tongue pressing against her teeth, waiting for Leo to open her mouth.

Sheila's car was in the driveway, but there was no answer when she rang the bell.

Eddie came around the corner. "So what's the deal? Is she home or not?"

"I guess not. Her car's here, but there's no answer."

He leaned over and pressed the buzzer three times quickly. "Is it locked? Did you try?"

"What?"

"The door, the door." He stepped in front of her, pulled open the screen door, and then turned the knob on the inside. There was a click and the door popped open about an inch. "S'open," he said.

"Now what?"

He pointed his head at the door and smiled. "Huh?"

"I don't think so, Eddie."

"S'okay. We're on a mission of mercy." Slowly he pushed it open. "Hello?" He poked his head through the doorway. "Hello?" Then a little louder. "Hel-lo-oh."

He put his hands on the door frame and leaned in. He turned his head to the right. "Anybody home?" He cocked an ear, paused, and then pushed himself away. "Nobody's home. Very trusting. Just go in. Leave the wallet on the kitchen table."

"I don't know, Eddie."

"What's to know? It's up a couple of steps up to the right. I saw it. It's easy. The kitchen's right there."

The kitchen was where Eddie said it would be, but when she stepped inside, the stairs leading into the rec room were directly in front of her. And all the rec room lights were on. She peered into the basement thinking for some reason that she might catch a glimpse of Sheila walking by. And that's when she noticed the book at the bottom of the stairs. It was a hardcover, and it was lying face down. Even from here she could tell that some of the pages were bent over on themselves. Sheila would never do that to a book, and she certainly would never leave it like that.

She turned around. Eddie was standing on the other side of the screen door. He was looking at his watch. "There's something wrong here," she said. "Didn't you feel it?"

He yanked open the screen door. "What?"

"There's something wrong."

"Like what?"

"I don't know." She turned back to the basement stairs. "Sheila? Anybody?" She listened. No answer. "This is too weird, Eddie. I'm going down."

"Where?"

"Into the basement."

He sighed. "All right, all right. I'll wait for you out here. But don't take all night."

What she found made her stomach turn over.

The basement had been done up real nice once with furniture and carpeting but now it looked like a tornado had come through. Books had been pulled off the shelves and thrown everywhere. Chairs turned upside down. The front of the TV had been kicked in. There were the pieces of what must have been a whole sound system—amp, CD player, turntable, cassette deck—and tapes and CDs and albums, all half under and half scattered around a wall unit where they must have once been stored before whoever had pulled the whole thing over.

She found the phone—the dial tone had long since fallen silent—and put the receiver back in the cradle.

"Holy shit."

"Eddie?" She turned around.

"What happened?" He was standing at the bottom of the stairs. He had his arms out.

"Somebody trashed the place."

"No kidding." He started picking through the stuff while Leo simply wandered around. "What's this?" he said.

"What?"

He had found what looked like a Walkman. "The little red light's on. You see?" He pointed. "It's a recorder, like for memos. I could use one of these."

"Let's see."

He gave it to her. "Somebody's hit the 'pause' button while they were still recording—instead of turning it off. That's why the red light's on. D'you see? It was on the floor there." He put his hands on his hips. "What a mess."

Leo went into a corner. She released the "pause" button and the tape started to turn. But there was only silence. She turned it off and pressed "play." There was distant music, some kind of synthesizer or electric piano, not very well recorded. She wound the tape back a little ways and started it again.

"George?" Sheila's voice drifted out of the machine.

Leo held the recorder up to her ear. The sound was tinny and full of tape hiss, but she could hear Sheila's despair.

"Mother...." It sounded like Samantha calling but from far away.

"It's okay, honey," Sheila called back. "Your father and I are talking. Don't come down. I need you to stay with Laurie. Okay? Your sister needs you to be with her right now." Silence. "How could you have done this, George? The girls are terrified. You're frightening the hell out of them. Not to mention me." Silence. "Are you going to smash that too?"

"This? I was going to leave you a message."

There was a click, a few seconds of silence, and then the poorly recorded music started again.

Leo turned the machine off and set it down. What kind of message was he going to leave? Whatever it was, Leo thought it would be full of hate. Because that was what she was surrounded by now. Hate. That was the message buried in the wreckage she and Eddie were standing in.

A wave of fear swept over her so strong it made her skin go prickly. "Sheila?" she whispered. Then she called out, "Sheila. Are you here? Is anybody here? Laurie? Samantha?" There was a hall leading off to the right. She stepped into it. She could see a laundry room. She went further and found some kind of workroom and a bedroom, a guest room maybe, and, at the end, a bathroom. But there was no one there.

"Let's get out of here, Eddie."

"Good idea." He took another quick look around. "Somebody walks in now our ass is grass. Come on. And don't leave the wallet. Anyone asks, there was nobody home."

They went to the St. Vital Hotel. It was the closest bar. They had a couple of beers. Leo wondered out loud if they shouldn't call the police. Eddie said no way. "They'd know we were there. Then they'd wanna know why we were there, and then how come this and how come that? No way."

She didn't argue with him. Part of her wasn't so sure calling the cops was a good idea either, but for different reasons. Eddie just thought someone had gone in and smashed up the place. Whoever it was might have been somewhere else in the house, upstairs maybe, he said, taking from the rich and all that. She didn't think so, and if she had, she would've called the police no matter what Eddie said.

By the time they left the Vital it was getting dark. They drove around for a while looking for a place to eat. Eddie would slow down and say, "How 'bout here?" Leo would shrug and they'd drive on. It wasn't that she minded most of the places. She didn't really care where they ate. She was worried about Sheila. Whatever had happened it wasn't good. What Eddie had said about somebody being upstairs had begun to bother her. What if what she was afraid of finding had been upstairs? She tried not to think about it. Eddie wouldn't drive her back to find out anyway, and she wasn't sure they would find anything. What had happened had happened in the basement, she figured. The kitchen had been neat when she glanced into it, nothing out of place, nothing turned over, just two glasses of milk not quite finished sitting on the table, as if Sheila had gathered the girls and left very quickly, too quickly for them to finish their milk and too quickly also to even stop and take her car.

The thing now though was the wallet. Sheila would need it, and what if she had realized where she'd left it and gone back to the store to get it? And it wasn't there. Or maybe she hadn't gone yet. Maybe there was still time. Out of a lot of choices Leo picked the one that made the most sense to her.

Eddie was tired of her shrugging at every burger joint and pizza place and had already told her they were going to the Kentucky Fried Chicken on Osborne, no arguments.

"Okay, sure, but—"

"What?"

They would be going right by the store. She would leave the wallet there in a place Sheila would find it. She told him to cut down the lane and park by the back door.

"What for?"

"I have to leave the wallet."

"Give it to her tomorrow."

"I might not see her right away."

"Okay, okay."

They went in together. The store was closed but the light in the back room was always on. Out front, the store itself would be dark except for some display lights in the windows. Still, you could find your way around easily enough.

Eddie said he figured he might as well take a look. "They got business books?" She said of course they did, and he wandered off, which was okay with Leo. She needed a minute to write a note to Sheila.

But he was gone only a couple of seconds. He came back walking quickly and glancing over his shoulder. "Leo," he said. "Leo, there's a guy out there."

"Cut it out, Eddie."

"No, I'm telling you, there's a guy out there."

"There's nobody out there."

"Did I forget to lock the door?" Behind Eddie at the other end of the receiving table stood a man. He was about the same height as Eddie—five eight maybe—but bigger around the chest and in the shoulders, heavier. He had a thick head of uncombed hair that came down past his ears. Even from here she could tell he'd been drinking. Everything about him seemed to droop. His voice was thick and he spoke slowly and carefully as if he had to think about forming every word.

But she recognized it right away. It was the voice of the man she'd heard on the tape in Sheila's basement only an hour ago.

Leo felt herself tightening up. "How'd you get in here?"

"I," he said, "used a key." He pushed himself away from the wall. "You must be the new girl. Leo."

"Yes," she said cautiously, as if it might be a trick.

"I'm Sheila's husband. George Stookner." He folded his arms. "I own this place."

"Sheila owns this place."

"It's the same thing. Marriage, Leo, is a peculiar institution."

Eddie started towards him before she could pull him back. "Mr. Stookner. I'm Eddie Valentine." He put out his hand. For a moment George stood there, arms folded. Eddie waited. He was a hard guy to put down was Eddie.

Finally George shook his hand. "So what brings you here, Eddie? Need some late-night reading?"

"I forgot to mail out a book," Leo said. She happened to be standing by the mail-out shelf. The wallet was on the counter. She had put it down beside a box. From where Stookner was standing he wouldn't be able to see it. "To a customer."

Eddie looked at the floor.

George shrugged. "So go ahead. Mail it out. Do what you came here to do."

The mail-out bin was empty. She stared at it. How much did he know about the way they did things around here? "I guess Kenny or Lisa must've seen it and mailed it for me."

George didn't look convinced.

She pulled down the scribbler they used to log the mail-outs. She was in luck. Two things had been mailed out that day. She went to show him.

"It doesn't matter," he said and turned away.

While he wasn't looking she slipped the wallet into the mail-out bin and put the scribbler on top of it.

"Come on, Eddie. Let's go." She opened the back door and waited for him. She didn't think Stookner would find the wallet unless he went looking and he had no reason to go looking. He might not have believed her but he wouldn't've known why.

"I'll be with you in a sec," Eddie said.

"Eddie."

"In a sec."

She didn't want to hang around any longer than she had to, not with Stookner there. He gave her the creeps.

"Wait for me outside," Eddie said, "in the car."

So she waited. Five minutes passed, then ten. Come on, Eddie, come on. She stared at the door as if that would make him step through it faster. What was he doing?

When he finally came out he got into the car and said, "He won't be long."

"Who?"

"Mr. Stookner."

"We're waiting for him?"

"Yeah. He's takin' a leak. He wants to see the u-drive. He's the man, Leo. You heard him. He owns the place. And even that's small potatoes. Get this. He also owns the biggest fuckin' recording studio in the city. Him and his partner. They do jingles, they do bands. Guys from New York City call him up. They're mega."

"And you believe him?"

"You saw the house. The guy's got money, cash, to put into things."

"He told you that?"

"He doesn't have to come out and tell me anything, Leo. I know when a guy's a player. You can tell."

"He's pissed out of his head."

"He's had a few drinks. So what?"

"Eddie, we gotta get out of here. Now."

"No way. This could be it. My ticket. I'm gonna walk away? Because he's had a couple of drinks?"

"Eddie, he's the one who smashed up the house."

"What are you on, Leo?"

"You remember the tape player? In the basement. . . . Don't shake your head."

"So what if he did? It's his house. Which reminds me. Where's that wallet?"

"I hid it."

"What for? Just give it to him. He's her husband."

"Are you out of your mind?"

"Quiet. Here he comes."

"Don't say anything about the wallet, Eddie. Please."

He got out of the car without answering her. "Okay, Mr. Stookner. Ready to go?" He folded the driver's seat forward and helped George Stookner into the back of the car.

Leo had never seen the gas station Eddie wanted to turn into a u-drive. He'd talked about taking her there but he never had. When they pulled in, to her it didn't look like much. Just an office with a couple of service bays attached. The concrete islands for the gas pumps were still there but the pumps were gone. The rest was an empty lot. The only illumination came from the street lights and there weren't many of those.

They were on King Edward Street slightly north of Ellice. It was a one-way, southbound, four lanes wide, which connected the northwest side of the city with the southwest. There was a big furniture discount store up the road, a warehouse across the street, and a bottling plant around the corner. Polo Park Shopping Centre was about ten minutes away in one direction and the airport was about ten minutes away in the other.

"Location's what's gonna make this operation work." Eddie waved his arms around like some crazy guy in a bad TV commercial. "Proximity to the airport, proximity to the major hotels in the area—the nature of the area itself." He listed them, bending back one finger at a time. "High traffic patterns, a good mix of light industry, a growing retail sector, professional sporting facilities—combined with free pick-up and drop-off service from my door to yours—make this place a potential gold mine for any u-drive operator smart enough to take advantage of the situation."

A growing roar in the sky made Leo look up. She saw the blinking lights of the airplane first, then its dark shape as it came in almost on top of their heads.

Eddie talked louder. "Location. It's what business is all about. And the physical plant is here. I got two service bays to carry out regular maintenance, lots of room to store cars—although I'm looking to have ninety percent of my cars on the road ninety percent of the time. But I mean there's capacity to handle peak turnover."

The plane disappeared behind a cluster of low, flat buildings. Eddie was still waving his arms in the air, but George was walking towards Leo.

"You see that hotel?" He had stopped a few feet away from her and was pointing down the road. "The Airliner. They used to have a bar in there. The Black Knight." He pulled out a small cigar and lit it. "I don't know what they call it now, club something or other. I used to have a band and we played there a lot. Sometimes we even had two-week gigs. Two weeks in a row at the same bar. You had to be good to get jobs like that, and we were very good."

The cigar smoke drifted past her, and for a moment Leo almost felt she knew what he was talking about. Then the whole sense of it slipped away.

Eddie walked over to where they were standing. "I can get the keys to the building if you want to have a look around, Mr. Stookner." When he didn't get an answer he started to pace. "Of course, it's up to you."

There was suddenly silence: no cars, no trucks, no airplanes, merely the sound of Eddie's shoes on the sand and gravel left over from last winter and maybe the winter before.

"I didn't hit her." George was a silhouette smoking a small cigar in the dark on an empty piece of land. It was almost as if he were talking to himself. "Or the girls," he said. "I wouldn't. I couldn't."

"I might be able to get the keys tonight," Eddie said. "I can make a phone call."

Another airplane filled the sky.

Leo kept her eyes on George, and he kept his eyes on her. He didn't seem as drunk now, as if he had moved beyond it, to a place where things were more clear.

"Maybe not with your fists," she said.

Eddie turned his face up to the dark aluminum shape. "Fucking airplanes."

SIX

"Leo?" It was a whisper.

She had the key in the front door of her apartment building. It was almost midnight. She and Eddie had driven George back to the bookstore. Then Eddie had driven her home.

Leo's building had an "A" side and a "B" side. A small court sheltered the two facing doors.

"Leo?"

The voice came from the corner behind her. It was thin and cracked, but it sounded familiar. She thought it was Sheila.

She turned, and a woman stepped out of the shadows. For a moment she didn't think it was Sheila after all. It was the way she held herself. Leo had never seen or even imagined a Sheila who didn't at least try to tower over everything and everyone around her. This woman seemed small, crumpled up. Then she came closer. "It is you," Leo said. Sheila's eyes had lost their shine, her skin its colour, her whole face its shape. "It is you," Leo said again, picking through the ruins of this Sheila for the Sheila she remembered. "How long have you been waiting?"

"I phoned but you weren't home, and the door was locked."

"Come inside."

"I wanted to see you. I'm sorry. Everything's so mixed up. I should really get back. The girls ... We're at my parents'."

"We can't talk here. Come inside." Leo knew from the store that Sheila drank more tea than coffee. She never bought tea herself but she had kept a sample tea bag that had come in the mail. "I'll make you a cup of tea."

Sheila waited by the door while Leo turned the lock. "But I can't stay long," she said as she followed Leo inside. "I wanted to see you, that's all." They were standing by the mailboxes. "I know you must hate me."

"No." Leo lowered her head. "Come on. I'll make you a cup of tea and we can talk. We should have talked before." Leo touched her arm. "But no, don't be ridiculous, I don't hate you."

Sheila sniffed back a rush of tears.

For herself Leo made decaf.

She sat on the couch. Sheila sat in the armchair across from it—knees together, pointed off to one side, and holding her tea in both hands. She had a caged-in look.

Leo sipped her coffee and looked at her over the rim of her cup. Whatever had opened up between them while they were standing by the mailboxes had closed again. She felt outside whatever ball Sheila had wrapped herself up in, but she also felt as if at least some of it was her fault. She didn't know what to say or how to say it. The room sank into silence. Leo tried to break it but whenever she started to say something the words felt wooden and unreal, and she stopped.

Sheila said nothing. Then, setting her tea down on the floor, she stood up and said, "I should go." But as she turned to leave, she knocked the cup over with her foot as if she had forgotten she had put it there only a moment ago.

Her eyes rose from the puddle of tea to Leo.

"It's okay," Leo said, and started for the sink to get some paper towels.

But Leo had not taken more than a couple of steps before she stopped. With a growing sense of alarm she watched as Sheila's face slowly at first but then more quickly began to collapse in on itself. Sheila put her hands over her face, dug her fingers in.

She turned towards the door. Leo grabbed for her and missed. Sheila bounced off one wall and then, with her hands still over her face, slid down the other one to the floor.

Leo knelt beside her, but Sheila was already trying to pull herself up. Her eyes opened, then almost closed, fluttered, then opened again.

Bent over, she staggered towards the door, but fell down again in a heap. This time she didn't try to get up, not right away. She just lay there twitching.

"Sheila." Leo reached for her, then pulled back. "Oh my God." Sheila rolled herself onto her side, tried to get up again, fell down. Her eyes were filled with panic. She kept opening and closing her mouth like a bird with no voice, and apart from the thumping of her body as she fell down everything happened in a chilling silence. It was as if Sheila were somewhere else entirely, screaming in another world, drowning in an ocean there, dying, and all Leo could see of it was this bumping into walls and this falling down on the floor of an apartment that for Sheila might barely exist.

Leo didn't know what to do. She had nothing to smother the fear. "Sheila." She grabbed her wrists. "Sheila!"

Leo paused for a moment, then leaned into the storm, the soft explosion, not knowing or even really thinking about what she would find. She put her head on Sheila's chest and her arms around Sheila's arms. Sheila twisted, brought her knees up, pushed at her, but Leo would not let go.

Sheila finally tired herself out and the calm that followed was the calm of exhaustion filled with only the sound of Sheila's fast, shallow breathing.

"Let me sleep," she said.

"Not here."

"Tired."

"Not on the floor."

"Tired."

"Stand up. Can you stand up?" Leo got her to her feet and helped her to the bed.

She curled up on her side. But it was a long time before her breathing slowed and grew deeper. She was still but she didn't go to sleep. Leo watched her from the sofa. Her eyes were open. They were blank and staring like they had been before but with the panic pushed back. Leo cleaned up the spilt tea and then lay down on the couch, just to rest, she thought. She left the lights on. She didn't think she would be able to sleep, but she must have drifted off because she found herself pulled out of a doze sometime later by a noise she couldn't figure out at first. She thought it was an animal, a cat maybe outside the window, softly crying.

She sat up. The noise stopped. Sheila was hugging Leo's pillow with both her arms and legs.

They looked at each other, then Leo lay back down again.

The next time she woke up Sheila was gone.

There was a knock at the door. Leo knew who it was. She had been waiting for that knock for days, perhaps weeks, without realizing it. She paused, but did not really hesitate.

It was the next day. It was a little after nine in the evening. She opened the door.

Sheila's smile flashed and then faded. "Can I come in?"

"Yes, of course. Are you okay?"

"I'm fine. I wanted to apologize for last night. What a performance."

"You were upset. Come in."

"Still . . . "

"Did you get your wallet?"

"Yes. Thank you. Lisa said what you'd done—you and Eddie."

"Tried to do."

"Anyways, here." She held up two Safeway bags. "I brought you this."

"What is it?"

Sheila carried the bags to the counter between the sink

and the stove. "It's what you need to make my favourite spaghetti sauce. You're always talking about those Italian things you read in the magazines."

Leo hadn't realized. "Do I?"

"I think I got everything." She started to take things out of the bags and set them on the counter. "Consider it a gift. And an apology and a thank you."

"I didn't do anything."

"You were there."

"So what do I do with all this stuff?"

She pulled out a piece of paper. "This is the recipe."

Leo looked at it. "Can you help me?"

"I have to pick up the girls."

"Oh sure, whenever, it doesn't have to be tonight. You could, you know, come over."

Sheila was reaching to put a bottle of olive oil in the cupboard. "If you like."

Leo put the ground beef in the fridge. "Did you and the girls stay at your parents' last night?"

"Yes. Did I tell you about that?"

"You said that that's where you'd come from."

"I don't remember a lot. I was pretty confused. What else did I say?"

"Not much. Where're you gonna stay tonight?"

"We're going home."

"Maybe it's none of my business . . . "

"It isn't." She closed her eyes. "I'm sorry."

"I know what he did."

There was suddenly nothing in Sheila's face. "What do you mean?"

"When we tried to get your wallet back to you. We came looking for you yesterday. I had your wallet. We went to your house. The door was open. I didn't know. I went inside. I was going to leave it someplace where you could find it."

Sheila continued putting things into the cupboard.

"Has this happened before?"

"Can we talk about something else?"

"Why do you stay with him?"

"You don't just throw your life away, Leo, and start over. It's not that simple."

"Is it because of the way you are?"

"It hasn't made things easy—for either of us. None of our friends know. My parents—they might have suspected . . . but I'm cured now, and I've got a husband and two of the most beautiful kids in the world to prove it."

"Does he know?"

"Oh yes."

"You're crying."

"I'm not crying." She drew the tip of a long finger under one eye and then under the other.

Leo took her hand before she could set it down, took her hand and slowly kissed the backs of her fingers.

Then she turned and went to stand in front of the couch.

She thought she might be making a mistake. What if, after all, it wasn't really what Sheila wanted? But it seemed like such a simple thing to do for someone, not that she really knew what it was she was going to do, because she had never been to bed with a woman before.

But she had made up her mind. And it wasn't simply because she thought Sheila had been handed a raw deal. For an instant at least she wanted to turn a corner and look at what was there. She pulled her tee-shirt over her head before she could change her mind.

She had her back to Sheila, and when she stepped out of her underpants and turned towards the bed, she was sure she had made a mistake.

But it was too late.

She lay down on her back and, turning her hips to one side, looked at Sheila. And it was all right. Sheila looked calm, almost serene. She held Leo's eyes for a moment and then allowed her own to move slowly down Leo's body, pausing at her breasts, at her belly, and at the furl of flesh in the hair between her legs.

Still fully dressed, Sheila sat down on the edge of the bed.

She leaned forward and stroked the inside of Leo's knee. Leo flinched without meaning to. Sheila looked back up into her face and gave her a little smile. Then she pulled away so that she was sitting upright once again. A moment passed. She stood up. "The light," she whispered. "Where's the switch?"

"On the wall there, by the fridge."

Sheila turned it off, and now the only light was the one by the door.

"That's good," Leo said. She lay down on her stomach and turned her face to the room. Sheila undressed where Leo had, by the sofa which was about four feet away from the bed. When she turned she was almost immediately standing over Leo, and Leo closed her eyes.

She placed her knees on either side of Leo's, and then she lay down on top of her, slowly giving her her weight as if Leo were eggshells, glass and mirrors, a bird.

The moment before their flesh touched, the craziness of what they were doing, the creepiness of it, flashed through Leo, and if Sheila had not already been on top of her she might have rolled away. Her skin crawled. She felt as if something had gone wrong. There was a cold fire in her bones drawing all the heat out of her flesh, making her feel unreal, making her feel like plastic.

And then Sheila kissed her—on the back of the neck. Licked the place she had kissed and kissed her again. She ran her hands over her shoulders, said how beautiful she was, and Leo felt okay again because it was Sheila, and Sheila only wanted to be kind to her.

Pushing her fingers through Leo's hair and deep into her flesh, she kissed and licked her way down Leo's spine and then paused in the small of her back. She made circles with her fingers around her buttocks and then touched the inside of her thigh. Leo wasn't ready, and she made a sound like "No," and Sheila stopped.

She lay back down on top of Leo, covering her. Her face rested in the crook between Leo's neck and shoulder, and her left hand kept slowly stroking her hair. Apart from that she was very still, drinking her in through her breasts, her belly, her groin, her legs, her arms.

When Sheila rolled away—satisfied or disappointed, Leo didn't know—she thought it was over.

But it wasn't.

Sheila was making a sound deep in her throat. Leo turned towards her. Sheila was half lying on the bed and half jammed up against the wall. She had two fingers inside herself, was moving them in slow circles while she held herself open with her other hand.

"Sheila," Leo said and realized it was the first time she had spoken her name since she had climbed onto the bed with her. Sheila seemed far away, she seemed alone, and just below the surface she seemed frightened. Leo put her arms around her, pressed her face between her breasts, tasted the salt on her skin.

Sheila's belly gave a little jump, and then another and then another. The noise in her throat strained and stretched. Leo freed her right hand and placed it over Sheila's, lightly, with hardly any pressure at all, a touch.

Sheila tensed. Leo tightened her arm around her. She twisted, and on a wind Leo couldn't see or feel, Sheila fluttered for a small eternity and then fell back gasping, her eyes wide and staring as if she were looking, not at the shadows that clung to the ceiling or even at Leo, but at something that wasn't even in the room, something that filled her with both joy and fear.

For a long time they clung to each other, hiding themselves in each other's hollows and folds, telling each other their secrets in kisses.

And it was a long time too before Leo allowed Sheila to make love to her. But she did, and she heard herself cry out and felt her hips thrust as the warm helplessness spread from the centre of her body to her arms and legs.

When it was over, they lay side by side with their arms around each other and drifted.

Leo wanted it to go on. She felt pleasantly used up.

But their drifting ended when Sheila said "I have to go."

Leo sat up. She felt a flash of panic and put the tips of her fingers to her mouth. "The girls. Oh Sheila, I forgot. They're waiting for you."

Sheila smiled and stroked Leo's arm. "It's okay. They like it where they are."

Leo went to find her bathrobe and Sheila got dressed.

At the door Leo turned her face up for a kiss and received several—on her nose, her forehead, her eyes, and on the smile that was spreading across her face.

And then she was alone with this strange warm feeling that didn't make any sense. And all the tough questions: who was she, what was she? Would there be a next time? And did it matter if there was or there wasn't?

GEORGE

ONE

He was staring into a clear blue sky. His head hurt.

And he was scared.

He sat up carefully. The river, gravy thick with mud, was nibbling at the edges of the bank only a few feet from the soles of his shoes. The water moved slowly enough near the bank, but the river was maybe a hundred yards wide, and out near the middle it ran fast and deep.

He figured he must have been in it, and not too long ago. His clothes and hair were damp and doughy with the mud of it. Perhaps he had stumbled along its edge or fallen down in the shallows. But he could have just as easily been out there in the middle where, as he watched, a water-soaked log tumbled near the surface for a moment and was then dragged under. If he had been out there he could have easily been drowned. If he had been out there he had simply been lucky, tossed up onto the shore and left to wake up in a muddy afterbirth.

But he could not remember, he couldn't remember anything.

A giggle made him turn and look up. A small boy was standing at the top of the bank. The boy laughed again, pointed. And then he was gone, a sudden emptiness against the blue sky.

From where he sat, the climb looked impossible. The bank seemed to go straight up, the crumbly clay soil held together in clumps by the tough yellow grasses that grew out of it.

"Stookie?" A heavy-set man was standing where the boy had stood, as if the boy had come back thirty years later, as if thirty years had passed while he had been casually looking the other way. The man wore a checkered shirt and had a walrus moustache. He knew the face—but the name, who he was, would not come to him. "What the hell you doing?" The man started down the bank sideways, moving carefully. "Stookie? For chrissakes." His flesh jolted every time he planted a foot. By the time he reached George his face was red, he was breathing hard, and there were dark stains under his arms. "Stookie?" He peered into George's face. "What the hell's a' matter with you? It's me. Eugene." He looked back up to the top of the bank and pointed. "Stephen saw you. What the hell are you doing here? For chrissakes, Stook, it's seven-thirty in the morning." He leaned closer. "Earth to Stookie. Beam me up, Mr. Scott." His face mushroomed into a big grin and then sagged again. "Come on, I'll help you up." When they were both standing the two men stared at each other. "Christ, you're a mess. What happened to you? You look like you been drowned."

George eased his arm out of Eugene's grip and walked to the edge of the river.

"Do we have a problem here, Stookie?"

A breeze blew through George's hair and clothes. "Why?"

"I don't know why. You tell me. I worked late last night, but Moira tells me Sheila was by. With the girls."

"And?"

"Apparently they were pretty upset."

George's stomach tightened. He stood there watching the river and everything in it, both seen and unseen, roll by. He had a sense of the day before. It was there, he could feel it, but he either could not bring it into focus or could not step back far enough to see it.

He turned around. "Would you come to the house with me?"

Eugene lifted his head. "What's going on?"

"I'm not sure."

Eugene seemed weary, as if he had grown tired of something that had been happening for too long. "If you like."

They crawled up the bank together. When they reached the top George saw the road some fifty feet away and across the road was the house where he lived with Sheila and Laurie and Samantha.

"I feel like a ghost," he said.

"Well, you look like somebody who's been dug up, I'll grant you that."

He looked back down at the river.

Eugene said, "What aren't you telling me?"

George was thinking of the dead bodies. It was a picture that had been in his head for so long it seemed to have been with him forever. The dead lay on the dry plain all the way up to the hills which had trapped them, and as he walked among them he always eventually found, and knew he would find, first Sheila and then Samantha and finally little Laurie scattered with the rest like so much rubble—and his heart broke, not simply over the fact that they had died, which was bad enough, but that they had died struggling on this desert of his imagination, that they had died in a way for him, and in a place where there was no love and no kindness, only the silence of hearts that had stopped beating and that would never beat again.

"What?"

"Something. You're not telling me."

"No." There was but he didn't know what it was. "No."

They went around the side of the house and stopped by the back door.

"D'you have your key?"

"I don't think it's locked."

"Sheila's car's not here, Stook."

"Try the door."

It opened. Eugene looked at him.

George nodded.

Eugene started to go up towards the kitchen. George said, "Down here," and flicked on the basement light.

Even before they reached the bottom of the stairs, Eugene said, "We'd better call the cops."

George sat down on the last step. "No." It had all come back to him.

"Stook. Stookie?"

He pressed his knuckles into his forehead and pulled his elbows together.

He had done this, he remembered doing it, he could see himself doing it, but he could not feel it. It made no sense. It was like listening to an argument going on in another language in another room.

"Why don't you want to call the police?" Eugene was standing over him, looking down at him.

Sometimes he woke up like this in a hotel room in another city or on the side of the highway in the middle of nowhere, and he always felt the same surge of panic. But this time he had stayed. Why? Why this time had he not climbed into his car and driven away, gone to a place where he couldn't hurt anyone, where he couldn't do what he had obviously done? And then the panic came rolling back, the shortness of breath, the sense that he was falling and would fall forever, the sense that he wasn't there.

"Why don't you want to call the police?"

You could always buy a new chair and make it comfortable again, eat popcorn with your kids on your knee again, squeeze in beside your wife and plan a vacation in it again. You could always buy a new chair.

"Stook?"

TWO

The yellow van is parked on the street. It used to be a school bus. Take maybe ten kids to school in the morning and home again in the afternoon. Through the windows he can see the tops of the seats.

Sheila is leaning against the side of it, arms folded, ankles crossed. She is looking out at him through long, sun-bleached hair. She is smiling.

Walking towards her he is vaguely wondering why she is driving a school bus. Or more exactly why she brought it here.

She pushes her hands into the pockets of her jeans. "D'you like it?"

He is twenty-seven. She is twenty-five.

Two weeks earlier he had stepped into the office of Shore Bus Lines looking to buy a second-hand bus or van.

Eugene was waiting for him outside. "How'd it go?"

"No dice." He climbed into Eugene's car. "They use them all, and if they retire one it's because they can't fix it. She said even then they usually keep it around for the parts until it's stripped and then it's sold for scrap."

"She?"

"The girl in the office."

The shocks were worn and the car dipped and swayed as they crossed the culvert to get back onto the road.

"You wanna try that other place?" Eugene said. "It's the last one. This isn't looking too good, man."

George was thinking of the girl. "Where is it?"

"A ways."

"What d'you think?"

In the office of Shore Bus Lines, it was the strangest thing. He could feel it happening even as he stood there telling her that he played in a band and that he was looking to buy a second-hand bus and asking if they ever sold any.

This falling away of space. So unexpected, so unplanned for.

She had looked up from her desk. Big pale green eyes in a long, suntanned face. Burning with a strange summer sun. Brawny, almost.

There was a can of Coke on her desk and a half-eaten sandwich on a piece of wax paper, and she was holding a thick paperback book in one hand with her forefinger in between the pages to keep her place.

She pushed her hair back. She was wearing a red shirt. She smiled. "You're not from the school board." Then she frowned. "Are you?"

He said to Eugene, "Let's leave it. We're not getting anywhere this way. We should make some phone calls tomorrow, try some of the dealerships."

"Maybe you're right."

But the next day he borrowed Eugene's car and went back to Shore Bus Lines alone.

She looked up from her desk and smiled. "You find a van yet?"

"Not yet."

Behind her there was an inner office. A man raised his head to see who had come in and then lowered it again.

Her elbows were on her desk. She put her hands together and leaned forward. "So what can I do for you?"

"You got any plans for tonight?"

"Tonight?" She began to move some papers around. "You don't waste much time."

"I'm sorry."

"No." She stood up. "I mean, it's okay."

"Have you ever seen us play?"

"I don't think so."

"D'you want to?"

"This is your band?"

"Yes."

"Where?"

"The Windso."

"Okay."

"I'll pick you up."

"I'll meet you."

Was this a no that only sounded like a yes? "Okay."

"What d'you play?"

"Bass guitar."

"D'you have a singer?"

"I'm the singer."

"D'you have a name?"

"George Stookner, but call me Stookie."

"I'm Sheila."

"Well, okay then, Sheila, tonight."

"Tonight."

She didn't come, and he was surprised at how disappointed he felt. He kept looking for her at the door and walked through the bar looking for her every time they took a break. But she wasn't there. Oh well, he thought, that's that.

But the next night as he was climbing off the stage, he saw her sitting at a crowded table. Tables were hard to find and almost as soon as he went over he realized she was not with anyone there.

He invited her to sit with the band. It was not the greatest place to watch them. They had a table tucked in the corner, and looking up all you could see of the stage was a narrow space between the building-block stacks of equipment.

"You're so loud." She laughed and put her hands over her ears. The strap of her purse slipped off her shoulder and caught on the bend in her elbow. "D'you always play so loud?" She sat down. "You must all be deaf." Still smiling, she shifted her eyes from his face to the rest of the room. "I'm sorry I didn't make it last night." She had put her hands together and was looking at them. Then she glanced at him and smiled again. "One of the drivers got sick and I had to go out on a run. By the time I got home I had this humungous headache. D'you know what kids can be like on a school bus?" She lifted one shoulder and let it drop. "Or I would've been here." She put her tongue on her upper lip and, with a quick turn of the head, took in her surroundings. "Are you angry?"

"No. Of course not."

"Because—I don't know—sometimes people get angry when you don't do what they want." She was watching him.

"I don't know anyone like that."

"Good," she said. "Then neither do I."

He introduced the other members of the band as they returned one by one to sit at the table before going back up onstage. The first was Doug Klassen, their drummer. Then came the keyboard player, Jimmy Long. And finally Eugene Baker, their lead guitarist.

She would not let him buy her a drink, but she stayed for the second set and the third. In between and after, they talked. He could not keep his eyes off her.

When she said she had to go, he walked her to the door. There he turned her face towards him gently with the tips of his fingers. "I don't have your phone number," he said.

Smiling and trying not to, biting her lip, she dug a piece of paper out of her purse and wrote it down for him.

"What is this?" George says. He tries not to think that maybe his prayers have been answered.

"What does it look like?" Standing in front of the yellow

van with her hands still in her pockets, she looks at him from behind the spill of her hair. She is tall and slim, almost willowy. "So?" She tosses her head to swing the hair out of her face and hooks it behind one ear, but she is holding her head on an angle and her hair slowly falls a few strands at a time over her face again. "Are you going to just look at it for the rest of the day or d'you want to take it for a test drive?"

"You're kidding?"

"I'm not kidding."

"Where'd you get it?" He is slowly walking the length of the van.

"I phoned around. D'you like it? Will it do, at least? The seats can come out to give you more room for your equipment."

"This is amazing."

"I had one of our mechanics check it out. It's got a lot of miles on it, but he figures it'll get you to Calgary and back at least twice."

There is a *Rolling Stone* interview that plays in George's head from time to time.

Rolling Stone: When did it all come together for you? Was there a moment you can put your finger on?

(Stookie doesn't answer right away. The hotel room is large. There are empty Chinese food cartons on a table, pop cans, beer cans.)

Stookner: We were doing okay. You know, we paid the bills. The three of us had this house back then so we split the rent, you know, three ways.

Rolling Stone: Three ways?

Stookner: Doug was already married and he and his wife had an apartment. Although he kicked in a few bucks once in a while to help out 'cause the house was like the band's house. It's where we rehearsed, where we kept the equipment. It was headquarters. It was the office. A nice big old house. Nobody bothered us, nobody complained. In Elmwood.

Rolling Stone: Where's that?

Stookner: Just a part of the city. But we did okay, you know. Wherever we played they sold enough beer to make it worth their while, which was what we were there for. But it was like we were stuck. Eugene and I had been playing the local bar circuit—sometimes together, sometimes in separate bands—for almost ten years. I was eighteen when I moved to the city. I knew exactly what I wanted to do. I had the dream. You know? I'd worked in my dad's store for maybe a year after high school to get some cash together.

Rolling Stone: So you didn't grow up in Winnipeg?

Stookner: No. In Dauphin. It's a little further to the north and west a bit.

Rolling Stone: And Winnipeg was the place to go?

Stookner: For a guy from Dauphin, yeah. But after ten years, it can grind you down. It was okay, don't get me wrong, there was a scene, and like I say we paid the bills, but we were getting stale, nothing was happening. We wanted to move on. You can be great in your home town but if nobody else has heard of you, it doesn't mean a whole lot. You know? Our manager had these gigs in Calgary and Edmonton lined up, but we had no way to get there. We were using Eugene's car and a U-Haul in the city, but it wouldn't've been any good on the highway. We needed a van or a small bus. But in those days the banks wouldn't touch us. Then I met this girl.

Rolling Stone: Sheila?

Stookner: Yes. I heard this horn out on the street and didn't think too much of it until Eugene told me I'd better come over and take a look out the window.

Rolling Stone: What was it?

Stookner: A van. Sheila had found us a van.

Rolling Stone: And three albums and five top-ten singles later . . .

Stookner: Yeah. We took it for a test drive, and by five o'clock that afternoon we had the plates on.

Rolling Stone: Was it a good deal?

Stookner: Sure, but that's not the point. It's simple things

like that which can make all the difference between bustin' out
and not. You know what I mean?

She rolls away from him and sits up on the side of the bed. In
the candlelight her back is a smooth arc from her hips to her
shoulders. He is not expecting anything bad to happen. It was
only a few minutes ago, wrapped in her arms and legs, chasing
the future buried deep inside her, that the heat of the sun had
stiffened his whole body. He could not have done anything
else except hold onto her even if he had wanted. The electric
snap at the base of his spine made his hips jerk and he took a
swan dive off the highest bridge he could find and thought, as
he fell, that he would fall forever into the river of Sheila's eyes
which were open and staring up at him as his were open and
staring down at her, until the very last moment when his arms
tightened and he pushed his face into the side of her neck, and
tasted oblivion.

But as the silence grows he begins to feel nervous. He
wishes she would turn around so he can see what she might be
thinking. He wants to know that everything's okay, he wants
to see the beauty rise in her face, he wants to see it, as he has
seen it before, dance on her smile.

Instead her hands are curled into fists. "There's something
I haven't told you." She turns her head briefly to look at him
but he cannot see her eyes through her hair. He can only hear
her voice. It usually rumbles like healthy timber. Now it
sounds cracked and full of holes as if some kind of worm is
slowly eating it up from the inside.

"I'm listening," he says. But he isn't. He's remembering
calling her every night from Calgary moments before the band
climbed up onstage for their first set. She was always there,
almost always picked up the phone on the first ring, and said
in a wondering, searching voice, "Hello?" They had arranged
none of this. He had simply called the first night. By the end
of the band's second and last week in Calgary, those five minutes

on the phone had become the centre of his day. Doing a little sightseeing, or working on some new songs with Eugene in the hotel room, even while they were up onstage—she was always there, always a part of it.

The band had enjoyed a good two weeks in Calgary, good crowds, and a good reaction both from the audiences and from the owners of the two bars they had played. On the Friday of their first week in town, one of the FM stations had interviewed them and broadcast one of their sets live. It was a real high. And you could hear it in the way they played—tighter, more intense. They had even begun to rehearse some of the songs Stookie and Eugene had been writing, working them out acoustically in the hotel room and then trying them out onstage.

Taking his turn at the wheel on the way back to Winnipeg, he felt as if they had crossed a bridge. He still really didn't understand how they had acquired the van. The financing was fuzzy. Frankly, it seemed too good to be true. His own fantasy was that a record company had already spotted them and was greasing the wheels for their success. It wasn't something he told the others, for obvious reasons. But however it had come to be, the van was theirs and they all felt this sense that it could take them anywhere. There was this sudden chance. All the way back they had begun to quietly talk among themselves about putting some kind of demo package together and shopping it around to the majors.

"Sheila," he said, staring down the tunnel of the high beams at three in the morning as they rolled east through Saskatchewan. The others were asleep. Glancing in the side mirror from time to time he would see the side of the U-Haul trailer they were pulling. "Sheila."

She gathers the sheet around herself and sits down in a chair in the corner. She is facing him now but he can't see her. There are only shadows—shifting, changing.

"I'm listening," he says again, bravely because he thinks he is inviting her to tell him something he does not want to hear. She has always been a little mysterious about herself, and as he feels his insides shrinking he realizes he knows almost nothing about her. He has never met any of her friends, hasn't heard her talk about them—or her parents. He doesn't even know where she lives. She always meets him somewhere, and she always drives herself home. She has a car that's less than a year old and he knows where she works. Beyond that all he has is a phone number.

He wonders—is she married, does she have a boyfriend, is she going away? Is she going to tell him this has all been a mistake?

He has always assumed that, in her material circumstances at least, she is like him.

She says, "You know that place where I work?" It is not a question, although it sounds like a question. He waits.

Moments before he could see her turning in the shadows like a prisoner looking for a way out. Now she is very still. From her knees up she blends into the darkness as if she is not there. "My father owns it."

He lowers his head, and nods as if he should have seen this coming. He feels smaller than he did thirty seconds ago. He feels toyed with. She is going to end whatever it is they have begun because her father is, loosely speaking, rich—and so is she. He wants to cover himself but she has the only sheet.

"They would like to meet you," she says. "My parents." Her voice is cold.

He opens his mouth but cannot find anything to say. Is it bad that her parents want to meet him? Does she not want them to? Is she afraid he will refuse? There is no up or down to this.

"I'd understand if you didn't want to." She pauses, and in the pause he hears her fear. It is like a bell ringing in the distance. Why is she afraid?

"Don't you want me to?"

"It's because of the van."

"What's the van got to do with it?"

"My father . . ."

"Your father?"

"I found it but he bought it. He asked me what kind of payments I thought you could afford and I told him."

"I don't get it."

She gives a little laugh. "Are you starting to feel trapped?"

"Should I be?"

"Yes." She rises out of the darkness and into the light from the candle, but she stays where she is on the other side of the room. "It's not fair, it's not fair to you. It's manipulative. My father's like that. It's one of the ways he gets things done. He manipulates people—to get them to do what he wants. So I'd understand if, I don't know, you felt threatened or anything, and if you wanted to stop, you know, seeing me."

He goes to where she is standing with the sheet wrapped around her. "Stop seeing you?"

"There are things you don't understand."

"Like what?"

"I just didn't think it would go this far. I didn't think it would come to this."

"What?"

"This. This. This conversation, the two of us here like this."

"Because your father helped us get a van?"

"You don't understand."

"You keep saying that. What don't I understand?"

"My father."

"Are you afraid of him?"

"Afraid? No."

"What then?"

"This is ridiculous, Stookie."

"I don't care about your father. Okay?"

"I don't want to see you get hurt."

"D'you want to stop seeing me? Is that why you're telling me this?"

She shakes her head. "No."

"Because I don't have any money? I'm a bad risk?"

"Oh Stookie." She moves towards him. "Don't think that." She puts her hands behind his head, pulls him gently forward. "Don't ever think that." Kisses him.

"Stay here tonight."

"I can't." Kisses him again. "I have to go to work in the morning."

"Go to work from here."

Kissing him. "We both need some sleep. What time is it?"

He finds his watch. "After three."

"I have to be up to go to work in four hours."

"Show me where you live."

"Tonight?"

"I'll follow you in the van."

"Tonight?"

The house stands on a leafy street. It is bigger than he had imagined—three storeys high—but older too. He thinks, colonial. The foundation is stone, the walls are brick. Everything else is painted white, including the two wooden columns that rise from the broad stone steps to hold up the porch roof.

He follows her to the front door. There is a big glass oval in it. No lights are on except for a disc around the doorbell button. She puts her key in the lock.

He had thought he was simply going to see the house she lived in and then say good night in the driveway. But he is standing with her at the front door. He isn't ready to say good night and she doesn't seem ready either.

"D'you want to come inside?" She takes his hand. "Come inside."

The first door leads to a second door. Everything is wood, a dark wood, old wood, polished. The space between the two doors is a mere few feet, a little room with nothing in it.

The second door isn't locked but there's a step up. She stops to warn him about it, and he realizes something has happened between the two doors. Her face shines with an excitement that might or might not have anything to do with him. It is similar to the kind of excitement he experienced as a ten-year-old boy when he stole a candy bar just to see if he could get away with it.

Walking towards her . . .

She is wearing a light cotton dress and tennis shoes with no socks. Her legs are bare. He wants to raise the dress up over her head. He wants to feel her body against his. But she is already turning away from him. For a moment he thinks she will disappear forever into the dark wood that surrounds them. But she holds out her hand. It floats, pale in the darkness, waiting for him, and when he takes it she pulls him to her.

They are face to face. She has made up her mind. She says in a whisper that is almost a kiss, "I'm going back with you." They are standing in a big hall just inside the door. "But let me get some things first." They have only the moonlight to see by. She frowns, sniffs the air. "My father's been smoking his cigars." Then, "Wait here."

She flees up the stairs so silently all he can hear is the swish of her dress.

"So you must be George." A chair turns in the next room, and all of a sudden he too can smell the smoke. The cigar glows for a moment, and he catches a glimpse of a face.

For a long time the man in the chair is no more than a shape. George steps into the room. "Mr. Shore?"

A hand comes out of the darkness. "George." It is warm and meaty in Stookie's grip. "It's a pleasure."

Shore stands up and turns on the light. He is like his hands. He returns from the light switch walking like a man who would rather drive to wherever he has to go.

He rubs the back of his neck. "This is a surprise. A pleasant one of course, but I hadn't expected the pleasure quite so soon. Sheila's told us so much about you. Please. Sit down." He gestures with his cigar to a chair near his own. "Would you like a drink? Scotch, rye? Something else?"

"No. Thank you."

"A cigar?"

"No thank you, sir."

"Call me Jack. . . . I do this sometimes"—he raises his cigar—"when I can't sleep. Sit down, George. Did Sheila tell you we wanted to have you over for dinner?"

"She said you wanted to meet me."

"Sit down, sit down. Chance has thrown us together a little early, that's all. I'm sure Mrs. Shore won't mind. Sit down."

He takes the offered chair. When Mr. Shore sits down he swivels his slightly from side to side, then puts one elbow on the armrest and leans into it. "I like to think of myself as an honest man, George, and a fair man. Mrs. Shore and I naturally place a great deal of interest in the well-being and happiness of our only child and daughter. And for the moment at least that well-being and happiness seem to be tied up in you." He glances into the hallway. "Where is she, by the way?"

"Upstairs."

"Waiting for you?"

George dips his head. "No. I'm . . . waiting for her."

"Don't be embarrassed. I tend to say what I think. I'm an honest man, George, and a fair man. Do you follow me?"

"I'm not sure I do, sir."

"Call me Jack." He puts his cigar between his teeth, closes his lips, and takes a long pull before blowing a cloud of grey smoke towards the ceiling. "I'll tell you flat out, George, I'm not much good with music. I don't understand it. I don't understand what you do and I don't understand why you want to do it. Quite frankly it baffles me. It even makes me feel a little uncomfortable. I mean, it's not a career I can imagine anyone choosing. It's not really a career at all, is it?—in any traditional sense. But I'm smart enough to know that all people are not alike. It would be a pretty boring world if we were, wouldn't it? But what I'm talking about here, George, is Sheila. That's what we have in common. Isn't it? Her well-being and her happiness."

"Yes, sir."

"Call me Jack. I don't intend to embarrass you, George. I don't intend to ask you a lot of personal questions which you may not at this time feel prepared to answer."

"Yes."

"But I want you to know if you are serious about my daughter I will do everything in my power to assist in making the both of you happy."

George nods. He doesn't know what to say or even what to think.

"Hell"—Jack laughs and turns the cigar between his thumb and first finger—"she's my daughter, George. I want her to be happy, I want what's best for her."

"We should talk about the van."

"Don't worry about it. A gesture, a token. Glad to help. You're serious too about this music. I can tell. I don't understand it, but I recognize your determination and I admire that. I like the way you go after what you want."

He sits back, rolls the end of his cigar around in the ashtray. When he lifts his head his smile has stiffened and he is looking past George. "Sheila," he says. "There you are."

"What are you doing up, Dad?"

George turns in his chair so that he can see her.

"Couldn't sleep." He holds the cigar beside his head. "George and I were just talking."

"What about?" She is not smiling.

"Things."

"What things?"

"Hush now, Sheila, hush now." He stands up and goes towards her. "You're going to get yourself all upset."

"What things, Daddy? What—things?"

"This Freya nonsense is over. It's all over. D'you hear me? It was a long time ago." He holds her by the shoulders for several seconds, then turns and takes a few steps back to George. "I expect you'll be wanting to go home now, George. Thank you for seeing Sheila home. Is this Sunday all right for you? Say around five o'clock. Nothing formal. We'll barbecue some steaks. Mrs. Shore will be looking forward to meeting you."

George tries to catch Sheila's eye on the way out, but her face is turned the other way.

Three

"Who is she, Stookie? Who the hell is this—broad—for chris-sakes?" Dee Dee Lavallee is standing in front of him. She wants to know, she has a right to know, and she's not leaving until she gets an answer.

"Dee Dee . . . "

"Cheesus, Stook. Why now? Did I do something wrong? It's humiliating is what it is. I have to hear it from Sarah. Fuck and double fuck. I'm so pissed off, Stookie. You have no idea." Dee Dee in her go-go boots laced up to her knees steps around him and walks into the house, Dee Dee in her tight jeans and leather jacket and with her long dirty-blonde hair. "Wait till I tell her—is she around? is she upstairs?—wait till I tell her that's my stuff hanging in your closet, Stookie, you no-good, big-time double-crosser you."

"Dee Dee, it's five o'clock in the morning."

"So? You're a musician, for God's sake. Since when did everybody start going to bed so early? Or did I catch you in mid-fuck. Huh? Or what?"

"Shhh." He holds a finger up to his lips. "Come into the kitchen."

"Is she up there? What's her name?"

"Sheila. No, she's at home."

"Some kind of rich bitch, is she? Got you wrapped around her finger?"

"No, Jimmy's the one you're gonna wake up."

"He still with that little pill-popper? Brenda?"

"Yeah."

"What about Eugene?"

"He's not here tonight."

"But what about him?"

"What, what about him?"

"I'm just asking, Stook. Don't give me such a hard time."

They go into the kitchen.

"I can't believe you didn't tell me," Dee Dee says.

"I haven't seen you."

"You've been avoiding me, Stook. Admit it. You went out of your way not to see me. I have to come here and bang on your door at five o'clock in the morning to talk to you, to get you to admit you're seeing somebody else."

"Dee Dee . . ."

"I know, I know. You never promised me a rose garden. And okay, sure, I stray."

"Stray? Dee Dee, you go from band to band to band."

"Why do you always have to exaggerate?"

"I'm not exaggerating."

"It was different guys in the different bands, Stookie. From time to time. Not the whole fucking band. And I always come back. Don't I?"

"Dee Dee . . ."

"I thought you wanted it casual. If you'd said something, if you'd complained, anything. If you would've let me know, Stookie."

"Dee Dee . . ."

"She's just another one of your airheads, Stook. This—whatever-her-name-is. And you'll get tired of her like you got tired of the others."

"Airheads?"

"Well, what d'you call that Debbie person? How long d'you live with her? Six months?"

"What's that got to do with anything?"

"And she threw you out."

"It doesn't mean she was an airhead."

"She threw you and your stuff out onto the street, for God's sake. Give me a break."

"We had problems. She wanted me to get a regular job. Every day we'd be fighting. I kept trying to patch things up."

"You're too nice, Stookie. Why don't you just call her a bitch and get it over with? I mean, really. She didn't know what she had. Give yourself some credit, Stook. I mean, I haven't been coming back here because I like the house you guys live in, believe me." She folds her arms—"So?"—and settles against the table. "How serious is it? Do I give you another week, another two weeks? How long?"

"I'm gonna ask her to marry me, Dee Dee."

"Marry you?"

"Yes."

"And d'you think she'll say yes? On a scale of one to ten."

"Eight."

"Have you met her parents?"

"Last week. They invited me for supper."

"To their house? Really?"

The kitchen door swings open. "Oh hi, Dee Dee."

"Oh hi, Jimmy."

"We got any aspirins, Stook? I got this fuckin' headache, man, and there's none in the bathroom."

"There's some in the cupboard, over the sink."

"What are they doing there?"

"Dunno."

After Jimmy goes back upstairs, Dee Dee says "Well," and shakes her head. "Married yet. Fuck me. I wish." She slings her purse over her shoulder. "But I'll see you around. Right? You're not gonna drop out of sight or nothin'." She looks hard at him. "Are ya?"

"No."

"Good." She starts tapping her foot. "So what's up with Eugene? Did you say he was seeing somebody or not?"

FOUR

There were crusty bread rolls on the table.

He took one and then offered the basket first to Laurie, then to Samantha.

"No."

"No thanks, Dad."

"Sheila?"

Her eyes moved across his face without stopping. "No thank you."

They were eating in the dining room. They had breakfast and, when they were all home together, lunch in the kitchen, but always tried to have supper in the dining room.

Samantha said, "May I be excused?"

"Yeah, me too," Laurie said. She looked cautiously at both her parents.

It seemed important to him that they all stay at the table until supper was over. And so he said, "You haven't finished what's on your plate," but in a nice way, with a smile.

Sheila sighed and said, "Run along if you like."

"Don't go too far," he called after them.

The back door slammed shut.

He looked at Sheila and she looked at him.

They were all going to go to the shopping centre together. The idea was that each of them would have a say in picking out the things that needed to be replaced.

"The insurance'll cover everything," he told her.

"The insurance?" She put down her knife and fork, carefully. "The insurance has nothing to do with it, George. What it has everything to do with is those two little girls who just ran out of here."

"What I meant—"

"You don't deserve them, George. You really don't."

"And you do?"

"I'm their mother."

"And I'm their father." He heard the anger in his voice, but as always it was as if it belonged to someone else. "I'm sorry," he said.

She turned her head. "I don't know if I can take much more of this, George. I mean, we've almost gotten used to your disappearances. One day you're here and the next we're waiting for you to come home for supper. I used to worry, but I can't keep on worrying, not unless you at least try to help yourself. But you don't. I used to tell the girls you'd had to go away on a business trip suddenly, but they don't believe me anymore. They know, George. They know Daddy's just gone—because you don't love them enough."

He slammed the flat of his hand down on the table hard. The bread rolls bounced. "That's not true."

"What is true, George? What is the truth? What you did to the house last week, what you do to me every day, day after day, what you do to the children, is that the truth?"

"The insurance . . . ," he said.

"Don't start."

" . . . won't cover it, I know. But it'll cover a lot of it. Some of it."

She stood up. "It's not insurance we're talking about, George. It's not things."

They went to Polo Park.

The idea was to walk through the mall and stop to look at anything they liked. But it was his idea. The others were merely going along with it—maybe out of a sense of duty or maybe out of a sense of hope.

He put his hands in his pockets and hung back, in no hurry, stopping when the others stopped, starting up again when they started up.

He had paused to look at a row of jars full of coffee beans. Some of the beans were darker than the others, but the only way you could really tell one jar from another was by the labels: "French Roast," "Vienna," "Dark Saigon." He had not even stepped inside. He had simply stopped to look in through the window.

He was about to say, "We should get some good strong coffee." He was thinking that he and Sheila, if not the girls, could drink it Sunday morning. They would buy enough for one small pot.

But then Sheila said, "Where's Laurie?" There was concern in her voice, a kind of mild surprise, but no panic.

He turned around, aware of a certain heightening of his senses. He thought he would spot her right away. He thought if he just looked hard enough he would see her. When he didn't, he felt a rush of bewilderment.

He saw Sheila looking at him. Her concern had turned to fear. She put her hand to her mouth. She spoke so softly he hardly heard her. She said, "She can't be far."

Samantha came closer. "She was here just a second ago. I saw her."

Sheila pulled Samantha in to her side. "It's okay, honey, we'll find her."

"Laurie," George shouted. His voice echoed off the tile and glass but at the same time seemed contained by it. A few shoppers turned to look. Most ignored him. "Laurie."

He started back the way they had come. "Laurie." He didn't go far but when he turned around he saw Sheila running down one of the aisles into Eaton's with Samantha right behind her. "Stay together," he called after them. "Samantha, stay with your mother." He didn't know if they had heard him. "Samantha."

"What's the problem, sir?"

Two men in blue suits with walkie-talkies on their belts were standing in front of him.

He almost went around them before they stepped back in front of him and he realized they were speaking to him. "It's my daughter, we can't find her," he said.

One of the men pulled out a notebook. "When did you last see your daughter?"

George opened his hands and gestured to one side. "She was just here. Right here. Here."

"How long ago?"

"A minute, two, maybe three."

"What does she look like?"

"She's a little girl."

"What colour is her hair?"

He felt frustrated. He took a deep breath. "Brown."

"What was she wearing?"

"Jeans, and a green tee-shirt."

"Anything on the tee-shirt?"

"A tree. It was from Earth Day. A green tee-shirt with a tree on it."

"Height?"

He held out his hand to just below his chest.

The man with the notebook looked and said, "A hundred and fifty centimetres."

"How old is she?"

"Six."

The other man began speaking into his walkie-talkie. "We've got a little girl. Missing. Six years old. Answers to the name of . . . ?" He released the talk button.

"Laurie—Laurie Stookner."

"Answers to the name of Laurie Stookner." He began to describe her using his partner's notes.

From out the corner of his eye and while she was still a long way off he could see Sheila bearing down on him. Samantha followed but was moving more slowly than her mother and without her mother's purpose. Sheila stepped in front of him while the security guard was still speaking into his walkie-talkie. "Why don't you do something?"

"I'm trying."

"Instead of talking to these idiots."

The look on her face made him nervous.

"Is this your family, sir?"

"Yes." He put his arm around Sheila but she pulled away. "My wife, Sheila, and our other daughter, Samantha."

"What have you done with her?" She levelled a finger at George. "What have you done with my little girl?"

The man on the walkie-talkie held his earpiece, apparently listening to what was being relayed back to him.

The other man was saying "There's no cause for alarm, ma'am. We're all here to help. From what your husband has told us, your daughter must be nearby. We've alerted all our security personnel to watch for her. We're checking stores, hallways, service areas—any place she might have wandered into or gotten lost in. We have every confidence that we will find your daughter in a very short time."

Why didn't George believe him?

The man continued, "A public address will be going out any second."

Sheila put her hand to her mouth and backed away.

"The best course of action for you folks to follow right now is for you all to stay here. First of all, so that when we find Laurie we know where you are and can bring her to you. Another reason is that when she realizes she's lost contact with you, she may well try to make her way back to where you were all last together. If you're not here, she won't have that opportunity."

Sheila wrapped her arms around herself. "I don't believe this is happening."

"We're going to start a search of this immediate area. With any luck at all we'll have found your daughter within the first five minutes. But please stay here. Okay?" He gave them a professional smile, which disappeared as he turned towards his partner. "Let's go."

George ushered Sheila and Samantha to a nearby bench. "He's right. There's no point in all of us wandering off in all directions."

Sheila sat down. "We'll wait here," she said, and turned her head away.

He put a hand on her shoulder and felt how stiff she was.

Samantha said, "I wanna go with Dad."

"No you won't." Sheila grabbed her arm so hard George wondered if he should say something.

"But Mum—"

"Stay with your mother, Samantha."

"But Dad—"

"She needs you. And I need you here together. And so does Laurie."

At first he stayed close by so that when he came out of a store he could see Sheila and Samantha on the bench where they had agreed to wait.

Sheila sat stiffly, staring straight ahead. The only time she moved was when she ran her hand up and down Samantha's arm. She looked almost resigned, as if Laurie's name had already been posted among the missing and she was feeling the pain and the horror of it.

In that numb vacancy there may have been only enough room left now for Samantha. In her inner heart of hearts where lived all that meant the most to her and which contained all that she could count on, he did not think he would find himself. In her heart of hearts he suspected he was dead—if he had ever been alive, if he had ever been more than a convenience, a means to an end, something to put in the window. Yet he loved her, still loved her and would continue to love her. It was the one warm spark in the lump of his failing flesh, something good, something true, something almost holy and that made him what he was. And he could no more put it out, he could no more stop loving her, than he could stop his children from growing up.

When he came out of the last store he could come out of and still keep Sheila and Samantha in sight, he went over to them.

Samantha looked at him expectantly. Sheila merely looked —with cold, untrusting eyes.

He said, "I guess the security guys haven't reported anything."

Samantha glanced at her mother and then back at her father. "Not yet."

"Look, I'm going to check a little further down. I might be a few minutes."

"We'll stay here, Dad."

"Watch your mother for me."

She smiled. "Okay, Dad."

He didn't really know what he was looking for. When he came to a door that said "NO ENTRY," he stepped through it on a hunch and found himself in a service corridor. Nothing fancy here. Concrete floors, windowless walls. For a moment he thought it was a dead end. But then he thought, why not? He hadn't had any luck anywhere else. So he continued on until he reached another door. He pushed it open, and before he realized it, he had stepped out onto the parking lot. The door went *k'thump-click* behind him. He turned around and found himself looking at the smooth surface of a firmly latched steel door.

He pried at the edges with his fingertips. His chest tightened with frustration. Then he thought, had Laurie come this way?

It was still a hunch, but he had stepped into the service corridor without anything stronger to go on. It was a little ball of light rolling around inside his head saying yes, maybe, yes.

But if she had come this way, was it by accident, had she wanted to come out here; and was she alone, or had someone taken her this way? He felt his heart pounding again, his throat tightening. Maybe she was out here, or had been out here a few minutes ago. Maybe.

After the air-conditioned mall, the day's stored heat rising off the lot grabbed him like a hot blanket. He tried to think. Looking around, he saw he was not very far from where they had parked the car. He had nowhere else to begin. He would go to the car, start there, retrace their steps.

He saw the top of her head before he realized what he was looking at. Moving from car to car, he thought he might only be seeing what he wanted to see, or a shadow perhaps or a reflection. But as he came closer he realized it wasn't a shadow or a reflection.

She was sitting behind the steering wheel, and still all he could see was the hair on the top of her head. But already he could smell the fresh clean shampoo scent of it, see her pale blue eyes full of surprise and wonder turning up to him, feel her soft and gentle fingers in his hand, hear her voice like a song punctuated with the sweet refrain of "Dad," "Daddy."

He paused by the back bumper and took a deep breath.

"Hi, sweetheart," he said as he laid his arm along the frame of the open window.

She looked at him as if not at all surprised to find her father alongside the car while she was driving down the highway. "Hi, Dad." Keeping her hands steady on the steering wheel, she returned her eyes to the front.

"You going somewhere?"

"Yep."

"Where?"

"On a trip."

"On a long trip?"

"Yep."

"By yourself?"

She shrugged.

"Well, okay, I guess. Will you send us a postcard when you get to where you're going?"

She glanced at him so quickly he would have missed it if he had blinked. "Sure."

"Did you bring your money?"

"I've got traveller's cheques."

"Traveller's cheques, even better. You sure seem to know what you're doing. You're very well prepared."

"Thank you."

"Okay then." He nodded. "D'you think maybe you could phone, just to let us know you're okay, 'cause we'll all be worried about you. You could reverse the charges, you know. D'you know how to reverse the charges?"

"Sure." She turned the wheel back and forth a couple of times.

"If you have any trouble getting through, the operator'll help you. Just press '0'." He paused and looked around. "Well . . . I just wanted to make sure you were okay." He leaned into the car and kissed her on the side of the forehead. "Bye for now."

He started to walk away.

From the corner of his eye, he saw her turn and look over her shoulder at him. As he continued to walk away, her head swung back slowly in a series of three or four jerky movements.

He made a wide circle around the car until he was approaching it from the front.

He stopped about a car-length away. He had been walking slowly as if he weren't going anywhere in particular. When he stopped Laurie still had her hands on the steering wheel. She leaned forward and peered at him.

If the car had been on the road he would have been standing at the curb on the passenger side, eyeball to eyeball with the younger of his two children who had wandered away probably not by accident and who was now pretending she was on a trip that would put as much distance between herself and the people she lived with as she could imagine. He hadn't planned any of this. He hadn't planned on finding her out here in the middle of a blacktopped parking lot, so when he smiled and put out his thumb as if to hitch a ride, the gesture was almost as much a surprise to him as it was to her.

But she didn't hesitate. She leaned over and pushed open the passenger door. He ran up and peered in. "Where you going?" he said.

"That way." She pointed.

"Me too."

"Hop in."

"This is mighty nice of you." He climbed in and shut the door.

"You'd better do up your seatbelt."

"You a fast driver?"

"Yep."

For the next minute or so, however, she seemed more interested in driving regally than quickly.

"Laurie," he began.

"That's not my name."

"No? What is your name?"

"Annie Oakley."

He put a finger on his cheek and looked at her through half-closed eyes. "I thought Annie Oakley rode a horse."

"Sometimes. But sometimes she drives a car."

"Like now."

"Yes."

"Well, Annie Oakley, have you seen a little girl in your travels? She's real pretty and has beautiful shiny hair that's a lot like yours. Her name's Laurie."

She had to think about this. Her eyes moved from side to side and her tongue came out. "Maybe."

"I'm her father."

"She said you made her cry."

"Did she? Not on purpose, I hope."

"She didn't say."

"What else did she tell you?"

She shrugged.

They sat for a while not saying anything, watching the road unfold in front of them.

"That's a big truck ahead of us."

She nodded.

"Maybe you oughta back off a little. Or maybe pass it."

"I think I'll pass it."

"Don't forget to signal."

"I won't."

He closed his eyes and waited. "Have we passed it yet?"

"Oh, a long time ago." She took her hands off the steering wheel and put them in her lap. "Dad?"

"What is it, sweetheart?"

"Are you going to leave us?"

He took a breath and held it against the rush of pain. "No, of course not," he said. "I would never do that."

She turned her head and looked at him. "Are you and Mum gonna get . . . like divorced?"

"What makes you think that?"

"I dunno. It's just that . . . sometimes you don't seem to like each other."

"Come here."

She moved across the seat and tucked herself under his arm. "How can I explain? Sometimes your mother and I—we disagree."

"Is that why you smashed up the basement?"

"No."

"Then why?"

"It's not easy being an adult, and some people aren't very good at it. Does that make any sense?"

"Aren't you an adult, Daddy?"

"I'm not a very good adult."

"Is that like when I get into trouble for being bad?"

"No. It's a lot worse than that."

"Yeah?"

"Can I ask you a question?"

"Yes."

"Have you ever been afraid of me?"

"Yes."

"Like the other day?"

"Yes."

"Are you afraid of me now?"

"No."

He pulled her more tightly against his side and she put her arms around his waist. "Your mother and I love you and Samantha very much, and we love each other very much."

"I don't like it when you yell."

"I know, honey, I know." They held onto each other. "Better now?"

"Better."

"By the way," he said, "who's driving the car?"

"It's okay. I parked on the side already."

"I see."

"Can we go home now?" she said.

"Sure. D'you want to drive or d'you want me to drive?"

"I'll drive."

"Okay."

In no time at all they were back where they had started.

"You're a pretty good driver."

"Fast. For sure."

"But not too fast."

"Of course I'm careful, Daddy."

"How did she get into the car?"

"She knew about the spare key."

"Was the car running?"

"No. Once she opened the door she put the key in her pocket."

Sheila turned onto her side and put her hand on his chest. "I wasn't much help to you today." She looked down. "I'm sorry. You hear all those stories about children being kidnapped right out from under your nose. It happens all the time. I didn't know what to think."

She was propped up on one elbow. In the darkness of their bedroom he could only see the shape of her face change as she went from relief to concern and back to relief again. And he could see her eyes. He couldn't read them in the dark, but he could see they were wide open—the way they were when she was happy—and he could see them moving over his face.

He reached up, cupped the back of her head in his hand, and drew her towards him. On this early summer night he had hoped for nothing more than a kiss. But her mouth opened to his in a way he had almost forgotten about.

FIVE

He was lying in a ditch. He turned his head. The front of the Volvo was less than five feet away.

He was trying to remember how he had ended up here.

Déjà vu.

In the sky a single cloud drifted between the tops of the pine and fir trees.

He pulled himself up onto his knees and looked around. The road he had driven off was narrow. It was a fire or service road. The trees crowded it along both sides almost everywhere, except here. He had been lucky. The ditch he had driven into was shallow. It looked like a natural depression, as if the ground had collapsed a few years ago perhaps and taken the trees with it. It had no real shape, a few rocks, some bush and scrub grass.

The air was cool. It was September, the Labour Day weekend. He knew that much. But was it Saturday, Sunday, or Monday?

He continued to kneel for a few moments, waiting to see if he could remember anything else, but the only thing that came to mind was an image of himself driving along the Trans-Canada Highway with Sheila and the girls, and Sheila saying, "You're going too fast, they won't be able to keep up," in a pleasant voice, not scolding, and Samantha saying as he eased up on the gas, "Does Leo know how to water-ski, d'you think?" They had been on their way to the cottage.

But when?

A wave of nausea came over him. He got to his feet, and his headache, which he had been half aware of a moment ago, now began pressing more forcefully against the inside of his forehead.

There was Tylenol in the glove compartment. He licked his lips. His mouth felt dry and scummy.

It was then as he turned towards the car that he saw the hand hanging out the open window on the passenger side.

Had he picked up a hitchhiker?

He tried to see in through the windshield but the face was jammed down too low in the seat.

The driver's door was open. He stepped around it and looked in.

Eddie.

He had his left hand clutched around a bottle of rye. It was the bottle George kept hidden in the trunk for emergencies.

He reached over, got the Tylenol, and dry-swallowed two extra-strengths.

"Whooos zat?" Eddie said. "Whooos z-air?" His face twitched. "Huh?" It was a few seconds before his eyes fluttered open. "Mr. Stookner?" He blinked. "Hi." He grinned, pulled himself up, and saw what he was holding. "Some hair of the dog?" He raised the bottle to get a better look and shook it. "I figure we got maybe a swallow each."

"Where are we, Eddie? D'you know?"

Eddie climbed out. "If you're asking, we must be lost."

"What happened?"

"I don't know. We went into town, had a few drinks."

"Kenora?"

"Sure, Kenora." He leaned against the front fender and opened his arms. "Where else is there to go?"

"But why?"

"You don't remember?"

"No."

"You and Sheila had this big fight. D'you remember that? Back at the cottage. By the way, that's a nice place you got."

"I remember coming down. And sitting around and eating hot dogs. Eugene got the barbecue going."

"Yeah, it was all that campfire kind of shit. You know? Everybody singing songs. It was a drag."

"But what happened?"

"Don't shit a shitter, Mr. Stookner." He lifted the bottle to his mouth and took a pull.

"Help me out, Eddie. Humour an old guy."

"Come on."

"I'm serious."

"Piss off."

"You said something about a fight. What kind of a fight?"

Eddie moved his head about two inches and then his eyes the rest of the way. "Well, basically . . . you and Sheila . . . "

"Yes?"

"You had this fight. You don't remember that?"

"All I remember is eating hot dogs."

"Not then. The next day. Yesterday." Eddie shook his head. "Man, you really are out of it. Or maybe you don't want to remember."

"What were we fighting about?"

"I think the both of us know that, Mr. Stookner."

"I'd had too much to drink."

Eddie flashed a grin. "Look, Mr. Stookner"—he came around to the front of the car—"having a few drinks is no crime. Sometimes you need a good soak." George saw Eddie's small pointed teeth, his pale face, the tiny wedge of vomit in the corner of his mouth. "It can be good for you. It's like getting laid, sometimes you just have to do it and forget about who gets hurt. It's nature's way."

"Nature's way?"

"Yeah, like the song. Come on, you had a few drinks. Forgive yourself, Mr. Stookner. Because both you and I know that ain't the problem, not the real problem. The real problem is something else, the real problem is something you don't even want to talk about."

George looked up at Eddie's face quickly and saw something a little too eager in it. He didn't know Eddie very well. He knew he was Leo's boyfriend, as far as that went, and he knew he dealt in cars and wanted to open a u-drive. Eddie had taken him back to the place where he wanted to open the u-drive once, and they had had a drink together on a couple of occasions to talk about it. Once he had even invited Eddie back to the house because it seemed a sociable thing to do, and then wished he hadn't. Eddie wanted him to buy into the u-drive. He came right out and said it, more than once. "Seed money," he called it, "to get me off the ground. A shrewd investment. Painless. For a man like you?" But George told him he didn't have that kind of money. He offered to talk to Jack. But Jack wasn't interested.

Eddie had refused to take no for an answer. His offer still stood, he said. There had been a number of phone calls. Eddie had been persistent.

"Forgive me, Mr. Stookner. It was just a little friendly advice." He held out the bottle—"You sure?"—and took another swallow. "Anyways, where was I?" He exhaled. "You and Sheila. There's not much to tell. The two of you were working so hard to pretend you weren't having a fight." He shook his head and tried not to smile. "But everybody knew. Every time one of you got near the other, we all held our breath. After a while Eugene's wife—what's her name?" He snapped his fingers but they didn't click. "Moira—she took the kids into town if only to get them out of there.

"It's a funny thing, Mr. Stookner. Leo's been bugging me all summer to take her to the lake. Normally I just don't have the time. There's the pressures of business and all—which as a businessman yourself you can appreciate. And besides, I'm not much for sitting on the beach. All that sand and water, it's boring. But when your invite came, through Leo of course, I couldn't refuse. I was hoping we might have the opportunity—much like this—to talk.

"Did you see what she was wearing yesterday?"

"Who?"

"Leo. Come on, Mr. Stookner. You saw. I know you saw. The black bikini. You were sitting on the end of the dock with a big glass of something at eleven o'clock in the morning—a big glass of something and it wasn't all 7-Up, Mr. Stookner—watching the boat out on the lake with Leo and Eugene and Sheila in it. They looked like they were having a good time. Leo's never water-skied in her life. But she got pretty good at it after a while."

"Is there a point to this, Eddie?"

"Sure there's a point. There's always a point, Mr. Stookner. And the point here is—the black bikini."

"Leo's."

"Exactly."

"I still don't see where we're going with this, Eddie."

"I'll tell you where we're going, Mr. Stookner. We're going to the heart of the matter."

"You've lost me, Eddie."

"The real question, Mr. Stookner, is why your wife would buy it for her. 'Cause I'll bet you dollars to doughnuts she did. Leo's got no spare cash. And if she did she would've bought herself a new one before now. She wouldn't wait till summer was over. Sheila bought it for her. To come out here. Like they planned it. And I figure you're thinking the same thing.

"Now picture this. Indulge me. Okay? Imagine them going shopping for it, imagine them going into the change room together while Leo tries it on, or imagine Leo putting it on for her somewhere a little more private. Huh? Think about that for a minute, Mr. Stookner. Or maybe you already have. It's a funny world, huh, Mr. Stookner? Yes, sir. It's a funny world."

"And you're the tour guide."

"The truth is sometimes difficult for us to see. Or to face up to. Sometimes we need help." Eddie shook his head. "D'you remember the phone?"

"What about it?"

"You ripped it out of the wall. You went into the cottage, ripped it out of the wall and brought it outside. . . . You don't believe me."

"Go on."

"You were pissed off. You dropped it in her lap. Said she should call her father, said she should tell him to come out here and arrange everything. Something like that. 'Like he always does,' you said.

"She turned to stone, Mr. Stookner, turned to fucking stone. And she gives you this look. Man, I'm tellin' you, daggers ain't the word for it. More like guided missiles, with nuclear tips, the whole arsenal, fire when ready. But they're gone, man, launched. And not a word. Slowly she sets the phone down on the ground beside her. She's sitting in one of those lawn chairs. I figured it was over. But you're a resourceful man, Mr. Stookner. You didn't bat an eye, just picked up the phone and started walking towards Leo, holding it out to her. Sheila moves then, I'll tell you, real quick. She shoots out of her chair, tells you to leave her out of it. By this time Eugene's moving in, but we're already on our way out of there."

"Where are the kids?"

"Gone already. Like I said, Moira took 'em all into town like earlier, your two and that little pudgy thing, their kid, what's-his-name, Stephen."

George stepped around the open driver's door and climbed in behind the wheel. "I have to get back."

"What for? If I were you I'd lie low for a while."

The keys were in the ignition. "I'm gonna try and back up onto the road. Can you push?"

"What were you and your wife arguing about, Mr. Stookner?"

"You seem to have all the answers, Eddie. You tell me."

"The answer—in one word, Mr. Stookner?—is obvious. The answer is Leo. She told me about your wife a long time ago, Mr. Stookner. She did. And Leo? She's only human, and she's like most broads, follows the path of least resistance. I can't blame her. I might do the same given the right situation. Still, it's surprising what you can get by spending a few bucks on 'em. It's their nature. They're all whores at heart. They go where the bucks go, and they don't give a shit."

"Are you gonna push, Eddie?"

"Whatever you like, but I'm telling you, I don't think anybody's gonna be too happy to see you."

"Maybe not."

"Then what for?"

"My kids are there, Eddie."

"Okay, okay. But which way? D'you know where we are? I don't."

"Back the way we came."

Eddie shrugged. "S'your funeral."

"Why'd you come with me?"

"That's what friends are for, Mr. Stookner." Eddie came over to the driver's door. "They help each other out. I couldn't let you drive out of there on your own acting crazy like you were. There was no telling what you were gonna do."

George started the car. "You ready? It's front-wheel drive."

"I know what it is." Eddie placed himself at the front of the car. They nodded at each other. George put the Volvo into reverse. It trembled slightly as the gears caught. He took his foot off the brake and pressed gently on the accelerator. The first few feet went smoothly, then he felt the front end start to sink. There was a scraping sound. The car jolted to a stop as if it had hit something. He let up on the gas, but Eddie's face was turning red as he kept on pushing. "Give her, Mr. Stookner," he shouted, "give her." He did. But the wheels merely spun. The car shook and the front end slewed suddenly to one side, pulling Eddie with it. It threw him to the ground. George put the transmission into neutral and set the brake. "Eddie?" He climbed out and found Eddie picking himself up out of the grass. "Are you okay?"

He got up and wiped the dirt off his clothes. "More or less."

"We're hung up on something."

They went down on their hands and knees and looked under the car.

"There it is." Eddie swept his arm from side to side. "D'you see it?"

"Looks like a rock."

"Yeah, but it's flat. D'you see? Most of it's buried." He pulled his head out from under the car. "You see the way it sits? If we try to go back it's gonna snag on the undercarriage—rip the shit right out of your exhaust and probably fuck up the front end too—if we got that far—which I doubt we would. But if we go forward . . . "

"Forward? Over this? The ground's too soft."

"It's a little spongy, but that way we get the back end clear. Then we go through the ditch and up the side. Piece a cake. Just don't stop till you're out."

"How come we didn't get hung up coming in?"

"Probably came in at a different angle. You can see the tire tracks. When you tried to back out you turned sharp to go straight up the side instead of taking the angle slow and easy. But we're hung up now, and unless you got a better idea, it's either forward and out or we start walking."

"Okay."

"You see, Mr. Stookner, I'm good with cars." He put a hand on George's arm. "I understand them."

"If this is about the u-drive . . . "

"You bet it's about the u-drive. That's my future, Mr. Stookner. That's my promised land."

"Not now."

"It's never now. Is it? For people like you. Is it? I'm looking at a man who lives in a big house, a man who has two cars, a couple of businesses, and a cottage by the lake. So don't you tell me the time is not now. I like you, Mr. Stookner, don't get me wrong. I have the utmost respect for you, and I would like to consider you as my friend, but this is business, and in business there is no place for friendship. It's bigger than both of us, Mr. Stookner, put together. It's like fate, and I am a man of destiny."

"I see."

"No, you don't see, Mr. Stookner. That's the problem. You don't see, but I do, and what I see, Mr. Stookner, is a man stalling, you stalling me, Mr. Stookner, on this u-drive deal, passing me off onto your father-in-law when you've known all along he ain't gonna bite—or maybe you're tellin' him not to. I don't know. But I ask myself, why? Why would an intelligent man like Mr. Stookner fuck me around like this when he knows my deal has to be done quick if it's to be done at all? I ask myself, how come? Is it because he thinks I'm a jerk? Some two-bit nobody who'll bend over for any Tom, Dick, or Harry?"

"Eddie, I told you already, I don't have the money you're talking about."

"Maybe, maybe not. But you can get it. For starters, you could probably shake a few bucks out of old Jack. Find a way."

"Why should I?"

"Because you been stringing me along, Mr. Stookner. And now you owe me."

"You're out of your mind."

"Do I have to spell it out for you?"

"Back off, Eddie."

"What I want is twenty thousand dollars up front and I want a line of credit for another twenty thousand at the bank of your choice."

"You are crazy, man."

"Draw up any kind of papers you want. It's a loan. I'm not asking for charity. Charge interest. I want it done right and I want it done legal, but I want it done by next Friday."

"I told you I don't have that kind of money."

"So cash in a couple of bonds, sell one of Jack's buses."

"Forget it, Eddie. There's no way."

"I'm not gonna let go."

"Then fuck off. Okay?"

"What you say?"

"Just fuck off. Is that plain enough for you?"

Eddie spun away and threw his arms into the air. "You miserable little piece of shit. Who the fuck d'you think you are, to talk to me"—he hit himself in the chest—"to ME, like that?"

"Eddie, you're dreaming."

"What the fuck is wrong with you, man?" He put his hands in his pockets but his elbows continued to flap. His anger had made him sweat, which forced some of the alcohol out of his pores. George could smell it. Eddie must have pissed himself at least a little during the night as well because he could smell that now too. "I don't dream, Mr. Stookner. I don't dream. I deal. I deal—big time."

"And what are you gonna deal for, Eddie?"

"It's simple. It's what deals are all about. You got what I want. Or you can get it. And I can give you what you want. Capiche?"

"You've been watching too many movies, Eddie."

"Shut up. Okay? Just shut the fuck up. And listen. For once."

"You wanna make a deal?"

"Deals is what I make, man. It's what I do."

"Your destiny, like what you said—before."

"Yeah. It's what I am. You could learn from me, Mr. Stookner. You could learn that business is the art of seizing the opportunity when it presents itself."

"And what opportunity is that, Eddie?"

"The opportunity to get Leo—how should I put it?—out of the picture, removed from the situation, banished, so to speak, from the hearth, expelled from the stage of your domesticity. It's Leo who makes you nervous. It's Leo who's ready to upset the old apple cart—if she hasn't upset it already."

"I'm gonna try and get us out of here, Eddie." George climbed back into the car. "D'you wanna push?"

"Haven't you been listening to anything I've said?"

"I heard every word, Eddie. And d'you know what it adds up to? A pile of shit."

"D'you think I'm making this up? Don't you know about your wife?"

"You leave Sheila out of this, Eddie. And if you even try to hurt her . . . "

"What?"

"This conversation is over. Now are you gonna push or are you gonna just stand there?"

Eddie stepped away from the car. "You're hung up on a rock, Mr. Stookner. If I push maybe you'll get out. If I don't, you're not going anywhere." He folded his arms.

"Suit yourself." George put the transmission into "drive" and took his foot off the brake. There was a brief scraping sound. The car moved an inch, maybe two, then stopped. He eased down on the gas pedal. The car shook as the wheels bit into the ground. The front end drifted to the right a little, and then the wheels caught, and the car moved forward about a foot. But he could feel it settling. He stepped harder on the gas. He heard the dirt thumping up into the wheel wells, but the car kept moving forward, slowly, and then a little faster and a little faster.

He swung to the left and started up the slope. The front bumper exploded through a small hummock of earth and grass, and although the car seemed to be trying to shake itself to pieces, it had enough momentum to keep going forward. Then, as he was about to reach the shoulder, it lurched to the right, and for a second he thought he was going to slide sideways back down into the ditch. But the back end swung around enough to keep it steady, and by then the front wheels had gripped and the car simply dragged itself over the edge and up onto the road.

The fire road came out onto a provincial highway, and almost right away George knew where they were. Half an hour later they were rolling up to the cottage.

All the way back Eddie hadn't said a word.

It was a little past nine-thirty in the morning.

Sheila was sitting in a lawn chair. She was wearing a large sun hat and sunglasses. Leo, dressed in jeans and a tee-shirt, was walking with the girls in the water along the edge of the lake. Eugene was scraping the grill on the barbecue and Moira was carrying a tray with glasses and a pitcher of iced tea down the steps and out towards the picnic table. Stephen was building a sand mountain between the grass and the water's edge.

It was like driving into a photograph. All eyes turned towards them, and then for a handful of seconds nothing moved.

"Daddy," Laurie cried out from the water. She started to run towards him. He and Eddie had left the car and were standing on the deck overlooking the lake. "Daddy."

He met her at the bottom of the steps, caught her under the arms and lifted her high into the air, and held her there against the clear blue sky and the sun and the trees. Samantha had followed her sister but more slowly. When he set Laurie down, she was standing a few yards away. "Hi, Samantha." She put her arms around him and pressed her face into his chest.

Laurie grabbed one of his hands and was trying to pull him forward. "Did you see any bears? Uncle Eugene said you might meet some bears."

"Son of a bitch," Eugene said, "were you out there all night?"

"We had a little accident, eh, Mr. Stookner?"

"Accident?" Eugene looked concerned.

"We got stuck. Nothing major."

Sheila got out of her chair. She walked past them and went up into the cottage. With her sun hat and dark glasses George couldn't see her face.

"Went off the road is what we did." Eddie seemed almost proud.

"Damn it, Stookie, you could've gotten yourself killed driving in the shape you were in. And Eddie, and whoever else happened to be around."

Stephen turned his attention back to his sand mountain.

Eddie started walking towards Leo. "Aren't you glad to see me?" he said to her.

Leo was still standing by the water. She wasn't looking at Eddie. She was watching George.

Moira set her tray of iced tea down. "I don't know how you can work with him."

Eugene said, "Don't start with that. Don't."

"This must be the last straw. Even for you."

In a loud voice Eugene said, "How about a glass of that iced tea, Moira?"

He found her sitting at the kitchen table turning an empty coffee cup around and around. The window above the sink was too small, and even on the brightest of days it was a dreary room. He reached for the light switch.

"Don't." She put her hand up to shield her face and then slowly lowered it when the light did not come on. She had taken off the sun hat and dark glasses.

He pulled out a chair across from her and sat down, but she stood up and walked over to the sink.

"I haven't always made things easy for you," she said. "Have I?" She was almost whispering, as if she were talking to herself. "Between my father and me"—she turned around—"we must've pretty well taken away everything you ever wanted."

"That's not true, Sheila."

"It's me, I know. The way I am, I mean. You can always tell when I'm interested in someone. Sometimes I think you know even before I do. But there haven't been a lot, Stookie. Very few, in fact."

"Stop it."

"You always assume the worst, even if it's just somebody I've seen in the street and will never see again. How do I give myself away? Do I seem happier? Or don't you even know that you know?" She walked to the end of the counter. "I must disgust you. Even my thoughts . . . must disgust you."

"Stop it."

She wrapped her arms around herself. "Leo is my lover."

"Stop this."

"My lover, George."

"Then get rid of her."

"Let me have this."

"No."

"I need her, Stookie." She turned her head from side to side. "I'm in love with her."

"No you're not. You just think you are. It'll pass. You'll get over it."

"I've never come to you before like this."

He stood up. "If you won't, I will."

"What?"

"Get rid of her."

"Where are you going?" She marched hard on his heels into Leo and Eddie's room. They had not brought a lot, but he threw whatever he could find onto the bed. Sheila tugged at him. "No," she said. "No. Don't do this, Stookie. No." He pulled off the sheet and dragged the bundle out of the cottage and flung it off the deck. Things were spilling out before it even hit the ground. "Eddie," he shouted. He had begun to sway, and he leaned on the railing to steady himself. "Eddie, pick up your things and get yourself and your girlfriend out of here. Now."

Eugene was still cleaning the barbecue. Eddie, with his hands in his pockets, was standing beside him. Moira was nearby at the picnic table with a glass of iced tea. Stephen's sand mountain had fallen down and he was building a new one. Leo was playing pat-a-cake with the girls.

They all stopped and looked at him.

"Eddie? D'you hear me? I've had enough."

He stood there listening to himself and watching himself as if from a great distance. He didn't know who this person was who had just dragged a sheet full of somebody else's possessions outside, and he didn't know who this person was who was yelling at them to get out.

He hesitated. "I . . . "

And still no one moved.

He turned around to look back into the cottage. Sheila was pressed against the side of the door frame. She looked terrified. She had one hand clamped over her mouth, and her eyes were open as wide as he had ever seen them.

"I . . . "

From behind him he heard Leo call out, "Laurie!" Too late she had reached for her, and now she simply watched, with the others, as Laurie walked up to him.

When she was about halfway there, when she passed between Eugene and Moira and Eddie, Samantha started walking towards him too.

What had he said to Sheila? To the others? What had he done?

Solemnly, the two girls climbed the steps to the deck and then stood in front of their father. "Don't send Leo away, Daddy," Laurie said. "She's our friend."

"Yeah, Dad, I mean, like, what are you *do*-ing?"

He was staring into middle space. A moment passed. Then he looked down at the two faces, Laurie, more like him, and Samantha, more like her mother. He ran his hand through his hair. "Your old dad's not feeling so good right now. Will you help me pick up Leo's stuff and take it back inside?"

They did, and once back in the room he realized how much he had left behind—obvious things like a hair dryer, a tote bag, and the large towel Leo had brought with her and which was hanging over the back of a chair. It struck him hard like a blow to the belly when he thought that not only would her smell be on it, but that Sheila at some point might have pressed it to her face to breathe in the smell.

Sheila had gone back into the kitchen. He didn't glance in when he left the cottage, and once outside he walked past the others without looking at them.

He dragged a lawn chair into the shade of the trees. He turned it towards the lake, sat down, lit a small cigar, and began to wait for the numbness to go away. How long would it be this time? A day, a week? Was it just the booze that made him feel like this?

The others started doing again whatever they had been doing. He sensed them moving and heard their voices, quiet at first, then slowly returning to normal. He felt as if he were somewhere else. Not twenty feet away, but somewhere else entirely, as if he were merely haunting them.

His head snapped back and he realized his cigar had slipped from his fingers. He had dozed off, and the sun had moved so that his feet, stretched out in front of him, were no longer in the shade. He pulled them back and then leaned over to pick up the cigar. He was wearing a long-sleeved shirt buttoned at the wrist, an old pair of cotton slacks, and the Hush Puppies he usually wore when he cut the grass. He was aware that the day had grown hot. Even Eddie had taken off his jacket and rolled up the sleeves of his once-white shirt. But George felt chilled, as if his arms and legs had been sitting in ice water.

He was patting his pockets for matches to relight his cigar. Moira was talking to Leo. He did not realize that he had something to do with their conversation until he saw Leo coming towards him with a glass of iced tea in her hand.

"Moira said you should have this." She held out the glass to him.

She stood stiffly, and several moments passed before he rose to his feet and took the tea. "I'm sorry," he said, "about this morning. And yesterday too. I'm afraid I haven't been a very good host. I hope none of your things were damaged."

She relaxed a little, shifted her weight to one foot. "No damage. Messed up maybe."

"You don't like me much, do you? I mean, as a general rule of thumb."

"Is there a reason I should?"

"Hey, Leo, get over here a sec." Eddie gestured with his head. He was standing with his hands in his pockets between the barbecue and the picnic table.

Eugene looked worried. He was standing behind Eddie. They had been talking a short while ago.

Leo turned and shaded her eyes. "What for?"

"Don't give me 'what for,' just get over here."

"I'm busy."

Eugene tried to say something to him but Eddie stepped away.

"Leo, I'm not gonna tell you again."

"Good. Now—d'you mind?"

She turned back to George, but George had his eyes on Eddie, and he was coming towards them.

"Leo and I were talking about her water-skiing, Eddie."

"She learns quick enough." He took her by the wrist. "Come over here, I wanna talk to you."

She shook him off. "D'you have to grab?"

"I wanna talk to you." He took her by the wrist again and this time she couldn't shake him off.

"Eddie, will you cut it out? You're hurting me."

He led her off into the bush and trees that separated George and Sheila's cottage from their neighbours', the Ackers. "What did you tell that little fuckhead Eugene about me? What did you tell him about my business?"

They had stopped at a small clearing a little ways in. George could hear them quite clearly.

"The u-drive?"

"You go behind my back to do this?"

"I didn't tell him nothing."

He pulled her up against him. "You don't tell nobody nothing about my business. Never. You understand? My business is my business."

George stepped into the clearing. "What's going on?"

"Stay out of this."

"Let her go, Eddie."

"Fuck you, man."

"Let go of her."

"Hey, this is private. Okay?"

"No, it isn't, Eddie."

He relaxed his grip and then slowly took his hand away. "Okay. Okay, Mr. Stookner. But she's got no right—no right."

"Cheesus, Eddie, I only told Eugene that you wanted to open that goddam, fucking u-drive of yours. I thought maybe he could be an investor or something—like what you're always talking about. I was trying to help, for chrissakes."

"Don't. Okay? Just don't."

"Leo?" It was Sheila. "What's wrong? I heard voices."

Leo glanced at her and then at the two men. "It's okay."

Sheila moved towards her slowly at first, then more quickly. "Your arm." She took her hand by the fingers and lifted it up. "Who did this to you?"

"It's okay, Sheila. Really."

"It's not okay." She ran her fingers over the roughened skin.

"She's tough." Eddie stood there with his hands on his hips. "She can handle it."

Sheila turned around slowly as if being called out of a dream. "Did you do this?"

Eddie shrugged and looked the other way. "It was an accident."

Sheila walked up to him. She was taller than Eddie by a couple of inches. "An accident?"

He refused to look at her. "It just happened. No big deal. I wanted to talk to her."

"So you grabbed her."

"Look, get off my case, lady." Eddie stepped back. "I didn't hurt her."

"Look at her arm."

"She's okay. What's with you guys?"

Sheila threw him a stiff look. "Come on, Leo." She put one arm around Leo's shoulders and started to lead her back towards the cottage.

Eddie waited for them to take a few steps. "Mrs. Stookner?" he said. "I wanted to ask you. How long d'you think you can keep up the charade?"

Sheila slowed down, then stopped.

Leo tugged at her. "Don't listen to him."

"What charade, Eddie?"

"Come on, Mrs. Stookner, I'm not stupid, you know. Don't you think I know what's going on?"

"I haven't the slightest idea what you're talking about, Eddie."

"I'll give you a hint."

Leo turned on him. "Shut up, Eddie."

"I'm talking about you and Leo." His grin spread slowly. "I'm talking about you fucking my girlfriend, Mrs. Stookner."

Sheila went still.

Eddie glanced from her, to Leo, to George, and back to Sheila. "A rumour, Mrs. Stookner? Just a nasty rumour? I don't think so 'cause I got this straight from the horse's mouth."

"You're lying." Sheila's voice had become a whisper.

"I'm not lying and you know it."

George stepped towards Sheila. "Tell him. It doesn't matter. He knows. Just tell him."

"Leo?"

"So what's it gonna be, Mrs. Stookner? Are you a dyke or aren't you?"

"I don't have to listen to this." But she didn't walk away. She turned and then turned again like someone walking the edge of a cage.

"Are you fucking my girlfriend or not? Yes or no? It's not a hard question."

"What did she tell you?"

"Enough."

Leo said, "Shut up, Eddie."

"What did you tell him?" Sheila had her thumbnail pressed against her lower lip.

"She told me, Mrs. Stookner. And we had a good laugh."

"Liar," Leo screamed. "Don't you see what he's doing?"

"Stop this, Eddie. Stop it, right now. Is it the money? I'll get you the money."

"You stay out of this, Mr. Stookner. You had your chance and you blew it. Timing, like I told you before, is everything. You guys have fucked me around for too long, and I'm tired of it." He turned back to Sheila. "So what's it gonna be, Mrs. Stookner? Yes or no?" He waited.

George said, "Tell him, Sheila. There's no point."

But all she did was stand there.

"Well then," Eddie said, "I guess Leo and I'll be on our way. Rumours are funny things, aren't they?" He took Leo by the arm. "Let's go."

She pulled free of him.

"Let's go," he said again.

Leo was staring at Sheila, but Sheila turned away.

Eddie put his hand in the small of Leo's back and gave her a nudge. "Come on."

They started back. Leo turned her head a couple of times to look, but Sheila was already making her way down to the beach. George watched her go. When she reached the water's edge she started along the shore in the direction that led out towards the point. He felt her loneliness, her away-ness, and felt even more keenly his inability to do anything about it. It was at times like this that he didn't exist for her. He was the shadow on the wall, the pattern in the carpet, the ticking of the clock—no longer seen, no longer heard.

He walked back to the cottage with this feeling growing inside him.

Eddie was loading up the car.

"Aren't you staying for lunch?" Eugene came around the corner carrying a plateful of hamburger patties. "There's enough for everybody."

"We gotta get back," Eddie said. "Hafta meet a guy this afternoon."

"Kind of sudden, isn't it?"

Eddie stepped around George, who was standing there watching all this, and threw the last of their stuff in the back seat. "Yeah, kinda."

Leo was sitting in the car. At the last moment she got out and walked up to George. She paused, and then she said, "You're okay, Mr. Stookner."

She didn't wait for an answer, she probably didn't want one. She got back in the car and a few minutes later they were reversing out onto the dirt road.

Sheila didn't come back to the cottage until the middle of the afternoon.

On the way home she sat pressed up against the passenger door. The girls were huddled in either corner of the back seat. They didn't play I spy or chatter or sing songs or read a book.

She went to bed as soon as they arrived home. George and the girls unpacked the car. They had soup and sandwiches for supper. The girls asked about their mother, and he said that she was going to be all right. They accepted his assurances with a mixture of hope and trust and maybe a little willing suspension of disbelief, and left it at that.

They watched TV until it was time for Laurie to go to bed. Samantha took her to brush her teeth.

George had an idea. It was probably crazy but he didn't know what else to do. While the girls were out of the room he phoned Eugene. Eugene, Moira, and Stephen had left shortly before them, and they had taken the boat. Eugene and George had winched it out of the lake and up onto the trailer together. Eugene was concerned and curious, but he had asked no questions, concentrating instead on the job of securing the boat to the trailer. He was still concerned and curious when he answered the phone that evening and George asked him if he would come to the house and look after the girls for a couple of hours.

Eugene said he'd be right over.

George explained to Samantha that he had to go out for a little while and that Uncle Eugene was coming over to sit and that if she or Laurie needed anything they should go to him and let their mother sleep. Okay?

Samantha nodded. "Eugene lets us watch TV," she said, but as if she was thinking about something else.

"Don't let Laurie stay up too late though now."

"I won't."

He copied Leo's address from the phone book. He wouldn't have been able to even get into her building, he realized once he arrived there, if someone had not used a popsicle stick to keep the street door from latching.

He found her apartment at the end of the third-floor hallway. Loud music came from the door next to hers. Behind her door, though, there was no sound. He knocked. The air was hot and stale. He looked down and saw a cockroach struggling over the carpet. He knocked again. There was still no answer.

Now what? He felt he had to see her. He didn't know whether it was for Sheila or for himself that he wanted to do this. What he feared most at that moment was falling into the great sea of the unloved and the unloving. Looking for Leo was like reaching out blindly to the only person who didn't appear likely to drown in that sea with him, with them. She was too young not to have hope. Wasn't she? If nothing else he wanted to feel her hope as Sheila must surely have felt it.

He knocked a final time and was turning to leave when he reached for his wallet and pulled out Eddie's business card. Eddie had pressed it upon him some time ago, and George had all but forgotten he even had it, until now. The only other place Leo was likely to be, George was thinking, was at the address printed on Eddie's card. He examined it under one of the hallway lights. He recognized the street number. It was not far from the bookstore.

He parked in Sheila's spot, but he had hardly climbed out of the car before wondering about the wisdom of what he was doing. If Leo was at Eddie's, trying to talk to her in Eddie's presence might create more problems than it solved. That is, if he would even let George talk to her in the first place. And what would he say to her? George didn't even know the questions he wanted to ask, let alone the answers he was looking for.

So he stopped at the doughnut shop to have a coffee and think things over.

It wasn't until he walked in that it dawned on him that this was where Leo worked. At that same moment he saw her, not working behind the counter, but sitting on a stool with a cup of coffee in front of her. She was talking to the woman behind the counter. The woman looked up when he came in, and Leo slowly turned on her stool to see who she was watching. She nodded at the woman that it was okay, and as he sat down next to her, the woman said "Look after yourself" and left them alone.

"We should talk," he said.

"There's nothing to say." Leo shrugged. "I got trashed. It's happened before—though maybe not quite like this." She sipped her coffee. Nearly a minute went by. Then she said, "I'm thinking of doing something. Can I trust you?"

"What?"

"I don't want to get you into trouble, but . . . buy me a doughnut." There was a gleam in her eye.

"Haven't you eaten?"

"It's not to eat."

Leo led him to the tenants' parking behind Eddie's place. It was a small, dark lot between the building and the river. They moved among the cars until they came to Eddie's.

She said, "You don't have to stay if you don't want."

"What are you going to do?"

She put the bag with the doughnut in it on the ground. She went over to the side of the lot and picked up a piece of broken concrete. "I'm going to commit a crime. It'll make you an accessory or whatever they call it."

He had an idea now of what she was planning to do. "I'll stay."

The piece of concrete was the size of a large fist. She held it in both hands. She smiled at him briefly. "Good," she said, and lifted it over her head and threw it through the back window of Eddie's car.

It made a lot less noise than he would've thought.

She stood there a minute looking at what she had done. He stood beside her.

"Is anybody coming?"

He looked around. "No."

"He's got one of those rear window defrosters. You know? The kind with the wires in it and everything. More expensive, maybe harder to find too. I hope." She picked up the bag and pulled the doughnut out. It was a big cruller. "His favourite," she said. She took a bite out of it, then held it up to George's face.

He took a bite. It was soft and sweet. He chewed slowly, watching her as she threw the rest of the doughnut through the hole in the window and then balled up the bag and threw that in too.

They walked away.

"Will he know?"

"He'll know."

They stopped at the sidewalk. "I'm this way." She nodded towards the bridge.

"I'll give you a ride."

"Thanks, but no thanks. I can walk. I usually do."

"Sheila's a mess."

"You're tellin' me." She looked around. "Is that why you're out here?"

"Sort of."

"I always thought you were a jerk. More than, actually." She put her hands in her pockets. "Anyways, gotta go." She turned and started to walk away. But she came back. "Tell her" —she shrugged—"tell her, I'm sorry."

Then she was gone, already halfway across the Osborne Street Bridge, running.

SIX

He came home one day early.

He had been in Toronto attending a recording industry convention. Both he and Eugene, even before they had opened their studio, had discovered that they had a lot to learn. And not just about the technical side but the business side as well. When they read about the convention, they decided that one of them should go. They flipped a coin.

The convention started Friday and ended Monday. He had planned to spend the Tuesday visiting record stores, but he was more tired than he thought he would be and the expense of staying over no longer seemed worth it. He was also feeling guilty about leaving Eugene to hold the fort by himself. So he phoned the airline to see if they could change his reservation.

They could, and he flew out of Toronto Monday evening.

While waiting for his flight, he found himself thinking about kids. It was something he was doing more and more lately. He looked for them, kids of all ages, all sizes—boys, girls. And when he found them, he glanced at the faces of their parents and wondered what it would be like to be a father. The thought of fatherhood, or more exactly the thought of Sheila's motherhood, filled him with a desire for her he had not completely anticipated.

They had talked about having children, but neither of them had made it an issue. They had been married for two years, and although the recording studio managed to keep its head above water, it was a month-to-month struggle to keep it afloat. He and Eugene were carrying a lot of debt, and a few uncollected bills could sink them if they weren't careful. Maybe it simply wasn't the right time to start a family.

He phoned Sheila from the hotel, and then from the airport, to say he was coming home early. But there was no answer.

He called too after landing in Winnipeg. This time at least he reached the answering machine. He left a message. She was, he thought, probably at her parents'.

But Sheila was not at her parents'. She was at home, she was upstairs.

At first when he pushed open the bedroom door, he didn't know what he was looking at. He did not recognize the woman lying on her back with a pillow under her head. He had never seen her before. And it took him a long time to realize that the other person—the person he had assumed to be a man—was, in fact, Sheila.

She turned her head slowly, almost curiously. Her lover had seen him first, and Sheila merely followed the other woman's gaze to where he was standing.

Sheila had long hair then and it covered the side of her face, but it did not cover her eyes. She said "Hi."

He just stared at her.

Slowly she lowered her head and buried her face in the mattress. She began to cry. She clawed at the sheets. She said, "No, no, no."

He spent the night in a motel room. He lay on the bed with his clothes on and stared into the incomplete darkness, sleeping for only minutes at a time. He did not feel pain or anger as much as he felt a kind of numbness as if he had been hit by something so enormous he hadn't even seen it coming.

He checked out at seven the next morning. He drove home. To what, he didn't know. His things piled up on the grass? The locks changed? But there was nothing like that. It was more subtle. He stepped up into the kitchen, feeling as though he were walking into someone else's house. The familiar was suddenly unfamiliar. Everything looked the same but the songs that used to quietly sing beneath the surface had stopped. There was silence and loneliness. There was desolation.

He sat down at the kitchen table. He would wait. It was still early. He had no idea if she was alone or not. He didn't really know if she was even in the house. At this point there were no limits to what might be. But the shock had begun to wear off and the feeling that was left behind was a kind of revulsion. It was almost physical, as if cold fish oil were slowly spreading over his skin.

He thought whatever they had, their marriage and whatever had breathed life into it, was over. But he also felt that they would have to look at each other so that they both knew what the other knew, they would have to sit down with each other and talk, at least a little. And so with the bravery of someone who thinks he has nothing to lose, he went upstairs to find Sheila and, if she was still there, her lover. He started out armed with anger and contempt but had to sit down halfway and put his face in his hands while he wept. Several minutes passed. Then he continued up the stairs but more slowly. His anger blunted, his righteousness drained. By the time he reached the top of the stairs he swayed as if he were teetering between emotional exhaustion and rage, and never knowing from one second to the next which one would have the upper hand. For a moment he thought maybe he should leave after all. What if he did something? He could not remember feeling like this before. But he was already at the top of the stairs and the bedroom was only a few feet away. He walked in. But she wasn't there, alone or otherwise. The bed was unmade, but there was no one in it. He went through the whole upstairs and didn't find her. The not-finding actually calmed him down. It was as if he were searching for his own death and finally said to God, "Well, I tried but it just isn't there," smiling bravely against the inevitable, holding onto this little pocket of time for as long as he could.

He finally went into the basement because that was the only place he had not looked. It was also where they kept their suitcases. If she had gone, surely she would have taken a suitcase. But that made no sense because her car was still parked outside and he hadn't noticed any of her things missing, but then he hadn't been looking for her things. He had been looking for her.

There wasn't much in the basement. They had plans to put in a bathroom and a shower and a bedroom, and generally fix it up into useable living space. But right now all that was down there was the furnace, the washer and dryer, empty boxes, and stuff they didn't want to throw away but had no immediate use for.

And their suitcases.

And Sheila who, wrapped in a flannel dressing gown, was cringing on the concrete floor beside the suitcases. He stopped. He had not expected to find her like this. He imagined her strutting, laughing, crowing.

Her hair looked thin and unwashed. There were deep hollows under her eyes. "They're coming," she said.

He didn't know what she meant. Who was coming? Her parents? Her father? Only after a moment did he realize it wasn't a threat. Whoever she thought was coming filled her with fear. They would hurt her, not him. "Who's coming?"

"They are."

He dropped to his knees and stared into her face. "Sheila?" It was as if most of her wasn't there. "Sheila."

"Don't let them take me," she said, "don't let them. With their knives and their teeth."

"No one's coming."

"Lock the door."

"Sh sh sh," he said, and very carefully folded her into his chest. "No one's coming." He began to rock her, and for what seemed like hours her arms remained stuck straight out like sticks.

"Stookie," she said, "oh Stookie, where were you?" He felt her arms tighten across his back. "Don't leave me, don't leave me." She began to weep. "I love you so much. You're all I've got. Oh Stookie, please don't leave me, don't ever leave me."

"I won't," he said. "I'm here," he said. "I love you," he said.

SEVEN

It could be threadbare from time to time, but his life before he was married fitted him like an old coat. It was simple and comfortable. He knew where all the pockets were and what was likely to be in each one.

Looking back, it wasn't their wedding day or any one moment of the days and weeks leading up to it that crystallized for him the changes that had taken place or were about to take place. No, the sense that he had traded in one life for another came on the trans-Atlantic flight to London where they were to start their honeymoon. They changed planes in Toronto. Their connecting flight left around eight o'clock the same evening. Everything went smoothly. They hadn't forgotten anything. They had their passports, their traveller's cheques, their hotel reservations, their rail passes. And they had each other. Wrapped up in their own cloud, they were constantly turning to each other. A coffee in the coffee shop, browsing through the Duty-Free held a strange, shared wonder that had much more to do with them being there together than the coffee shop or the Duty-Free or even the airplane that was waiting out there for them somewhere on the tarmac.

At least that was the way it was for him. That was the way he remembered it.

Once airborne they were given drinks and then a meal. After that came the movie, and they were asked to pull down their window shades. He wondered why. It was pitch dark outside.

They were sitting on the right-hand side of the plane. Sheila had the window seat.

Later, while the movie was still on, someone a few rows ahead lifted his shade, and George was astonished to see that the window was full of light. But at two o'clock in the morning? Sheila was dozing. He had tried but had been unable to get to sleep. He lifted their shade a few inches and saw a bright band of light, and realized why they had been asked to lower the blind. He closed it again.

The movie finished shortly afterwards and he pushed the blind completely up. He was not alone. Others were doing the same and peering out. He wanted to show Sheila this miracle, but he didn't want to wake her. So he watched by himself the morning rise up in front of them in the middle of the night.

It was during those few moments that he felt as if some hand had arisen and wiped away not only time but his own past, as if he had crossed over into the morning of some strange new day where nothing would ever be the same.

Sheila opened her eyes.

"Look," he said.

She blinked and turned to the window. "What time is it?"

He listens to the tinkle of glasses in the washer, the smack of billiard balls, the muffled sounds of people talking, laughter, the clamour of the jukebox. He smells stale beer, feels the sticky beer rings on the table, and breathes in and out the fine haze of lingering cigarette smoke.

He is sitting with Sheila and Eugene.

Doug has gone up the street to the 7-Eleven. His wife phoned and left a message at the bar for him to bring home a loaf of bread. Jimmy, crouched between two chairs, is visiting friends at another table.

People come and go.

"You just like us 'cause you think we're gonna be famous." Eugene's hand is curled around a draft glass full of ginger ale.

The room is full. People are waiting up to an hour to get in.

Sheila laughs. "I like good music," she says.

Eugene bangs his glass on the table. "We make good noise, Sheila. Not good music, good noise." He laughs. "How many times do we have to tell you? You tell her, Stookie. I gotta go to the can."

She waits until he's gone. "He's a good friend to you."

"We go back a few years."

She puts her chin in her hand. "Have you finished reading the book?"

The book is *Middlemarch*. She has loaned it to him. She has already loaned him and he has already finished *Vanity Fair* and *Bleak House*. She has promised him Aldous Huxley and D.H. Lawrence.

"Almost."

It is not a book he would have picked up for himself. But he enjoys feeling his mind stretch. It is a part of what is happening to him. But he is still comfortable in his old coat. Some of the pockets have surprises in them now but it is still his coat and he still wears it with no thought of a day when he might not wear it. He is happy enough simply to live in the eyes of this woman who has accepted slowly, almost methodically, his heart, his body, and most of what he considers to be his soul.

Doug returns as Stookie, Jimmy, and Eugene are climbing back up onto the stage to start the second set. Doug puts the loaf of bread down on top of Stookie's amplifier where it will sit for the rest of the night.

In the middle of the first song when there are no lyrics to sing, Stookie, feeling the sound with his body as much as he hears it with his ears, turns to watch Eugene do what he does best. What he sees and hears and feels never ceases to amaze him.

Eugene plays with the ferocity of a charging elephant. The loose flesh on his upper arms swings as he moves back and forth. His guitar sits on his round belly like a strange, flat animal on a small hill, and he is hunched over it, listening for the sound inside himself and then tearing at the strings to get it out.

Still climbing up and down the ladder of his bass riff, Stookie steps towards the mike to pick up the next verse and feels a shyness creep over him. Sheila is out there just beyond the starkness of the lights glaring down on them. A smile tugs at his lips and he knows he will remember this night for the rest of his life. He will remember the ordinariness of it, and it will stand for the days when he was most happy, when nothing seemed impossible, and when death seemed a long long, long long way away.

"It's the future I'm thinking about, George. Your future. Some security for you. I think the idea fits in very nicely with what you're already doing. And builds on it. The two things don't have to be mutually exclusive."

"I don't know, Jack. It's not anything I've considered before."

George and Sheila's father are huddled in a corner of the Skyview Ballroom at the top of the Marlborough Hotel. It is George and Sheila's wedding reception. All the speeches have been made and the guests are dancing.

"A recording studio could be a nice little profit centre for you, George. I've done some homework and the business is there."

"I'd have to talk to Eugene."

"You're partners?"

"In most things."

"In a venture like this a partnership might be the best way to go."

"And Sheila, I'd have to talk to Sheila."

"Absolutely."

"Have you said anything to her?"

"No. It's just an idea I've been trying to work through in my head. I haven't spoken to anyone about it. Except for the few phone calls I've made to get a feel for the situation and its viability."

"And?"

"There's an opportunity here—for the right person."

"Okay, but I need time. To think."

"About what?" Jack takes a sip from his drink and watches his son-in-law's face carefully. "Don't be squeamish, George. We're all family here."

"Well, for instance, where am I going to get the money for something like that? It would be a bundle, and I don't have anything to offer a bank that would make them even listen to me."

"You'd have my name." He pauses to let this settle in. George has not entirely failed to anticipate this line of discussion. Jack makes circles in the air with his drink. "And of course I'd like to invest substantially myself in any endeavour that involves the welfare and happiness of my only child and daughter. Money isn't the problem, George." He raises his eyebrows and, lifting one finger off his glass, touches it to George's chest. "The only question here is your will to make it work. The only question here is your desire. We'll find the money. The money is not the problem."

"A wonderful party, Jack." George's father is standing a few feet away. He's holding a drink and smiling. He's a round jolly man, a pharmacist who owns his own drugstore. He and George's mother have come in from Dauphin for the wedding and are staying as guests at the Shores' house. George's mother, a small woman who goes to the hairdresser once a week, is dancing with a provincial cabinet minister. His parents are overwhelmed with George's new life. They have been worried about him ever since he left home but have always encouraged him in whatever he wanted to do. But they never expected this. Sheila has told him that his mother and hers are getting along famously. The Stookners arrived at the beginning of the week and his mother and her mother have gone for long walks together and on even longer shopping expeditions. George's brother, Jerome, is here too. He is dancing with the maid of honour. George asked him to be the best man. He is a rigger in the Alberta oil fields and he was hard to get a hold of. The message "Phone your brother" finally got through to him via the company office. Over the phone Jerome shouted his congratulations. There was a lot of background noise. He turned away to tell whoever was with him that his little brother was getting married. "When?" he said. Then, "I'll be there." As it turned out he flew in less than an hour before the rehearsal. George was waiting for him at the airport. They hadn't seen each other since the Christmas before last when they had both gone home for the holidays.

"An absolutely wonderful party." There are tears in his father's eyes.

"I'll leave you two alone." Jack touches the senior Stookner on the arm as he steps away.

Father and son embrace. "I'm so happy for you, Son. I'm so happy for you."

SHEILA

ONE

He said it like a frog croaking. "Faggot." It was one of Petey Macauley's standard jokes. When people ran out of things to say he would drop it into the lull. "Faggot." And everybody would laugh.

Including Sheila. Petey was a funny guy. He didn't have to work at it. He just was. He had watery blue eyes set in a freckled face and red hair that stuck out on either side of his head. At parties he drank Club beer until he passed out.

He was one of Sheila's old friends from high school. They were both in second year, and between classes they'd hang out with a bunch of different people at the University of Winnipeg's fourth-floor cafeteria, called the *buff*. It was a broad, well-lit area where you could have a coffee, get something to eat, and even find a corner to study in if you didn't want to go into the library.

"What's up?"

Jill Franklin, Roger Lemay, Andy Lichinsky, and Rosemary Thompson were at the table when Sheila sat down. It was Friday afternoon and the place was starting to feel empty.

Roger said, "Jill's broke again."

"All I was saying was—"

"She went skiing over Christmas." Roger smiled. "Whistler, no less."

Sheila removed the lid from her coffee cup and took a sip. "Expensive?"

"And I didn't even pay for my plane ticket."

"Her parents," Rosemary said, as if to say "I wish."

"It was a Christmas present."

"Don't forget," Roger said, "there's broke and then there's broke."

Andy was rolling a cigarette. "You seen Petey?"

"He said he was going to the Mall for a beer."

"It's such a dive." Rosemary picked up her lighter and waited while Andy leaned his cigarette into the flame.

Sheila laughed. "Petey'll go anywhere for a beer."

"I wouldn't mind a beer." Andy held his cigarette out at arm's length and admired it.

"You're burning," Jill said.

"What?"

She reached over and flicked a glowing piece of tobacco off the lapel of his tweed jacket. "Ash."

Roger said, "I could use a beer too."

And so it was decided.

The bus depot was across the street from Manitoba Hall. They went in through the bus bays and then followed the corridor to the beverage room of the Mall Hotel.

"Hi, Petey," Rosemary said. "We've come to join you."

Sheila helped Roger drag a table over.

There was an army parka hanging off the back of the chair next to Petey's. They all thought it was his. But when Jill tried to sit in it Petey said, "Chair's taken." He reached for his beer. "And there's books on the floor there somewhere, eh."

"Who you havin' a beer with, Petey?"

"I ran into her on the way over."

"Her, no less." Jill sat down in the chair one over, folded her arms on the table, and leaned forward. "Who's the lucky girl?"

"Freya."

She pulled back. "Freya Delaney?"

"Why not? She likes to talk, she enjoys a good laugh."

"Where is she?"

"I was powdering my nose."

Sheila had taken a chair at the other end of the two tables. She lifted her head to see a pale, thin young woman standing next to Petey. She had short, straw-coloured hair and almost no figure at all. She was wearing jeans and a green paisley shirt.

"Miss me, Jill?" Freya said.

"Like shit."

Petey leaned back until he was looking straight up at Freya. "Sit down." When she didn't right away he said, "You were here first."

Freya wasn't carrying a purse, not even a small one. Maybe it was on the back of her chair, but when she had returned from the washroom, both her arms had been swinging freely and there was nothing hanging from her shoulder. It would have been an insignificant detail if it had not caused Sheila to feel a ripple of desire. It was as if a hungry voice had whispered in her ear. That Freya should not be carrying a purse made her seem more like a boy, which she wasn't, which somehow made her seem more like a girl, which she was but different.

Freya sat, and Jill came over to take the seat beside Sheila. The waitress, with her tray tucked between her wrist and hip, was taking their orders.

"Ignore her," Jill said, "and she'll go away."

At first Sheila thought she was talking about the waitress, but the waitress was already walking back to the bar. "Who?"

"Freya. Just ignore her."

"But why? What's wrong with her?"

"Anybody hungry?" Andy stubbed out his cigarette and stood up. "Potato chips?"

"Go for it," Roger said.

The beer arrived, and then Andy returned a few minutes later.

"Okay, I got barbecue, I got salt 'n' vinegar, I got ketchup, I got sour cream and onion, I got . . ." Andy tossed the bags of chips onto the table one by one.

Everything was fine until their waitress came back to see

if they wanted another round. Great, Sheila thought, she could use another beer, and was about to hold up her empty bottle so the waitress could see the label. But the waitress wasn't looking at her. She was looking at the bags of potato chips. "What's this?" She pushed at one of the bags. "Where'd you get these?"

Everybody looked at Andy.

"Next door," he said. "The bus depot. In the shop there."

"We sell snacks at the bar."

"But these don't cost as much." He looked at the others for support. "Right?"

"Listen, honey, when you're sitting at my table you buy your snacks from the bar. If you want chips I'll get 'em for you. How many, what flavour?"

"But I already bought these."

"D'you wanna talk to my manager?"

"We just want to order some more beer, I think. Don't we? Another round all around?"

"I'm gonna get my manager."

She walked away.

"What's her problem?" Petey said.

Freya pulled one of the bags towards her. She put a chip in her mouth and slowly crunched it.

The manager was a short man with short black hair, a shiny forehead, and a tired-worried look on his face. "What seems to be the problem?"

The waitress and a big guy in a black tee-shirt were standing behind him.

The bar wasn't full but whoever was there turned their chairs to watch.

"We don't know," Andy said. He laid out a cigarette paper, but when he tried to put a line of tobacco down the centre of it, he ended up with more tobacco on the table than on the paper. He looked at what he had done, then he looked up at the manager. "The waitress here started asking us about potato chips."

"Florence tells me you bought them next door."

Andy nodded. He looked around and they all nodded.

"D'you think that's fair?"

Andy pushed the spilt tobacco to the edge of the table and tried to catch it in his pouch. "Fair?"

"Did Florence tell you that you had to buy your snacks from the bar?"

"After I went and got these? Yeah. You should have a sign or something."

"D'you want me to toss 'em, boss?" This from the big guy.

Sheila glanced at Freya and saw her set a chip on Petey's shoulder. He laughed quietly. Then he took the chip, put it in his mouth, and washed it down with a swallow of beer.

The others sat there. They were waiting it out like you would wait out a lecture from your father—about forgetting to put gas in the car maybe. That kind of thing. It was a game of patience, and if you were patient everything would turn out all right in the end. There were a few sighs, a few glances up at the ceiling, but other than that they just listened.

Except for Freya. And maybe Petey.

"When you come in here," the manager was saying, "you buy your beer from the bar. You don't bring in a six-pack or whatever and sit down at one of my tables and ask for an opener. When you go into a restaurant you don't sit down at a table and bring out a sandwich."

"Not only that, Clifford, they leave shit for tips."

"Florence?" He held up his hand. "Please?"

"University students. Ha. Bums, more like it. All they want is a handout. Everything for free."

"Florence?"

Florence looked around, tapping her foot. "I want them out of here, Clifford."

Clifford said, "Look. What I run here is a business. I got rent to pay, wages to pay, I have to pay for the lights, the tables and chairs, the carpets, taxes. So to stay in business I have to make money, and to make money I have to sell things to the people who sit at my tables. It's as simple as that. You're thirsty? You buy my beer. You're hungry? You buy my snacks. Hell, I can even get you a cheeseburger. Does this make sense to you?"

It was a rhetorical question. He waited for the rhetorical answer. He didn't get it.

"Bullshit."

There was a moment of confusion. No one seemed to know who had spoken. Everybody looked at everybody else. The big guy stepped forward. Florence clicked her tongue. "Bingo," she said softly.

"It's all bullshit." Freya put another chip in her mouth. She crunched it down and swallowed. "What this guy's saying, it's crap."

"Now let's not get excited here," Andy said. "The man has a point."

Petey said, "What point is that, Andy?"

"Oh Christ," Andy said.

"Can I see some ID, Miss? Young lady?"

Freya laughed. "He thinks I'm a young lady."

The big guy started towards her. "It's okay, Tony." Clifford held up his hand. "I am obliged under the liquor laws of the province of Manitoba—"

"Don't you think you're making a big deal out of nothing?" Freya stared up at him. "I mean, a few bags of potato chips? Come on. How 'bout if we promise never to do it again?"

"I wanna see some ID, from all of you, on the table, now."

"How about we finish our beer, take our chips, and go?" Freya said. "How about that?"

"I'm not making deals here. I am enforcing the law as required of me by the Manitoba Liquor Control Board."

"Okay." Freya found her purse. "I don't have a driver's licence. But here's my birth certificate. And my medical card. And my student card with my picture on it. Will that do?"

A few minutes later Clifford had seen all their ID's. As he handed back the last one, Sheila realized that Freya had made them call his bluff. The question was, once again, what was he going to do about the chips?

He stepped back, shook his head. Then he turned to Florence. "Clear the table," he said. "Get rid of those goddam potato chips."

"Pleasure." Florence went to work, starting at the end where Sheila was sitting. They all watched as she picked up the bags and dropped them onto her tray. Sheila felt resignation in herself and sensed it from the others. They would finish what was left of their beers, wait five minutes, and leave. But they would leave humbled. It wasn't something they would be laughing about next week or be able to talk about even a year from now without feeling uncomfortable.

The last bag, half eaten, was sitting in front of Freya. Florence reached for it, but before she could pick it up Freya grabbed her wrist. Florence had not expected this. But the smugness stayed on her face. She obviously thought Freya would give way. She didn't, and as her grip on the woman's arm tightened, Florence seemed to become first confused, then irritated.

The rest all happened very quickly.

Freya said, "Keep your fuckin' hands off my potato chips."

Tony lurched towards them.

Then Sheila and the others—Roger, Petey, Andy, Jill, Rosemary—all stood up. One of the tables tilted. Two glasses and an empty bottle of beer fell to the carpet. Florence staggered back, tripped on something, and fell down.

Clifford nodded. "Her," he said, and Tony grabbed Freya under the arms and yanked her out of the chair. He put her in a full nelson and started walking her to the door. She tried to windmill her arms but all she could do was flick them uselessly back and forth. "Let go of me, you bastard. Let go."

The others were all standing back as if from an explosion.

"He's gonna toss her," Andy said.

Sheila grabbed Freya's parka, got her own coat, and went after them.

She could hear Tony laughing. "Y'wanna fuck with me y'fuckin' little bitch? Huh? Y'wanna fuck with me?"

He pushed open the lobby doors.

There was the sudden sound of traffic on Portage Avenue.

Then he sent Freya sprawling out onto the sidewalk—out onto the frozen ruts of ice and snow and the layers of sand and grit and salt.

And into the cold.

The late afternoon shoppers and people going home from work saw the place she'd been tossed out of and stepped around her.

She got up, wiping the grit out of her hands and off her knees.

Sheila helped her into her parka. "You okay?"

She nodded and started back towards the hotel. "My books," she said.

But Tony was there before she even reached the door. He had her books in his arms. For a moment Sheila thought he was going to walk up to her and hand them over. Enough damage had been done, and fair's fair, the hotel had made its point. That's what Sheila thought. Tony didn't. He threw them at her.

Some opened up like stunned birds and fluttered to the ground, some simply fell.

Tony went back inside as Andy and the others were coming out. Petey brought Freya's purse with him and gave it to her.

Jill put her arm through Sheila's. "Come on. We're gonna walk up to Sorrento's for pizza."

Freya started picking her books up off the sidewalk.

For a moment Sheila allowed herself to be led away. "What about Freya?"

"What about her? She made the mess, let her clean it up."

Of the others only Petey hung back. The rest were halfway up the block.

Sheila picked up two of Freya's books.

"We're not gonna wait for you, Sheila," Jill said.

Sheila put the books on top of the ones Freya had already collected, and turned around. "What's with you? Freya's the only one who stood up for us in there, the only one who put up any kind of fight. And now you're just gonna walk away?"

"She doesn't know," Petey said.

"Doesn't know?" She walked up to him. "Doesn't know what?"

"She's a dyke," Jill said.

"Faggot," Petey said.

"And her name? 'Freya'? It's some bullshit thing she made up. It's really Alice. She likes girls. Tits turn her on. Because she doesn't have any."

Sheila turned her head. She opened her mouth to say something—what, she didn't know—but Freya was already crossing Portage Avenue, walking towards the Bay, not serenely but steadily, with her books clutched to her chest.

They ate pizza and drank beer at Sorrento's, and Sheila almost forgot about the girl with the slim hips and the paisley shirt.

She laughed as hard as the others laughed when the conversation ran out and Petey said "Faggot."

"Hi."

Sheila was reading in the library. She lifted her head. "Freya."

"I wanted to thank you for trying to help me out last week."

"Thank me? Hell, we should be thanking you. I feel kinda bad."

"I got kind of carried away—literally, I guess." She laughed. "But I got so pissed off at that guy. What was his name?"

"Clifford."

"Yeah, him. He was probably right and all that stuff, but still. It bugged me. You know?" She nodded a couple of times. "Anyways, you're trying to study. I'll get out of your hair."

"No. Actually I was thinking of going down for coffee. D'you wanna come?"

"No offence, but you probably don't want to be seen with me. People would talk." She shrugged. "It's the way it is."

Sheila felt the blood rush to her face. "All I meant . . ."

"Relax. I know what you meant." She smiled. "Besides, I have a class."

"Maybe later."

"Whenever."

"No, I mean it. I'd like to talk to you."

Freya thought for a moment. "Okay. Tomorrow afternoon, three o'clock, at the Aberdeen. I'll buy you a beer." She started to leave and then stopped. "On your way out. Of the library? Check out the photographs on the mezzanine. You know that little area where they display stuff? Tell me what you think."

After she was gone Sheila was left with the sound of Freya's flat, almost nasal drawl in her ears and the pressure of her eyes on her face. The body rush that had slammed through her when she looked up and saw her standing there had begun to fade—the sweat to dry—but the memory was slowly settling into her bones.

Was this what she wanted? What she really wanted was to be left alone. But did she have a choice? She had almost unconsciously assumed—like her friends—that she'd somehow, somewhere, sometime get married, have kids, and step sideways through the rest of her life.

She thought of Petey trying to put his soft thing into her in the laundry room at Rosemary's house. It was at a party during the summer between grade eleven and grade twelve. They were both drunk. Petey did his best and she did her best to let him, but all she remembered was the embarrassment of it all and the pain. And then later after going back to the party being terrified of the moment when Petey would reappear. But he never did. Not in the next half-hour anyway. She started to worry, so she went back to the laundry room a little later and found him passed out on the concrete floor with his pants around his ankles and a little pool of semen drying on his belly. His thing had gone down to a little thumb-end—as if it wanted to hide in the scratchy hair that surrounded it. She tried to wake him but he wouldn't wake up. She wiped his belly clean with a towel from the clothes hamper. She pulled his pants up and left him there to wake up when he was ready.

She didn't see him again until a few days later. He didn't mention what had happened, and never did, and she wondered if he even remembered it. He got so drunk sometimes, he could be like that.

On the mezzanine of the library there was an area where small shows by painters and photographers were mounted for a couple of weeks at a time.

The present exhibition was all black-and-white photographs by different people. She was nervous about what she was going to see. She expected to find scattered among the pictures images of women loving women—subtly maybe, or maybe not, she didn't know. It left her feeling a little disappointed that Freya would be so obvious. Yet she felt she should at least look. She had said she would, and Freya might ask her about them.

If Sheila showed up the next day at the Aberdeen, that is. The thought of not going had crossed her mind.

The photographs were interesting, but Sheila didn't find anything that she had expected to find, and it was not until she was about to leave that she saw what Freya had wanted her to see. Each photograph had the name of the artist on a small rectangular card next to the work. It had never occurred to her that Freya's photographs were on show—she didn't even know she took photographs—until she saw her name on one of the cards: "Freya Delaney."

She looked back up at the photograph she was standing in front of with a sense of surprise and wonder creeping over her. It was a picture of the sun rising on a clear morning over a burnt-out house. The one beside it was Freya's also. She took it in all at once and then searched for the details. It showed a beautiful sunny day through a broken window as seen from the centre of a dark and gutted room. She moved to the next one with anticipation. It was the last of Freya's photographs. It was the only one with a person in it and the one that stayed with her the longest: a boy standing over a dead dog which was lying in the road. The boy had just turned his grief-twisted face to the camera when Freya snapped the shutter.

Freya was waiting for her. For a moment coming out of the bright sunshine into the beverage room of the Aberdeen Hotel, Sheila could make out nothing more than the dark shapes of tables and the few people sitting at them. And then she saw one of the shapes waving at her.

"Hi." She sat down and slipped out of her coat.

The waiter was there almost immediately. Freya had two glasses of draft in front of her, one half full, one untouched. She looked at Sheila. "Draft?"

Sheila let her eyes graze Freya's. "Yes. Please." She was nervous. She put her hands between her thighs. Even as she set off from the university, Sheila had thought about not coming. She could have wandered into the Bay or simply caught the next bus home. But she had too many questions about herself, she realized, not to come.

"Is draft okay?" Freya said after the waiter had gone.

"Draft is fine."

Freya's eyes wandered, then rose to Sheila's and held them.

"Draft's fine. Really."

"Thanks for coming."

"Thanks for getting here first."

"D'you want to go somewhere else?"

Sheila looked around. "No." It was cleaner than she thought it would be.

"It's really an okay place. It's dark and quiet and nobody bothers you. I study here sometimes. You can buy a cup of coffee and stay here all afternoon. I've written term papers here."

The waiter came back. Sheila reached for her purse. "I'm buying," Freya said. "I said I would." She handed him a couple of dollars and the waiter thumbed the change out of a coin dispenser on his belt. Freya put the change on the table. "You can buy the next one."

Sheila held up her glass and touched it to Freya's. "Deal." She took a sip. "I loved your photographs."

"Did you go and see them? I don't think anyone knows they're there."

"They're very powerful. I can't get them out of my head.

How long have you been taking pictures?" It wasn't the wrong thing to say, but she got the feeling Freya didn't like to talk about her pictures. She stiffened ever so slightly and Sheila's compliments, even though she meant them, sounded hollow, even to herself.

"Awhile," Freya said.

"When I saw your name I nearly flipped out. They're really good." She reached across the table and put her hand on Freya's. "Really."

Freya's hand was cold. It turned under Sheila's, and as Sheila drew back her hand, Freya's fingernails lightly scraped her palm.

Freya rested the side of her head on the closed fist of her other hand. It was hard to tell in the dim light, but there seemed to be colour in her usually pale face. "Thanks," she said. She smiled. "Thank you."

For the next few weeks it was the Aberdeen at two, the Aberdeen at three, the Aberdeen at four-thirty, and on Fridays the Aberdeen for lunch. Sheila had never met anyone like Freya. The more she came to know her the more she sensed, between the anger and the pain and the suspicion, a quiet power.

And yet Freya said very little. Her father was the president of a hospital, her mother was an orthodontist. She had a brother in Malaysia working for CUSO. Freya's major was art history, but she wanted to take photojournalism somewhere, maybe Carleton, she said, if they had a photojournalism course. They talked about these and other things, but there were long pauses in their conversations. A quarter of an hour might tick by without a word passing between them. They might look at each other and laugh or just look at each other, or one of them might move the other's draft glass to the end of the table and wait for the other to pull it back, and then move it again. It was a teasing, peculiar kind of friendship which Sheila felt herself being drawn into.

By the time she realized she was drowning in it, it was too late.

Freya said, "D'you like pizza?" It was a few minutes to four on a Friday afternoon. "Homemade?"

They were in the Aberdeen.

"Like, at your house?"

"My parents are going to some banquet thing."

Sheila looked at the pale face watching her from the other side of the table. "Sure." She pulled a dime out of the change. "But I have to call my parents. They expect me for supper. They'll have a bird if I don't call."

Freya pushed the rest of the coins into the middle of the table for the waiter. "There's phones in the lobby."

Freya's house was not a whole lot different from her own. It wasn't quite as big but it was big enough. Her parents were already gone by the time they arrived. Freya pulled a box of Chef Boyardee Pizza Mix out of the cupboard and told Sheila to look around while she mixed the dough.

It was a clean, modern house. There was nothing remarkable about it except that this was where Freya lived.

After they had eaten, Freya took Sheila downstairs to show off her studio.

It was separated from the rest of the rec room by a long curtain. She pulled it aside to let Sheila pass through, then stepped in behind her and pulled it shut.

It was a bare space. The floor was plain concrete. There were a couple of pod lamps on stands, some drop sheets, a moveable screen, and a yellow extension cord that was as thick as her thumb but wasn't plugged into anything. At the end of the bare space there was a plywood wall with a door in it, and on the door the kind of sign you'd buy at a stationary or hardware store that said "KEEP OUT." Only when she came up close to it did Sheila see the words "This means you, Dad" scrawled underneath it. Freya keyed open the padlock and stepped inside. "Darkroom," she said. There was a small fridge inside. She pulled out two beers and opened them on an opener nailed to the wall. "This is where I keep my stuff." She handed one of the beers to Sheila.

"Can I see?"

"There's not much to see." Freya gestured with the beer bottle. "There's the developing tray, a sink, the chemicals, fixer, paper."

"This is where it all happens, I guess."

"Sort of." She leaned against the doorjamb and let the beer bottle hang at her side. Sheila was the width of the door frame away. Freya leaned over and kissed her quickly on the lips. Then she turned, took about five steps, and stopped.

Sheila's whole body itched, her skin crawled, her bones ached. She stood in the warm, still, everlasting, silent wind of Freya's kiss, and burned. But even here, even now she heard a voice in the wind screaming that Freya was a dirty bitch. It was far away but Sheila could hear it howling all the names she didn't want to be called: *queer*, *butch*, *dyke*. She could have walked out, pretending to Freya, to herself, and to the whole world that she wasn't what Freya was. She wasn't no goddam fucking dyke. But she was, and what she wanted more than anything else was to lose herself in the face and hands and body and in the eyes of this person who had been brave enough to reach for her with a kiss.

Sheila was sitting with Jill and Roger and Andy and Rosemary in the fourth-floor buff.

Rosemary said, "Can I try one of those?"

Andy was rolling a cigarette. "I'll make you one."

"All's I want is a puff."

"I'll make you one."

"Anybody seen Petey?" Roger said.

No one had. But it was mid-morning during the middle of the week and no one expected even Petey to have gone for a beer.

"He's got some kind of job, I think." Andy licked the cigarette paper and sealed in the tobacco. He handed it to Rosemary and started another one for himself.

She pulled a face. "You expect me to smoke this?"

"Here." He pinched off the extra tobacco at each end. "I admit it's not like store-bought, but if you don't want it—"

"No, no. You'll have to show me sometime."

"It's pretty simple. You take your paper . . ."

"He works pretty late apparently."

"Who's that?"

"Petey. This job he's got. Delivering. But he won't talk about it. All I know is he uses his own car."

"Maybe he's delivering pizza."

"Maybe. Or chicken."

"I don't think he has a class till the afternoon." Sheila looked at her watch. "But I do." She put the lid on her coffee. "I'll see you guys later."

"Sheila?" Jill looked up at her and smiled. "Who's the lucky guy?"

At first she had no idea what Jill was talking about. "Guy?" she said, and then panicked.

But Jill went right on. "He's such a secret, Sheila. Aren't you going to give us a hint? First name even?"

The others were looking at her.

"What are you talking about?"

"It's written all over your face."

"My face?"

"All the classic signs. Distraction. Preoccupation. Is it serious?"

"I don't know what you're talking about."

"It's not a prof, is it? Please God, don't let it be a prof. Especially a married one. He'll only break your heart, Sheila. They always do."

"I have to go."

As she walked away, Jill called after her, "Sheila, don't get mad. We're happy for you. We're your friends."

"Delivering what?" Roger said.

"Who?"

"Petey."

"I dunno. It's at night. Sometimes late."

Freya leaned over her and brought the clock closer to her face. "It's almost eleven." She rolled out of bed and started to get dressed. "Sheila? Please?"

Sheila moaned. She wanted to curl up in Freya's arms and go to sleep. The last thing she wanted to do was get dressed and go outside. It was cold. She would have to scrape the ice off the windows of her mother's car and then sit in it while the engine warmed up. "You said they wouldn't be home till midnight." She dropped her feet over the side of the bed.

"It's the one-hour rule, Sheila."

"Right. The one-hour rule."

"One hour either side of what they tell me. One of them's late getting home—the dry cleaning's not ready, whatever: they don't get away on time."

"Right."

"That's not so bad. But at the other end, they're not enjoying themselves, something happens, the party or whatever breaks up: they come home early."

"Right."

"Besides, I told John we'd stop by."

Sheila pushed herself off the bed and started looking for her clothes.

"In the corner," Freya said.

"Thanks." She started to get dressed. "This isn't a party or anything, is it?"

"At John's? No. But I said we might drop by. He wants to meet you."

"Does he know?"

"Sure, of course. He's my friend. He's a really cool guy, Sheil. I met him at this photography club I used to belong to. He's shown me stuff. He helped me set up my darkroom."

"You told him about us?"

"Yes. He's very together."

"I don't think I could do that."

"What?"

"Tell somebody about us."

"Maybe you just don't know the right people."

"I wish we could just go out and be normal. Don't you?"

"We do, we are."

"What would they do, your parents, if they found us together?"

"Like this? I don't know. They'd probably be confused."

Sheila finished dressing and lay down on the bed to watch Freya put the rest of her clothes on.

"Don't fall asleep."

"I won't."

Freya zipped up her jeans. "What?" she said.

Sheila patted the bed. "Come here."

"The one-hour rule, Sheila."

"Like we're not gonna hear them come in? And we're dressed, aren't we? All we have to do is stand up."

Freya lay down beside her.

"Give me your hand. . . . Not like that."

"How then?"

"Like this."

"Like that?"

"Yes." Sheila stroked the backs of Freya's fingers. "So you never told your parents."

"I stopped trying. They just think I'm a little weird. Art weird. You know? What with my photography and everything. What about your parents?"

"What about them?"

"D'they know?"

"My dad'd kill me."

"What about your mom?"

"She'd hand him the gun."

"Naw."

"Metaphorically speaking."

When Sheila started the car she had to keep her foot pressed gently on the gas to prevent the engine from stalling.

Freya scraped the windows. She climbed in saying, "Your mother needs a new car maybe."

"She doesn't use it much. Besides, it's okay once it's warmed up."

"Can we stop at the Travelodge for a six-pack? I don't like to show up empty-handed."

"Sure."

"What's wrong with this thing anyways?"

"Compression. A couple of the cylinders are down. And the carburetor needs work."

Freya laughed. "Oh right, the old thingamajig."

"Carburetor. My dad's on the lookout for a rebuilt. They'll drop it in at the shop. But he doesn't seem to be in much of a hurry."

"What's a 'rebuilt'?"

"It's an engine that's been . . . rebuilt."

"D'you work there much? In the bus place?"

"In the office, during the summer, yeah." She took off her glove and put her hand over the front window vent to see if the air was getting any warmer. She put her glove back on. "Can I ask you something? You don't have to answer if you don't want."

"What?"

"D'you ever go to bed with a boy?"

"No." Freya shook her head. "I mean, why would I?"

"Just wondering."

"You?" When Sheila did not reply, Freya continued, "There's no magic pill, Sheila. You can't change what you are."

"But I liked him. It wasn't like I didn't. It wasn't like he was just some guy."

"Sheila, there's liking someone and then there's . . . liking someone."

"I know." She checked the heater vent again. The air was starting to get warmer. She put her glove back on and slipped the transmission into "drive." "You said you want to go to the Travelodge?"

"To get the beer? Yeah. You know where it is?"

"I know."

"It's behind the Canadian Tire."

"I know where it is."

"Don't get mad. Honestly, sometimes the tiniest little thing can set you off."

"Me?"

"Yes."

"Me?"

"Yes."

"That's a laugh and a half."

"What d'you mean?"

"You don't know everything, you know."

"I never said."

"You just act like it."

"I do not."

"The one-hour rule?"

"What about it?"

"It's so . . . pompous. You're just as scared as I am—of your parents, of everybody. You just talk like you're not."

The silence that followed made Sheila feel guilty. "Freya?"

"Yeah?"

"I'm sorry."

"It's okay. I was thinking."

"What about?"

"This girl I knew."

"Who was she?"

"Somebody I had a terrible crush on." Freya let out a small, painful laugh. "I don't know what made me do it."

"What did you do?"

"It was stupid. I was going to school over here, eh. I never tried to hide what I was but I don't think anybody really knew. I wasn't exactly active or anything. I was quiet, went to class, didn't say much. I had friends, you know, played a little basketball. Nobody got nervous because I was in the locker room or anything. I was the one who got nervous. Anyways . . . she wasn't even in my homeroom. We had French together, and when we passed in the hall she always said hi to me. It got so I'd find ways to be in the hallway when she'd be there. I was addicted. It was like my glimpse of heaven. I mean, she had a boyfriend and everything. But it was like I didn't care. I was on this crazy suicide mission. I thought about her all the time, I thought what it would be like to be with her. You know? I didn't care if I got hurt, I just wanted her to know how I felt."

"You didn't."

"I did."

"How old were you?"

"Seventeen? We were both in grade eleven. I was pretty naive. I know it doesn't make any sense."

"It never does."

"I haven't told anyone this. Not even John."

"But what did you do?"

"I gave her flowers."

"Flowers?"

"A dozen roses. From a real florist. They cost a fortune. All my babysitting money for like two weeks."

"You didn't." Sheila pulled out onto St. Anne's Road heading south.

"I did. I wanted her to know. I'm not sure what I expected her to do. I never thought beyond the point of just giving her the flowers."

"What happened?"

"I went to her house. Right? And her dad answers." She pointed straight ahead. "Don't go down Fermor. Go one past and turn left on Niakwa so you come in the back way. It's easier."

"What did her dad do?"

"Looked at me kind of funny."

"Did he call her?"

"Oh yeah. After a moment. I could see him trying to figure out who I was. I'd never been there before."

"Did he ask you in?"

"No. He told me to wait there."

"Where?"

"On the porch. This was like at the back, okay?"

"And?"

"She comes to the door. My stomach's in knots, my knees're weak, the usual. I can see her through the screen. She looks surprised to see me. But she smiles, says hi. I mean, we never hung around together or anything. She opens the screen door and for a second it's like she's trying to decide whether she should invite me in or step outside. I don't think she'd even seen the roses yet, not really seen them. In any case she steps out. 'These are for you.' I give her the flowers. 'Oh, how lovely. Who're they from?' I nod a couple of times like some simpleton with his head on a spring. 'Who sent you with them?' 'They're from me,' I say. She says, 'Oh,' and it's like the smile kind of like freezes on her face. 'Oh,' she says, then, 'Thanks,' and goes inside and closes the door."

"And that was it?"

"I wish." Freya didn't say anything while they made their turn. They drove along behind the Canadian Tire. "It's just up ahead on the left." Sheila saw the vendor sign a moment later. "Pull up outside and wait for me. I won't be a sec." She was back in less than a minute. She put the beer in the back and climbed in. "Go out the same way. Turn left onto Fermor and then left on St. Mary's."

Sheila turned the car around. "If that wasn't the end of it, then what was it?"

Freya said, "It was like just the beginning. I went by her house the next day. You know how you do. Because you want to be near her. Where she lives and everything. I was going down the back lane. And I found the roses. They were sticking out of a plastic garbage bag. But that's okay. What the hell, who're you going to complain to? God? Nobody else is gonna listen, are they? It hurt, sure, but that's love. Right? It hurts. That's part of the game. You get stomped on. I could handle that. It's no fun, but you expect it. No, the bad part started right after that, and I hadn't counted on it. You might say I should've seen it coming. But it was something between her and me, private. It didn't have to involve everybody else in the whole universe. Come on, I gave her some flowers. I mean, what's the big deal here?"

"You can't have it both ways, Freya."

"You would've thought I'd set off a bomb and tried to kill everybody in the school. People I didn't even know coming up to me and calling me all the usual names, all that bullshit. Phone calls at home to my parents. They didn't understand. They didn't get it. Thick, you know? Come here—Mom, Dad—let me draw you a picture. My dad thought it had something to do with the hospital, abortions or something, I don't know, so he did what any practical father would do, he got us an unlisted number. Abracadabra."

They turned onto Fermor. "So what happened?"

"Finally? I got kicked out of school. It's funny, all your friends, the people you think you know, they melt away. Sure, a couple of people hung in there for me, and I appreciated it but they couldn't save me from the others. And one teacher. Most of the teachers tried to pretend it wasn't happening."

"You got kicked out of school?"

"Yeah."

"But why?"

"Because, well. I figured if they were gonna label me, I'd play the part. So that's what I did. I blew kisses at the girls, I winked at the female teachers."

"You didn't."

"Sure I did. It got me beat up a couple of times but it didn't stop me."

"You got beaten up?"

"Roughed up maybe."

"And they kicked you out?"

" 'A disruptive element,' 'anti-social,' 'does not get along with the other students.' They had all sorts of phrases. 'Perhaps a different environment would be more conducive to your daughter's well-being. . . .' They just wanted to get rid of me. And my parents still didn't get it. They gnashed their teeth and pulled their hair. I felt sorry for them. Nothing like that ever happen to you?"

"Which part?"

"The coming out part. Where you have to decide."

"No."

"One day you're gonna have to."

"Don't go political on me. Okay?"

"I'm not going political. This isn't politics."

They turned onto St. Mary's Road. A block later Freya said, "We're here."

John's apartment building was a three-storey walk-up. He opened the door wide enough to peer out.

"Hiiii," Freya said in a rising voice. John smiled and stepped back to let them in. He and Freya gave each other a hug. Then Freya was turning to her. "This is my friend, Sheila."

"So this is Sheila." His smile was fresh and open. "Come in, come in."

Sheila lifted the six-pack. "Hi."

"We won't stay long," Freya said. "I know you're gonna start getting busy soon."

"No. Don't worry about it. All work and no play. . . . I've been trying to catalogue my slides. I'm thinking of going into the postcard business."

"Really?"

They sat down.

"We'll see. Got any views of the city I could use, Freya? Downtown, the zoo?"

He was a little older than they were. He turned to Sheila. "Are you a photographer?"

She shrugged. "I'm just a student."

Freya pushed her leg. "Don't be so modest, Sheil. She gets straight A's all the time in everything. It's sickening."

"Take a look at this." John reached a little hand-held slide holder towards her. "Tell me what you think. It's nothing like Freya's work. It's not art. Hold it up to the light. If that was a postcard, would you buy it?"

It was, Sheila realized as she took the holder, the first time she and Freya had been together like this in the company of another person. She didn't put the holder up to her eye right away. She wanted to enjoy the moment, let it sink in.

There was a knock at the door. She lowered the viewer and glanced at Freya. Freya touched her lips. Shhh.

The one odd thing about John's apartment was that he had what looked like a dozen or so cases of beer stacked up against one wall. They were twenty-fours, and Sheila thought they must be empties, or why else would Freya have wanted to stop for a six-pack on the way?

John answered the door. He spoke to somebody for a moment and then two guys walked in. They ignored Sheila and Freya, grabbed a case of beer each, and walked out.

Judging by the money in John's hand they definitely were not empties. He brought two cases out from his bedroom to replace the two that had gone out the door.

"We should get going." Freya stood. "You're gonna start getting busy. Saturday night and all?"

"Been busy since eight o'clock. But you're right, it'll get busier." He looked at his watch. "Vendors are just starting to close."

Sheila wondered how many cases he had in the other room.

"I've had a guy on the road all evening. You just missed him. He was taking out his third order. People party, they run out. They don't want to go to the vendor even if it is open. They phone me. I deliver."

"Who's driving for you now?"

"A new guy. Friend of a friend of a friend."

"Don't work too hard, John."

"It was nice meeting you," Sheila said.

"The pleasure," he said, "was all mine."

Once outside Freya said, "Well?"

"He's a bootlegger."

"Among other things."

Sheila didn't know why she liked the idea of knowing someone who was a bootlegger but she did. "He seems like a nice guy."

"He's always been there for me."

"Maybe we could take him out for pizza or something sometime."

Sheila's locker was in the basement of Manitoba Hall. Jill and Rosemary shared a locker one aisle over. The room was all concrete walls and tile floors. Voices carried, especially when there weren't many people around. When Sheila went to get a book the place was almost deserted.

But not entirely. She heard a locker door close. And then two voices. She was turning the dial on her combination lock.

The voices moved to the end of the aisle. She recognized them now. It was Rosemary and Jill. The clasp on her lock sprung free and she pulled open the door. The book she was looking for wasn't on top where she thought it would be. She tried to find it quickly so she could catch up to them.

Then Jill said, "But you know her better than I do. You went to high school together. Junior high even. Would she really do something like that? I mean, it could ruin her whole life."

Sheila's first thought was to dismiss the automatic reaction that they were talking about her. Why would they be? Only to lean into her locker hoping that they wouldn't see her when she realized a few seconds later that they were.

"Why does it have to be anybody at all?"

"Oh come on, Rosemary. She's got that secret smile."

They had stopped at the end of the row.

"Well, the only guy I know she ever dated was Petey."

"Petey? Somebody actually dated Petey?"

"Petey's okay."

"But to date him, Rosemary."

"Well, maybe they didn't exactly date, but they were, you know, like . . . tight."

"How tight?"

"Tight enough. She never really went out with anyone special other than Petey. Not that she wasn't popular and everything. You know the way she is, she's so . . . nice. Everybody likes her. She's always been like that. Always had a million friends. Smart. On the debating team. Drama club. Ran track at the provincials. Anyways, what's wrong with seeing a prof?"

"Nothing, I guess. Unless he's married. It's just that she won't talk about it. She's hiding something."

"She's no fool, Jill."

"I guess. Anyways, whatever it is'll have to wait. I got a class."

"Me too." They walked out into the hallway. "I'm not trying to make a big deal of this," Jill said before they were out of earshot. "I'm worried about her. That's all."

John did not want to go out for pizza. Business was good and there weren't many nights he wasn't glued to the phone till three or four in the morning. So Freya and Sheila brought the pizza to him.

They stayed until around ten o'clock. They both had an early class in the morning and were getting ready to leave. There was one piece of pizza left. Freya told John to have it for breakfast. Then the phone rang and he turned to get it.

Sheila had her back to the door. She heard it open. She knew it wasn't Freya. She could feel her standing a few feet behind her, waiting to say goodbye to John. Someone was coming in. It wouldn't be a customer. Customers knocked and waited for John to answer the door. Then it occurred to her it was probably his driver.

John looked up from the phone and waved him in. "How'd it go?" he said after he'd hung up.

"Fine." The guy had hung back by the door while John was on the phone, and only now started forward.

She knew the voice. She was about to say hi. She could feel the smile on her face. Then she remembered who she was with, and her spine turned to ice.

"You got any more orders for me, boss?" Petey stepped up and put the money he had collected down on John's desk. "Better count it."

John leafed through the bills. "Take a load off."

Petey Macauley sat down. He brought his head up slowly and let his gaze turn to the two women standing near the door. He nodded at each of them. Then he got up and went into the kitchen. "Where to now, John?" he said when he came back. He was holding a beer. "Where to now?"

Neither Sheila nor Freya said anything until they got into the car.

"It was Petey, Freya. It was Petey. Cheesus. I can't believe it."

"It was gonna happen sooner or later."

"He'll tell. He can't help himself. It'll just come out—he won't even mean to do it."

"You're embarrassed."

"If only we hadn't gone to John's."

"But we did."

"And why Petey of all people?"

"Would you've preferred Jill?"

"Of course not."

"I still love you."

"Oh, Freya, don't say that."

"Because of Petey? Nothing's changed."

Sheila rested her head on the steering wheel. "Oh, Freya."

Petey Macauley said it like a frog croaking. "Faggot." And everybody laughed.

TWO

Freya. . . .

Sheila stepped out of the cottage and started walking through the darkness towards the lake. There was a breeze off the water. It pressed her nightgown against her body and made the hem flutter out behind her. She stopped and turned, a kind of one last look, and saw the cottage, lit only by the moon, high up on its rock shelf, dark and sleeping. Those inside would be sleeping too, the ones she was leaving behind, the ones she did not want to remember.

But she stopped only briefly. The water pulled her forward, the sheer weight of it, the darkness of it, the mystery of it.

There was someone out there waiting for her.

She waded in until the water came up to her knees. "Freya," she said, and stumbled forward, "Fraaay-ahhh . . . ," her voice swallowed up by the water, immense enough in itself, but which was just a shallow, island-dotted pool left over from a 10,000-year-old glacial lake that once had straddled the continent.

"Mummy." Laurie running, in her nightgown almost floating down the steps. "Mummy."

Sheila turned in the water's grip. "Laurie, honey. Sweetheart."

"Mummy." She was waving frantically. "Wait."

"What is it, sweetheart?"

"It's not Freya, Mummy."

"Of course it is."

"No it isn't. It's Leo. Don't you know?"

Sheila sat bolt upright. The sheet fell away. She was breathing hard and fast. Her heart was pounding. She put her feet down on the floor and pressed her hands to her chest.

She was in Leo's apartment, in Leo's bed. But Leo wasn't there. She grabbed the edge of the mattress and tried to slow her breathing. Her clothes were on the chair where she had dropped them. "Leo?" She was sweating. The air was cold on her back and on her shoulders.

There was a noise in the hall. She held her breath to listen but all she could hear was her heart. She pulled the sheet around her. The door opened. They would find her like this, sitting on the edge of Leo's bed, naked. They would find her. Then parade her through the streets, collecting as they went the stones they would use when they finally formed the circle.

The door closed.

"Sheila?" Leo put her keys down on the TV.

"I can't...I can't..." She tried to stop gasping long enough to speak. "Catch my breath." She felt Leo's weight on the bed beside her. Then her arms around her.

"What's wrong?" Leo said. "You were sleeping. I just went out to get some milk. For your tea. Sheila? What is it? You're shaking."

The blinds were drawn. It was Wednesday afternoon, their afternoon to be together. Sheila made an excuse to get out of the store—said that she had to see a rep or was going home to work on catalogues. It was Leo's early shift, but Leo still didn't get away till two o'clock. So they didn't have a lot of time. Occasionally they had a quick lunch out and then went to Leo's apartment, but more often than not Sheila picked up a bottle of wine and something from the deli and was waiting around the corner for her when she got off work.

"Sheila. What's wrong?"

In a nutshell?

Sheila had lost control.

More and more Leo was leading her. The comfort and the safety of their Wednesday afternoons, which for Sheila had isolated her feelings in a kind of circle and had given her an emotional routine, broke down almost as soon as she had become aware that it was a routine. She should have realized that Leo didn't think that way. For Leo circles did not exist. She just didn't see them, or, if she did, walked out of them as fast as they were created. Without the circle, Sheila's feelings for her had begun to bleed into the rest of the days of the week.

The circle may not have existed for Leo but she had broken it for Sheila a few days earlier like this:

"I'm sorry I had to call you." Leo sat down in the back of the bookstore and wheeled her chair over to where Sheila was working. She was making up the bank deposit. Lisa or Kenny usually did the end-of-day and then dropped the money in the night deposit on their way home. Leo was working with Lisa that night, but Lisa had taken ill suddenly and had had to go home early. Leo knew how to close up but she didn't know how to do the banking. Sheila counted out some twenties and wrote a figure in the deposit book.

Leo, with her shoulder pressed against Sheila's upper arm, was watching what Sheila was doing. "Why don't you teach me this stuff?"

"Not tonight."

"It looks simple."

"The deposit? It is. But then there's the blue book."

"What is the blue book, exactly? I've heard Lisa and Kenny talk about it, but nobody's ever shown me how to do it."

"It's where you compare what's rung through the register with what you put in the bank. They're supposed to be the same."

"Are they?"

"Mostly."

"Teach me the blue book."

"Another time. I'm very tired, Leo."

She could feel Leo's face turn from the desk towards her. "How tired?" Leo kissed her on the cheek. Sheila lost count. Leo licked her throat, and Sheila stopped counting altogether.

Sheila did not want to smile, tried not to smile. It was the first time Leo had kissed or touched her first. It was the first time that she knew for sure it wasn't just her wanting Leo but that it was Leo wanting her. The realization filled her body with sex almost instantly. Everything opened.

"How tired?" Leo undid the top few buttons of Sheila's shirt and kissed her high up on the chest. Sheila wasn't wearing a bra. Her breasts were small enough that she felt she didn't always have to. When Leo found Sheila's nipples already stiff it seemed to excite her and she went after them with her tongue, lips, and teeth. Then she went back up to her neck, then down to her breasts again, back and forth.

She put her knee between Sheila's legs and then lowered herself onto her thigh. Leo whimpered and, still kissing her, began to rub herself against Sheila's leg.

Sheila stood up, half angry, half determined not to let this happen. Leo staggered a few steps, a look of surprise on her face. Then she walked back to Sheila like some punch-drunk boxer. Sheila grabbed her wrists. Leo's face was flushed and puffy. Sheila pulled Leo's hands together, but Leo kept coming at her until she had pushed her up against the wall. Sheila heard herself say "Oh Christ" as Leo began to tug Sheila's clothes off. She did it with a clumsy determination, stopping every few moments to kiss Sheila on the mouth while Sheila's hands moved from Leo's shoulders up into her hair and back to her shoulders again. Sheila's breathing had become ragged, she felt heavy, she felt stuck to the wall. As she lifted her foot for Leo to pull off the first pant leg, she put her head back and closed her eyes.

They ended up lying in each other's arms on the floor in a bed of their own clothes. Sheila felt a physical contentment, but at the same time she felt unsettled, as if she had been asked to make a decision that she did not want to make, a decision that, she worried, she might have already made and not realized it. It was only when Leo's fingers stirred up a second wave of desire that Sheila glanced at her watch and saw what time it was. She stood up quickly and started to get dressed, leaving Leo on the floor staring up at her. "I still have to do the deposit," Sheila said. She tried to smile but her mouth didn't move.

Leo pulled herself to her feet. "Let me help."

"No." Then more softly, "It's okay."

Leo got dressed while Sheila finished counting the money. Sheila was fretting about what George would say when she got home, fretting about the look she might get from Samantha, if George had not already insisted on her going to bed. Laurie would be asleep even if he had let her stay up.

"I'm sorry," Leo said. Sheila could feel her standing off to the side. "Sometimes I forget you've got, you know, responsibilities. And all I want to do is have fun."

"No, it's me. It's my fault." Sheila stared at the money in her hand. "It just seems that there's never enough time."

"You've got a family to look after. What have I got? Eddie."

"Does it bother you?"

"What?"

"My family."

"You've got a great couple of kids. You can't ignore them. I wouldn't want you to."

"George and I . . . in case you're wondering . . ."

"I don't."

"Haven't for a long time."

"You don't have to tell me, Sheila."

"I want you to know."

"I know already. Okay? It's the same with Eddie. Boy, is he pissed off." She shrugged. "Are you finished counting the money? Because I can drop it in the night deposit. You go home. Do the blue book in the morning. Can't you?"

"I was going to drive you."

"I'll walk. It's a nice night. I'll make the deposit and bring the key back here tonight. Go home."

"This isn't your responsibility."

"Sure it is." Leo went to her purse. "And oh yeah. By the way." She pulled out two keys on a key ring and put them down on the table. "These are for you."

"What are they?" Sheila picked them up.

"For my place. This one opens the outside door and this one opens the door to my apartment. You know, in case you have to pick up stuff and stuff, if I'm not there."

Before she went into the house Sheila pulled Leo's keys out to look at them. She sat in the car holding them for almost five minutes, then put them in her purse and went inside.

Leo had said "Everything's okay" when they had parted, and all the way home Sheila desperately wanted to believe her.

The first time she saw the white Dodge Colt with the blue vinyl roof she didn't think too much about it. The second time she tried to remember where she had seen it before.

It was parked on the side street that angled behind their house. She was putting out a bag of garbage. The car was parked across the street. She stopped at the garbage can and then took a couple of steps out onto the road. The driver turned, and that's when she recognized him. It was Eddie. She hadn't seen him often, but she had seen him enough to know who he was. Apart from his connection with Leo he had somehow latched onto George.

He looked at her for a long time. Then he slowly reached for the keys to start the car. And drove away.

It was almost as if he had wanted her to see him.

And there were other times too when he had been parked outside the bookstore.

She was thinking about this as she sat in one of the lawn chairs watching George and Eugene and Moira and Samantha in the boat out on the lake taking turns water-skiing. Laurie and Stephen were playing on the narrow strip of beach at the bottom of their property. She was keeping an eye on them. Laurie, however, seemed more interested in the water while Stephen kept going back to his sand pile and his collection of collapsed castles, hoping perhaps he could figure out what had gone wrong with each of them before starting on another.

It was the August long weekend. In another month it would be Labour Day and the summer would be over. By Thanksgiving they would have closed up the cottage for the winter.

She wondered whether or not she and Leo would still be seeing each other when there was snow on the ground. Already she missed her. Not that they usually saw each other on the weekends. Most weekends she spent with George and the girls—and Eugene, Moira, and Stephen—here, at the lake. She simply missed her, wanted her here, wanted to hear her voice, wanted to sit across from her at the big picnic table where they always ate lunch and supper as long as it wasn't raining and the mosquitoes weren't too bad, wanted to hear her laugh, wanted her to be included—wanted, even, to introduce her to their neighbours, the Ackers.

There was a good piece of Canadian Shield rock and scrub between the Stookners and their neighbours to the other side. But the Ackers and the Stookners shared a stretch of the mud road that branched off to their respective cottages which were set back a couple of hundred feet or so from the highway, and the two families were, if not great friends, acquainted in a pleasant sort of way. George and Mr. Acker always had a chat when they opened the cottage for the summer. This was usually on the Victoria Day long weekend. The Ackers came down a number of times during the winter as well to skidoo mostly or to go ice fishing. Mr. Acker hired a local contractor to plough his driveway. Every year he told George about the man's services and every year George said that he didn't think it was necessary. They simply did not come out to the lake in the winter. But the Ackers did, and they always made a point of checking on the Stookner place to make sure nobody had broken in. Mr. Acker had George's phone number but fortunately he had never had to call.

The Ackers were prepared for anything. They had flashlights, candles, a battery-operated radio, and a Coleman stove. In the summer they left the cottage stocked with canned and dried food, bottled water. They had a chemical fire extinguisher, extra gas, chains for their car in case it snowed in July, and a rubber dinghy so that if their boat sank with all hands on board someone could come out and rescue them.

They also had a rifle. Mr. Acker cleaned and oiled it every weekend. It stayed at the cottage all year round because Mr. Acker didn't see the need for a weapon in the city. But out here? Yes, sir. It was because of the bears. Every year while George and Mr. Acker renewed their families' friendship and self-interest over a few drinks behind the Ackers' place, Mr. Acker would take George and Sheila inside and show them where he kept the rifle and the ammunition. Both families had keys to each other's cottage, and Mr. Acker wanted it to be perfectly clear to both George and Sheila that if they ever felt threatened by a bear or anything else for that matter, and the Ackers were not down for whatever reason, that they should not hesitate to let themselves in and take the rifle and use it if they had to. Mr. Acker wanted to give them lessons. He gave his fourteen-year-old son lessons, but both George and Sheila declined.

Mr. Acker would always grin and say, "You're right, you're right. As long as you understand the principle of something, necessity is usually, not always, but usually, the best teacher. There's nothing like a little panic to focus the mind. Am I right or am I right?"

That was Mr. Acker.

Sheila arrived at the studio a little after two. George had taken the Volvo in for service in the morning and she was going to drive him to the garage to pick it up. Eugene normally would have taken him but he was stuck in the editing room trying to finish a package of commercials by a three-o'clock deadline. The work had come in late the previous afternoon and Eugene had promised to get it done. By noon George could see he was going to be pressed for time so he had phoned Sheila and asked her if she could slip away from the store for a little while.

There was a long-haired young man with a ring in his nose sitting at the reception desk when she walked into the office. "Mrs. Stookner," he said. "How's it going?" He was one of the trainees who played in bands or who simply walked in off the street or out of some other job and said they wanted to learn the business. Today it was a boy, tomorrow it might be a girl. George and Eugene had them doing everything from answering the phone to working the audio room. Every time she came here, which wasn't often, there seemed to be a platoon of them chasing some project or deep in a conference about how to get just the right sound out of something or someone. The guy at the reception desk this afternoon might be in the dubbing room tomorrow. To Sheila it all seemed like chaos. It was what George and Eugene spent their days surrounded by, and George, as much as he loved anything, seemed to love the out-of-control-ness of it all. Eugene put up with it because it seemed to work. Mind you, they hadn't worked any other way and probably didn't know if they could.

"Is he in?" she said.

The young man with the long hair and the ring in his nose smiled with such clear-eyed innocence Sheila had to look away. "He's in the audio room. Follow me."

"I know where it is." She hadn't meant to be rude. She smiled. "The phone might ring."

"Gotcha," he said.

She stepped carefully into the audio room. They were recording. Two actors on the other side of the window were acting out a scene that sounded like a mini public-health drama. George left a young woman, who didn't look too much

older than Samantha, in charge of the sound board, and walked
with Sheila out of the building and into the parking lot.

"Sorry to drag you away," he said. He had the preoccupied
air about him that he always seemed to have after leaving the
studio.

"It's all right. It gives me a bit of a break."

"Uh huh," he said.

They got into the car. On the way she said that she had
invited Leo and Eddie to the cottage for the Labour Day weekend.

"I feel sorry for her sometimes. She never gets a chance to
go to the lake. I guess they've got no lake to go to."

"You invited them both?"

"Yes. Is that okay? D'you mind?"

"No. Maybe I'll invite some of my lot from the studio down
too and we'll be one big happy family. Would that be okay?"

"I thought you liked Eddie."

"Frankly? He's starting to become a bit of a pain."

"Who stepped on your toes today?"

"Sorry. I'm a little pissed off. They come in—you know
who I mean—late yesterday with their jingles half finished,
the timelines all over the place, and Eugene has to straighten
it all out because they have a deadline. It's annoying, that's all.
But it's what we do. Fix things, make them air-able."

"So is it okay about the lake?"

"Sure, whatever. How can I refuse?"

"You can't."

"Exactly."

They spent ten more minutes in the car but neither of
them said anything.

Leo. . . .

Sheila stepped out of the cottage, heading towards the
lake. It was the middle of the night. The water was smooth
and dark. She could feel the air cool on her skin. She had

come out of the cottage dressed in jeans and a shirt, but now she wasn't wearing anything.

She crossed the ground to the beach and waited. Leo was wading out of the lake towards her, her skin silvery in the moonlight.

"Mrs. Stookner?"

She turned her head and saw Eddie. Laurie and Samantha were standing on either side of him. He was holding their hands.

She tried to step in front of Leo so the girls wouldn't see but it was useless. They saw. In that one instant they saw everything.

She opened her eyes. A dream. Another bloody dream. Her nightgown was up around her hips. She pulled it down and sat up.

She looked at the clock. Seven-thirty. The girls were up. She could hear them in the kitchen downstairs. The toaster popped. Then she heard George say, "Would you like another glass of milk, Laurie?" He hadn't come to bed. He had probably slept in the spare room in the basement.

He was drinking again, and with the familiar knot of guilt and rage winding itself up inside her, she started down the stairs.

LEO

ONE

Leo's apartment was a brick oven. It was the middle of August and she still didn't have a fan big enough to move a feather around, let alone this hot heavy air.

But she was like that. She put up with things. Besides, a good fan would've cost eighty or a hundred bucks, and there was always something else she could think of to spend eighty or a hundred bucks on.

She could put up with a few hot days.

Sheila never complained, but then she had other things on her mind when she was here, the kind of things that made you sweaty whether the room was hot or not. Besides, the real hot days never seemed to fall on a Wednesday. Until today.

Maybe the heat had something to do with their not being able to find Sheila's shoe.

Leo was sitting in her armchair with it cradled in her lap. It was a grey pump with a low heel.

A few hours earlier they had both been looking all over for it. Leo had found it behind the TV about ten minutes ago—completely by chance. She had happened to catch a glimpse of it as she turned from the sink after washing her supper dishes, or it might've been there until the next time she cleaned behind the TV, which could've been a while.

She had sniffed it cautiously. It was almost new and it had that leathery, new shoe smell. So she had brought it closer and breathed in the smell more deeply, wondering what part belonged to Sheila and what part belonged to the shoe. She had thought of touching her tongue to it but didn't.

Now she was simply holding it. It bugged her that she couldn't phone Sheila and say she'd found the shoe. She would've enjoyed quietly laughing with her about it, she would've enjoyed hearing the surprise in her voice, "Where was it?"

"Have you seen my other shoe?" She was carrying the one she had around with her. She was almost dressed but hadn't done anything up.

Leo knew Sheila had to leave soon, and she felt a moment of nasty pleasure at the thought that Sheila might get held up for a few minutes, that she might not be able to leave when she wanted. It had crossed her mind that if Sheila had been a man, married with a wife and two kids, and visited her on Wednesday afternoons as Sheila did, and had to leave by a certain time so as not to be late getting home—what would she think?

Leo climbed off the bed. She picked up her underpants and tee-shirt from the floor and put them on. "It's by the door maybe." She didn't think her apartment was big enough to lose anything in. "D'you want some tea?" She plugged in the kettle.

"It isn't there either."

Now they both started to look. "It can't be far."

"You keep saying that."

"Well, it can't. Come and sit down. Forget the shoe for a minute. We'll have our tea and then have a good look."

But before they had a chance to have a good look, almost before they'd had a chance to taste their tea, Eddie showed up. He never just knocked or used the doorbell. He pounded with his fist or the flat of his hand hard enough to make the walls shake. "Hey, Leo. Open up. It's me. Eddie."

Leo was used to it and sighed. Sheila wasn't and shot to

her feet. "It's okay," Leo whispered. "The door's locked. Keep quiet and he'll give up in a minute."

Sheila was staring at her as if that would make him go away. "Does he have a key?"

Leo shook her head.

He rattled the knob and then pounded again. "Hey, Leo. Come on. What're you doin' in there?"

Someone who must've been standing beside him said, "Maybe she's not home."

Leo didn't recognize the voice until Sheila said, "That's George."

"Leo, open the door. Open the door, Leo." Now he pressed the buzzer.

"She's not home, Eddie. Let's go."

"Where the fuck is she, man?" Eddie's voice trailed off as they turned and started down the hallway.

Leo listened.

Sheila whispered, "Are they gone?"

Leo said "Shh." She thought she heard the front door close but it was two floors down and at the opposite end of the building. She listened for another minute. Nothing.

"Could he be waiting out there?"

"Give it another sec and I'll stick my head out."

"And what if he is there?"

"I'll pretend like I was on my way to the store."

"But he'll know you were here."

"So? I was asleep. I was in the shower. What's he gonna do once I step out and lock the door?"

But he wasn't there, and they didn't bother to look any more for the shoe. Sheila left in her stocking feet. Leo would've loaned her something—a pair of slippers even—but everything she had was too small.

So when Sheila called later that night Leo was all ready to tell her she'd found the shoe, but Sheila never gave her a chance.

"George, the fool," she said, "brought Eddie home for supper. We barbecued burgers in the back, and now they're out there drinking beer and smoking cigars. Leo, you have to get him out of here. I'm terrified he's going to say something."

"What's he gonna say?"

"I don't know. He just makes me nervous. Can you come over? Get a cab? I'll pay for it."

"How's George?"

"What d'you mean?"

"Is he acting funny?"

"No. He seems fine. Wherever they went Eddie must've done most of the drinking. I think he wishes Eddie would leave as much as I do but he doesn't know how to do it. He keeps saying he'll drive him home but Eddie's not taking the hint."

Leo wasn't sure how she was going to make Eddie leave with her. But she called a cab anyway, and twenty minutes later she was sitting on the couch with Laurie and Samantha watching *Snow White*. Before she arrived George and Eddie had moved into the basement to play a game of cribbage. Sheila was making popcorn.

They had central air and as she stepped into the house the coolness filled her with relief. No wonder Eddie didn't want to leave.

"This is my favourite," Laurie said, meaning the movie. "Daddy bought it for me for my birthday."

Samantha picked up a magazine. "We've seen it like a zillion times."

"Don't be rude, Samantha," Sheila said. She spoke over the waist-high divider separating the kitchen and the living room.

"I'm not being rude, Mother. I'm being realistic." She put down the magazine. "D'you wanna see my room, Leo?"

"Samantha, I'm not going to tell you again." The popcorn was popping in the microwave behind her. "You said you wanted to watch the movie and that's what we're going to do. You can show Leo your room after. When we have an intermission. Okay?"

Samantha came over and sat down beside Leo. "Is he really your boyfriend?" she said quietly.

"Eddie?"

"Yeah." She crinkled her nose. "'Cause I think you could find a better one."

George came up from the basement. He stepped up to Sheila, who was still in the kitchen, and put his arm around her waist. Leo watched the way she settled against him and felt a moment of confusion. This was not what she had expected.

She heard Sheila say "Leo's here" and watched his face as he turned in the direction Sheila was looking. He nodded, but his expression gave nothing away.

"How's Eddie doing?" Leo said.

And then he smiled. It was a complicated smile full of warmth and regret and a kind of acceptance of things she had not expected. And she would've smiled back if she had not felt so unsettled.

"He won the first game," George said, "but then I'm not a very good cribbage player."

"I'll take him home." She had stepped into the kitchen. "I'm really sorry about this."

He shrugged. "I enjoy his enthusiasm."

"I'm glad somebody does."

"What about the movie?" Laurie said. "You're gonna miss it, Leo."

"Maybe we can watch it together another time. You can invite me. But right now I have to go and see Eddie."

"He's a stinko," she said without taking her eyes off the TV. She giggled. "A stinko."

Leo started for the basement stairs. As she stepped away from it, she felt the simple ease of the family behind her. George's appearance only seemed to bring them closer. She hadn't expected that either.

Eddie was sitting at a table surrounded by a cloud of smoke. He had in front of him an ashtray, a deck of cards, and a cribbage board. In one hand he had a bottle of beer and in the other a cigar the size of a small tree. He raised it to her and said, "Hey, Leo. Where you been? Tried to get hold of you earlier. Mr. Stookner invited me to this barbecue thing, eh. I thought you might've wanted to like join us."

"Come on, Eddie. Let's go. I think you've worn out your welcome."

"Me? Me?"

"How many beers you have?"

"A few."

"A few too many."

"I was invited."

"They've got kids in the house."

"So?"

She sat down across from him. "This isn't the way to treat people, Eddie."

"I'm a guest, Leo. I didn't crash the place." He looked pale even for Eddie, who looked pale all the time.

"Where'd you get that?"

"This?" He lifted the cigar off the table. "Mr. Stookner. You know how he smokes those little ones sometimes? Well, he brings out this box, says they're for special. This is what was inside. Fuckin' monsters, aren't they? But, hey, you don't refuse a man's hospitality."

"But you don't smoke, Eddie."

"I do now." He grinned, and then his eyes clouded over.

"Come on, let's go outside. I think you need some fresh air."

"I'm fine."

"I don't think so."

"My head maybe, a little. You got an aspirin?"

"Yeah." She opened her purse. She had almost forgotten she'd brought the shoe with her. She thought she might have a chance to give it back to Sheila tonight. She pushed it aside and felt for the little box of aspirin she always carried around.

"What's that?" Eddie said. "Looks like a shoe."

"It is."

"What are you doing carrying around a shoe for?"

"I dunno."

"You got a shoe in your purse and you don't know why?"

"I was gonna take it in to get fixed."

"Let's see."

"What d'you wanna see it for?"

"Give it here. I know a guy who fixes shoes."

"No you don't."

"Sure I do."

She gave him the shoe.

"Looks okay to me."

"It pinches."

"Since when d'you wear shoes like this? Put it on. Where does it pinch?"

She grabbed the shoe and put it back in her purse. "Across the toes."

He tried to look shrewd for a moment and then the cloudiness came back into his eyes. "I gotta take a piss," he said.

"Don't you want the aspirin?"

"Later."

He went for the toilet in the basement. Halfway there he started to run. He got the door closed, and she heard a gagging sound followed by a big whoosh, then another whoosh, and Eddie said, "Oh man, oh man. Oh shit."

He stayed in there a long time, probably sitting on the edge of the bathtub wondering if he was going to be sick again—or maybe curled up on the floor.

While he was in the bathroom Laurie and Samantha came down the stairs with soft drinks and a bowl of popcorn.

"I thought you guys were watching the movie," Leo said.

"Intermission." Laurie held out the bowl. "Did Eddie leave?"

"He's in the bathroom."

"D'you want a 7-Up?" Samantha said.

"Not for me, thanks. As soon as Eddie gets out of the can we gotta go."

Samantha opened a soft drink. "What's he doing in there?"

"He doesn't feel so good."

"Stinky cigars." Laurie held her nose and pulled her face

back and forth. She laughed. Then she stopped and said, "Daddy took us on the train last year. Didn't he, Samantha?"

"Yes. And Mum too."

"But it was Daddy's idea."

"I didn't want to go." Samantha sipped on her drink.

"What train was that?"

"It was an old steam train, like the kind they used to have a long time ago?"

"The Prairie Dog Central," Samantha said.

"Did you have fun?"

"It was hot," Laurie said, "but Mummy had a Thermos of cold lemonade. And sandwiches. I helped her make them."

"So did I."

"We both did."

"Dad took us up to look at the engine."

"It was humungous."

"He told us how it worked and everything. It was pretty neat. He asked the engineer how fast it went and all kinds of stuff like that."

"It was scary."

"There was like steam coming out all over the place."

"A teakettle."

"Yeah."

"Boom," Laurie said.

"No. Don't you remember, Laurie? Dad said there was a valve that would open if the pressure got too high."

"Where?"

"In the boiler."

"Boom," Laurie said again and grinned.

"The steam."

"Hisssss."

"Dad said we could go again if we wanted. Or maybe take the train to Vancouver. Go through the Rockies. Have you ever been through the Rockies, Leo?"

"No."

"Mum said she thought that was a pretty good idea. Dad even got a timetable from the station."

"But not on the steam train," Laurie said. "It doesn't go to Vancouver."

"Dad said we could have our own room if we wanted. And we'd eat in the dining car."

"And see the mountains."

The bathroom door opened. Eddie looked white. "I'm gonna," he said, staggering towards the stairs, "go outside, for a little while."

All three of them watched him make his slow, painful way up the stairs.

"But we didn't go," Samantha said.

"To Vancouver," Laurie said.

"Not yet anyways."

"They say the mountains are beautiful," Leo said.

Laurie whispered, "Bee-yoo-ti-full."

"You'll get to see them," Leo said, "but right now I better go see how Eddie is."

He wasn't good, but at least she didn't have to watch him fall down, because he had already passed out on the grass by the time she stepped outside.

She sat down several feet away from him, in case he spewed again. No telling what kind of range he had, or if he might not lurch to his feet and dump a pre-digested meal on her head.

The screen door was closed but not the inside door and a few minutes later Laurie and then Samantha walked by on their way up into the kitchen—to get more popcorn, another can of pop, and to settle in to watch the rest of the movie. Samantha stopped on the way and stuck her head out. "Everything okay?"

"I think so. I'm just waiting on Eddie here."

"D'you want me to get my mum or dad?"

Leo shook her head. "It's okay." She still had Sheila's shoe but didn't see any way of giving it back tonight. "We're gonna go soon."

"All right."

Eddie coughed.

"If you change your mind . . . "

"Thanks."

Eddie coughed again. Then he groaned and rolled over onto his back. She glanced at the door. Samantha was gone.

She pulled her knees up to her chest and thought about Sheila and George and Laurie and Samantha all sitting together in the living room and eating popcorn, sipping on cans of pop, and watching the movie George had given Laurie for her birthday. They all seemed so far away, Sheila seemed so far away.

But that was the way it was, wasn't it? Her problem was to get Eddie home. That's what she was doing here. That's why Sheila had called her. To do a job. To clean up a mess.

At that moment someone, she had no idea who, closed the back door. A second later the porch light went out and she was sitting in the dark. Forgotten.

She looked up at the kitchen window. The blinds were drawn. A blank sheet of glass with a light behind it. "You know, Eddie, I think I liked it better when they were fighting."

He groaned and flopped his arms like a dead man's. Then his eyes opened and he tried to sit up. "Oh man," he said, and, putting his hand to his forehead, fell back down onto the grass again. "I feel like shit."

"Time to go, Eddie."

"Help me up, will ya?"

She helped him up.

"You got any money?" he said.

"Why?"

"I gotta get home." He pulled out his wallet and gave it to her. "Take a look."

She looked. "What am I s'pose to be finding here?"

"Have I got any money?"

"A little. Why?"

"For a cab."

"No cab's gonna pick you up, mister."

"You gotta help me, Leo."

"Where's your car?"

"Fucked if I know."

"How'd you get here?"

"Came with Mr. Stookner."

"What am I s'pose to do?"

"Leo, you gotta help me. I've never felt so fucking lousy in my whole life."

"Okay, okay. We'll walk out to St. Mary's Road and see if we can flag a taxi down. Otherwise we're gonna have to take the bus."

"I don't ride no buses, Leo."

"You got any other ideas?"

"You gotta help me, Leo."

"I'm trying, Eddie. I'm trying."

They got about a block. She didn't have to carry him, just sort of keep him going in the right direction. He heaved once, but all that came up was a little bile. It hung from his lower lip, it seemed like forever in a long string that reached past his knees before it finally broke off.

He was bent over while this was going on and she was holding onto the back of his shirt to help him keep his balance.

He must've seen her out the corner of his eye. "Somebody's coming," he said.

"What?" She turned her head. It was Sheila. Leo was surprised at how angry she felt. She wanted to walk away. If it hadn't been for Eddie she would have.

"Leo." Sheila waved at them. "Leo." She was out of breath when she caught up. "I'm so sorry. I didn't know you'd gone. I thought you were still downstairs."

"Eddie thought the fresh air might make him feel better."

"Are you taking him home?"

"Trying to."

"Wait here. I'll get my car. I'll drive you."

"We were gonna get a taxi."

"Don't be silly."

"He might be sick again."

"I'll get a pail. You can sit with him in the back."

Thanks, Leo said to herself, thanks a lot.

But he didn't even retch, although she made sure he kept

his head over the bucket the whole way. When they got to his place she and Sheila laid him down in a chair, put a pot in his hands, and left a glass of water on the coffee table where he could reach it. He looked as though he had recently lost ten million dollars on the Vancouver Stock Exchange, money he didn't have, money he owed to ten million guys with baseball bats, ten million guys who were on their way to his place right now.

"You'll live." Leo pinched his cheek. "Won'cha, Eddie?"

He tried to turn his face away.

"Won'cha?"

He pawed at her hand. "Cut it out, Leo." His voice sounded like dry wood rubbing on dry wood.

"There's ten million guys out there with baseball bats, Eddie, and you owe them all money."

"Fuck off." He had no voice left. "Fuck off."

"If you need anything call me and I'll bring it over before I start work. Okay?" He nodded. "Are you going in to work tomorrow? D'you want me to call in sick for you?" He shook his head.

All the time they were taking Eddie home Leo hadn't looked at or talked to Sheila unless she had to. Now on their way out of the building Leo kept her distance. Sheila didn't seem to notice. She was miles away, she seemed relaxed, happy even. Leo should have been happy for her, but she wasn't.

Still, Leo didn't feel like walking home, not from Eddie's place, not after tonight. Sheila owed her a ride at least.

And then there was the shoe.

The city was drifting through a long prairie twilight. Pale shadows had begun to gather close to the ground while the sky was still strangely lit up with pinks and reds.

They were walking towards the car. "Why don't we go for a coffee?" Sheila asked. "We've got time."

"No thanks."

"No?"

Leo waited for Sheila to unlock the passenger door. "I'm kinda tired," she said, and tried to hide her face.

"Leo?" Sheila pushed the hair on Leo's forehead to one side. "You're crying."

"It's just a little hay fever." She should've turned away but Sheila's fingers felt too tender, too cool, too much like a caress. So, hugging herself, she simply stared at her with eyes that had probably already turned an ugly red. "It happens every summer."

Sheila laughed. "You don't have hay fever. Come on, get in the car."

She got in the car. It made her even angrier that Sheila thought this was so funny, that it was somehow cute. "You think you're so goddam smart," Leo said. "You know? You think you're just so goddam smart." She put her elbow on her knee and jammed her fist into her mouth.

Sheila seemed startled. "Leo, what's gotten into you?"

She couldn't keep her knee steady. She pushed her hand into her hair. "Is this how it ends?"

Sheila swung around all loose like a puppet with its strings cut. "What?"

"Is this how it ends?"

"What are you talking about? Leo?"

"I must seem like shit to you. Oh, she's just a piece of trash, she doesn't matter. Did you ever fuck one of your friends, Sheila? Did you ever fuck anybody who's read as many books as you or lives in a house as big as yours or drives a car that's newer than yours? Did you?"

"Leo? Leo, don't." Sheila's hand drifted from her mouth slowly out to Leo and then back to her mouth again.

"Does it turn you on that I'm this dumb straight chick who works in a doughnut shop?"

"Leo, please. Stop it."

"And now you're going to go home to a house and a family and all is forgiven, and I'm going to be left out here. In the dark. By myself."

Sheila tried to put her arms around her.

"Get away from me," Leo screamed at her. She smacked her hands and arms, turned away from her, and pressed herself up against the side of the car door.

"It's not true, Leo, it's not like that." Sheila's face was only inches away, hovering. Leo could feel her breath on her neck. "It's not true." The touch of her hand. The side of her face pressed into the broad part of Leo's back, as slowly Sheila slipped her arms around her.

Leo turned. For a moment all she could see was the top of Sheila's head. But when Sheila finally looked up, they stared at each other.

The kiss that followed was not an easy kiss. It was a kiss filled with longing and pain.

Later, after they had pulled away from the curb, Leo said, "I found your shoe."

"Where was it?"

They were crossing Portage Avenue on the way to Leo's apartment.

"I brought it with me." Leo pulled it out of her purse. "It was behind the TV."

"How'd it get there?"

"You throw your stuff around."

"Do I?"

"Yes. Anyways, here it is." She put the shoe on the seat next to Sheila's purse. And with it she put everything that kept them together and everything that kept them apart.

Leo suddenly knew what she was standing outside of. She had never seen it before, until tonight. A circle of warmth. It was so domestic. Her heart ached for it, yearned for it. And as she stepped into her apartment, alone, she knew that she would always be on the outside of it. It didn't belong to her. To others maybe, to those who sacrificed and made the right choices, but not to her.

On the Labour Day weekend, Eddie picked her up at her apartment Friday after work. Leo had switched her Saturday shift so she wouldn't have to be back at work until Tuesday. She tossed her things into the back of his car, except for the

Safeway bag which she put down carefully on the floor behind her seat.

"What's that?" he said.

"A pack of smokies and some eggs."

"You didn't say we had to bring our own food."

"It's only polite, Eddie."

"'Cause I wouldn't last more'n a couple hours on one pack of smokies."

"Eddie?"

"Huh."

"Try to behave."

"What I can't figure out is why we all have to meet at their house. I can find my way."

"They want us to. Okay? It's not such a big deal. They want us all to start off together."

"We're going to the lake for crying out loud, not setting off across the Sahara Desert."

"Eddie, will you quit it?"

"Okay, okay." He put the car in gear. "I bet their cottage is bigger than my fucking apartment."

"I'm sure it is."

"There's money there, Leo, and don't let anybody tell you different."

"We're going to go and enjoy ourselves, Eddie. Okay? Have a nice time. Okay?"

"Whatever you say, Leo. Whatever you say."

TWO

"I'm not going back." Sheila was standing in Leo's apartment. "Not tonight, not tomorrow. Not ever."

Leo stepped around her, dropped her purse on the couch, and peeled off her jean jacket. "What d'you want me to say?" She glanced around, looking for a suitcase or an overnight bag. She wanted to believe her. But there wasn't even a carryall.

She tossed the jacket on the couch. "Look, you can stay the night. Okay? And we'll talk in the morning."

"I'm not going back, Leo. I told you."

"Don't. Okay? Just don't. You're all fucked up inside, Sheila. I know. I've seen it. Maybe this is a tough time for you, but it's a tough time for me too. Okay? So don't come over here and talk like this when both of us know goddam well you don't mean it."

"Is that what you think?"

"Yes."

"Okay."

"Okay what?"

"We'll talk in the morning."

"It's all bullshit, Sheila."

"I don't blame you for being like this."

"It's all bullshit, and you know it is."

"I'm here, aren't I?"

"I just don't believe you."

"Will you believe this?" Sheila got her purse. "Here're my

car keys." She put them in Leo's hand. "All my keys, they're all there. Keep them. Hide them if you want."

Leo stared at the ring of keys. She was thinking about Laurie and Samantha. She was even thinking about George. "And tomorrow?"

"We might have to go away for a few days."

Five minutes earlier Leo had been standing outside her apartment door listening to the phone ring. Normally she would've hurried to answer it before the ringing stopped. This time she waited, this time she hoped the ringing would stop.

She thought it might be Sheila. She had spent the whole day dreading the moment when she would walk into the 'Nut and order coffees to go, acting as if nothing had happened. It drove her crazy—Sheila's habit of smoothing everything over with a bland kind of whatever-do-you-mean look.

But she hadn't shown up, and Leo had left work feeling restless. She thought she didn't want to see her. She had spent the whole Labour Day Monday locked in her apartment thinking that, and then the whole day at work. But now, listening to the telephone ringing on the other side of the door, she wasn't so sure.

Going to the lake had broken something inside her. Perhaps it was hope, or the ability to believe that she meant something to Sheila that was, at least, worth suffering some embarrassment over. Sheila never seemed to consider that Leo might feel any awkwardness about their relationship.

She began to hurry with the key. Maybe, if she could talk to Sheila, listen to what, if anything, she had to say . . .

She pushed the door open and flung herself towards the phone.

But it wasn't Sheila calling, and she knew it wasn't Sheila even before she picked up the phone, because Sheila was staring at her from less than three feet away. She had let herself in.

"Answer it," Sheila said. She spoke slowly, solemnly.

200

"What do I say?"

"Answer it."

It rang two more times before she picked it up. "Hello?" Leo listened.

"Who is it?"

Leo shook her head.

"Is it George?"

She nodded.

They talked for less than a minute.

"Yes," Leo said. "I will. Of course. Bye."

Sheila leaned forward. "What did he say?"

"He doesn't know you're here."

"But what did he say?"

"That you weren't at home and you hadn't been at the bookstore, and did I know where you were, had I seen you?"

Leo was still looking at Sheila's keys. She picked through them, glancing at the ones with the different coloured liners along the grip. "Why d'you think we might have to go away?" Maybe Sheila had brought some kind of suitcase after all, and Leo simply hadn't seen it.

"Don't you think it's a good idea?"

She shrugged. "I guess."

"I've been on the phone to Lisa and Kenny at the store. I've told them I won't be around for a little while, and I've arranged for part-time people to fill in for me."

"Didn't they ask what was going on?"

"No," she said, leaving no room for any more questions about that. "Are you hungry?"

Leo put Sheila's keys down on the television. Was this for real? Leo watched her, trying to figure her out.

"I hope so." Sheila walked to the counter between the sink and the stove. "Because I started a salad already." She stood up half a tomato and finished slicing it on the breadboard. The other half lay in circles beside it.

Leo hadn't noticed the food. "Where'd you get all this stuff?" She picked up a piece of cheese and popped it into her mouth.

"The store."

"Ask a stupid question." It was the kind of salad Sheila had always said she would make if she ever had the time to make it and they had the time to eat it: full of nuts, thinly sliced cucumber, green and red peppers, cheese, green onions, radishes, kiwi fruit, tiny shrimp, and tomatoes all mixed up with a dressing that Sheila made from oil and vinegar and spices. Leo said, "This is fabulous."

"There's wine in the fridge. Would you like to open it?"

A part of Leo—sullen, suspicious—still wanted to be angry, but it was fading. Sheila was in her apartment, she had handed over her keys so she couldn't go anywhere, it was after five o'clock, and she was making them something to eat.

And now wine.

A kind of happiness, not quite sure of itself, began to rise like a thin mist from the floor.

Leo opened the bottle, poured them each a glass, and then put up the TV tables. She set out plates and forks and a paper towel each. She didn't have serviettes. She did all this slowly and carefully because she had become suddenly self-conscious and if she tried to work too fast her hands became tangled.

It felt strange not having to rush, not having to count the minutes before Sheila would have to dash out the door.

"Can I help?" Leo said.

"It's almost done."

"What about the dressing?"

"It's ready." She pointed to a bowl.

It also felt strange thinking that Sheila would be here in the morning, that they would wake up together. That thought alone took away her sense of emptiness that often came with the night. It was nice to think that she would not be by herself. When she used to be with Eddie she sometimes felt that, after they were done, there was nothing much else to stay for.

They were sitting side by side on Leo's couch and eating from their TV tables.

The phone rang.

Leo went on eating.

Sheila said, "Aren't you going to answer it?"

"No."

"No?"

Sheila had large feet, not delicate or pretty feet. Without slippers, even through her stockings, you could see the calluses on the sides of her big toe and the way her little toe on the left foot bent inwards and almost sideways under the toe beside it. Leo was wearing white socks. She put her foot against Sheila's and then slowly slipped her toes over Sheila's toes.

Sheila laughed.

The phone rang half a dozen more times and then stopped.

"My stuff's in the car."

"What stuff?" Leo was sitting on the floor with her back against the bed. So that's why she hadn't seen any kind of case. It was in Sheila's car. She got up on her knees and moved towards Sheila, who was sitting in the armchair. Leo shared out the last of the wine between them.

"My toothbrush, deodorant, a change of clothes."

"Oh, that stuff," she said as if the thought had never crossed her mind.

The last thing Leo saw as she turned out the light was Sheila's keys sitting on top of the TV.

She stood for a moment in the dark. The room was full of the smell of food and the smell of Sheila's delicate perfume.

There was no turning back, Leo realized suddenly, and just as suddenly realized that she did not want to turn back, would have refused the opportunity to turn back even if it had been offered to her.

She stepped away from the wall and started across the floor, thinking how you take one journey with you into another journey into another, forever and ever.

Leo woke up from a dream about a column of bears marching like soldiers through the forest.

She glanced at the clock. 8:03. She was alone, but the space beside her was warm. She listened. The people next door were moving around. She could hear cupboard doors open and close and the tap go on and off.

She looked down. Beyond her feet the sheets hung off the bed like a layer of skin.

Then she heard it, out of all the traffic noise and next door's moving around and somebody's radio across the hall, the sound of the bathroom fan in her own apartment. Then the shower came on, and she let herself sink back into the bed for a minute before she got up and plugged in the kettle. While waiting for the water to boil, she got out the bread so she would be ready to put it in the toaster. She had some jam in the fridge.

They had never had breakfast together. She put on a long tee-shirt that came down to her thighs and got ready to not exactly cook for her—although she had some eggs if Sheila wanted—but to make her something to eat.

She kept the blinds drawn, but behind them the morning light was full in the window.

The water boiled. She made tea. Then she sat down to wait.

When the bathroom door opened, Leo felt her stomach drop. What if Sheila wouldn't look at her or what if her eyes were cloaked or cloudy? How could she offer her toast and tea for breakfast and say that she had eggs too if she wanted, and orange juice, if that wasn't what Sheila was thinking about, as if toast and tea and all the rest were completely beside the point?

Sheila was towelling her hair as she stepped into the room. She was wearing Leo's dressing gown. It was a ratty old thing that she had gotten from her mother's. She hardly ever wore it. Normally it hung on a hook on the back of the bathroom door. There was a moment, a heartbeat, when everything stopped. Then Sheila smiled, and said "Good morning," in a thick, morning-after voice Leo had never heard before.

And suddenly she felt terribly shy. "Good morning."

Sheila came over and gave her a little kiss. The intimacy was almost too much for Leo. It was as if she were so full of sugar that she could feel it turning to crystals in her arms and legs. "I made tea." She had to move against the syrup in her veins. "I have toast. D'you want eggs?"

It wasn't until Sheila gave her a hug and squeezed out some of that sugar, made her share it, that Leo felt she'd be able to butter the toast without sending it flying off the breadboard.

Sheila's plan was pretty simple. "I thought maybe we could go to the cottage," she said. "We'd have the whole place to ourselves. I don't even think the neighbours'll be down."

They were at the kitchen counter eating their toast, standing up and holding their plates under their chins.

The idea of getting out on the highway seemed good to Leo.

But it was all pretty vague. Still, you heard about people running away together all the time. Besides, they weren't exactly running away. They were going to the lake to figure out what to do. Weren't they?

Before they left Leo phoned in sick. She hated lying. She hated it even more when Betty told her to take care of herself and not worry about anything.

They pulled up at the cottage well before noon.

You could stay here for a long time, Leo thought as they unloaded the car. There was food in the cupboard and in the fridge, and there were books and the radio. There was even a propane heater.

Around lunchtime Sheila pulled bread, margarine, and half a lettuce out of the fridge. She took a tin down from the cupboard. "How's tuna sandwiches sound?"

"Great."

Sheila opened the fridge again. "I know there's mayonnaise in here somewhere. Here it is." She closed the door with her foot and said she would make the sandwiches if Leo would go next door to see if the Ackers were there. "I think they should still be away. I can't remember. They went somewhere," she said, "Europe or something, South America maybe. But if they are there I think we should know."

"And what if they are?"

"They haven't seen you before. Tell them you're looking for the marina and got lost."

"The marina?"

"Ask for directions."

When she returned Sheila was waiting for her on the deck with their sandwiches. "It's all locked up tight," Leo said. "They've even got the shutters on."

"Good." They went down the steps and sat at the picnic table. "Help yourself." Sheila pointed at the plate of sandwiches. Leo took a half and bit into it.

But Sheila hardly touched hers. Her gaze drifted out to the lake and stayed there as if she were watching for something. She finally came back to herself and said, "I'm going to make some tea."

Leo caught her hand as she went by. On the surface it was a question that might have appeared to come out of the blue. "Are you okay?" she asked.

But it wasn't on the surface that they were talking to each other, and Sheila seemed to know exactly what she meant. "I'm just a little tired." She gazed down at Leo for a moment, then slipped her hand out of Leo's and started back towards the cottage.

It was after she had been gone for a few minutes that Leo thought maybe she should have stayed with Sheila, helped her make the tea, kept her talking. Even in the car on the way down Leo had felt her drifting away, as if a part of Sheila were trying to hide from something.

Sheila seemed to be aware of it herself. In the car she had taken Leo's hand. It was awkward with the bucket seats but Leo had ducked her head under Sheila's arm, and for miles they drove with Leo's head pressed against her side. It was as if they were lashed together then, as if that were the only way they could stay afloat. The day had been bright enough and sunny enough, but Leo felt that if she looked quickly to the horizon she would see a great darkness boiling up from the edge of the world.

Later, while they had been unpacking the car, Sheila had seemed to suddenly emerge bright and cheerful. She smiled, talked about how much she liked it out here, how peaceful it was, and she bothered Leo with passing caresses and more than once laughed out loud at something Leo said. But these were like islands, too small and too far apart to tell what, if anything, joined them all together.

For Leo, however, nothing about what they were doing seemed submerged. Just the opposite. Behind her eyes there were pictures—imaginings—as if from a dream she had woken out of and then forgotten, until now—a dream of lush forests full of green hills and overflowing rivers, all of which seemed to have broken out of the basement of an old house, leaving stairways, rooms, and hallways scattered among the trees, connected, but not as they used to be. And in this dream she was standing at the edge of a grassy cliff. She never meant to jump. Being in the forest was enough. But she leaned over to look and found herself falling towards a river. She thought she might die if the water was too shallow and drown if it was too deep. But it was neither, and as she waded towards the shore she could hear the boards creak under the weight of someone coming up the stairs.

She reached for her sandwich and was surprised to find that the bread had gone a little dry. It had been out in the air too long. It was still okay and she finished it, but it made her realize she had lost track of time.

Sheila had gone in to make tea. But how long ago? She picked up the plate with the rest of Sheila's sandwich on it and went inside to see what she was up to. She took the sandwich because she thought Sheila might want to finish it, but also because she was remembering Eugene's lecture the other day on how important it was not to leave food around because of the bears.

Sheila was in the bathroom. The door was closed. Leo paused long enough to see the band of light underneath the door and to catch the sound of the fan. She went on into the kitchen. Sheila had set out their cups and put the tea in the teapot, but she had not yet put the water on. The teapot was small and round, with a chip in the handle. Until Leo had come out to the lake on the long weekend, Sheila had been the only one to ever use it.

Wrapping Sheila's sandwich in wax paper, Leo put it in the fridge. Then she filled the kettle and set it on the stove. It had a whistle in the spout, and when it boiled she stood, arms folded, and let it sing for several seconds, hoping Sheila would hear it and know the tea was ready. But if she heard, she didn't come out, and Leo stood by the teapot letting the tea steep and tried not to worry.

She left the kitchen, figuring that she would give a little knock on the bathroom door. But halfway there she thought Sheila would think she was being silly, and walked up to the living-room window instead.

The trees shaded the cottage from the afternoon sun but it made the rooms a little gloomy. A few feet away, maybe ten or twenty at the most, the sunshine floated like a warm, yellow ball in the spoon of uneven ground leading down to the water.

She wished Sheila were somewhere she could see her.

She turned away from the window and looked towards the

bathroom. In the sudden change of light, the darkness bubbled for a moment.

It wasn't much but it was enough to make her walk quickly up to the bathroom door. The tea would be an excuse. She had her knuckles raised to knock. It was going to be a light knock and her throat was already tensing for a singsong "She-la. Tea's ready." But she never got the words out. Because before she spoke, before she knocked, she listened, and what she heard made her step back.

She went into the kitchen and took her tea down to the dock. Sheila had been crying, with her hands over her face, it sounded like, muffled like that, sobbing.

"There you are." Twenty minutes later Sheila sat down beside her on the end of the dock, all loose and girl-like.

Leo looked at their reflections staring back up at them from the water.

"Thanks for making the tea," Sheila said. Her reflection smiled, then disappeared behind her cup.

The next day they went into Kenora to buy groceries.

They had slept late, or at least they had stayed in bed late, and when they finally got up they were lazy about heading out. So when they pulled into town they decided to have lunch first.

They ate and talked and had a glass of wine, and were happy in such a quiet and comfortable way that Leo was thinking maybe she had imagined hearing Sheila crying in the bathroom, or maybe it was just something that Sheila had to get over—because after she'd come down to the dock she seemed better.

Sheila paid for their groceries using a credit card. She had also paid for lunch with it. If Leo had asked her about it she knew Sheila would have said, "What choice do we have?" And she would have been right, but hanging around Eddie had given her a mistrust of things like credit cards. They could be traced.

So the sight of an OPP cruiser car in the parking lot of the grocery store made her pull back. Sheila either didn't see it or wasn't worried about it. She kept on walking towards the Rabbit and only stopped when she realized Leo had fallen behind. "Leo?" She smiled. "D'you want me to bring the car around?" Leo shook her head. She ran to catch up to Sheila, holding the bags she was carrying out in front of her so they wouldn't swing, and they walked back to the car together. As Leo climbed in, she glanced over at the OPP cruiser. The two policemen were walking towards a restaurant. Lunchtime. Leo closed the door.

It got her thinking, though, and she couldn't imagine that a similar thought had not crossed Sheila's mind. George must have figured out by now what had happened even if he had not figured out where they'd gone. She had been wrong about him, but how wrong she wasn't sure—just a little bit, or a whole lot? But sooner or later, he was going to check out the cottage or ask the OPP to do it for him. They had at best—what?—one more day, two?—before they'd have to go forward or go back. But either way, to what?

Yet despite these uncertainties, Leo was happy in a way she had never been happy before. There seemed for her and Sheila a way forward, if they could just steer through these first few days. They might have to make things up as they went along, but she thought they could do it. It never occurred to her that Laurie and Samantha wouldn't eventually come and live with them at least part-time. Here, miles away from anyone, it seemed simple enough. But then Leo's past hardly weighed upon her at all. There was very little in it that she wanted to look back on. For her, the weight of her life lay buried in the future.

But the present was okay too. Helping Sheila put the groceries away, doing these simple, around-the-house kinds of things, lifted her up on a gentle wave of longing that had no centre, nothing you could point to. It was like the beginning of a never-ending question that had no answer.

Leo didn't remember to call the 'Nut to tell them she was still sick until they were back at the cottage, and by then it was too late. The phone hadn't been fixed. It probably hadn't even been reported. She decided not to worry about it.

"I'm going for a swim," she said. "Coming?"

They were sitting outside on the grass between the cottage and the lake.

Sheila put down her book. "I didn't bring my suit."

"Neither did I." Leo got out of her clothes and walked down to the water. She went in up to her knees and then turned around. Sheila was picking her way across the uneven ground. "What if somebody comes?"

"Who's gonna come?"

There was a pause. Sheila was standing at the very edge of the lake now. They both knew the answer and they both chose to ignore it.

"They won't." Leo crouched and splashed water onto her arms and shoulders. "They won't," she said again, and then, cupping her hands, stood up and threw all the water she could hold at Sheila. As the ball of water broke in the air she laughed and turned and headed away from shore.

Behind her she heard the sound of water churning, and then a splash. A moment later Sheila glided past on her stomach. She gave a little kick, her legs dropped, and she stood up. The water was up to Leo's chest; it wasn't quite so high on Sheila.

Sheila had this really loopy look on her face. "What?" Leo said. She felt herself smiling. She cocked her head. "What?"

Sheila submerged, disappeared without a ripple. Leo tried to follow her shape under the water but lost her in the surface shine. Leo restlessly kept turning, trying to guess where Sheila would come up. She guessed wrong. Something touched her legs, and a moment later the water was pouring off her as she rose out of the lake on Sheila's shoulders. Leo clung to her head to keep from falling off.

"Ready?" Sheila shouted.

"For what?"

Sheila laughed. She was holding Leo's ankles. She started

wading towards the shore. Leo had no idea where they were going. But it wasn't far. As soon as the water dropped to Sheila's waist, she leaned back, pushed Leo's feet out, and dumped her.

Leo screamed.

A moment later she opened her eyes to see a water-obscured Sheila reaching down to haul her up. "You okay?" Sheila said, trying not to laugh. But she wasn't doing a very good job of it. She had that grin on her face, and it seemed even loopier than it was before.

"Your turn," Leo said.

"Oh?"

"Uh-huh." Leo found a grin to match Sheila's. "Uh-huh."

They messed around like this for almost half an hour, until exhausted they dragged themselves back to shore. They collapsed on the sand and lay there trying to catch their breath. "Oh man," Leo said after a while, and rolled onto her back. She draped her arm over her face to shade her eyes. She listened to Sheila's breathing as it returned to normal. A little later something moved in front of the sun, and she pulled her arm down to find Sheila leaning over her. "We should get into the shade," Sheila said, and began brushing the sand off Leo's stomach. She was close like she was when they made love. Her small breasts sloped towards Leo, the nipples pointing. Leo reached up to kiss her, to taste the water and the sun she could smell on her skin.

Leo woke up, blinking. She had been dreaming of the bears again, a column of them, marching like soldiers through the forest. Except now they seemed closer.

"The bears." She shook her head. What had bears to do with anything? She rolled over, hoping that by snuggling up to Sheila she could make the unsettled feeling from the dream go away. But Sheila wasn't there, and what had been a vague uneasiness turned into a rush of panic.

She sat up, peering into the darkness. The bedroom door was open. Through the doorway she could see a soft light coming from beyond the living room. She followed it into the kitchen and found Sheila sitting at the table.

She was dressed and her keys were in front of her.

"Y'going somewhere?" Leo had wrapped the comforter around her when she had climbed out of bed. It was chilly at night. She pulled it tighter and sat down in the chair across from Sheila.

"No." She pushed the keys into the middle of the table. "They're for you."

"Sheila, come back to bed."

"You go." She let her eyes drift away. "I won't be long."

"I don't understand. What's wrong? This afternoon ..."

"I don't know."

"Things'll look better in the morning."

"I'm no good at this, Leo. Any of it."

"Okay, so a lot has happened in the past couple of days. Things'll work out. We'll make them work out."

"It's too late, I've gone too far. For everybody, for you. My father ..." She stopped.

"Maybe you haven't gone far enough." Leo got up and filled the kettle.

"What are you doing?"

"I'm gonna sit up with you."

"No no."

"Yes."

"This isn't your problem."

"How can you say that? Why d'you make it like I'm not involved? I hate that. I'm involved. Okay?"

"You can still go back."

"I'm not going back. I love you for chrissakes, Sheila. What d'you think I'm doing here?"

Leo rinsed the teapot. "We're going to sit down and talk this out." Or wait it out, she thought to herself. She was convinced if they could make it through to the morning everything would be okay. She stared out the little window over the sink while she waited for the kettle to boil. Sheila had started to say something about her father. She had never met Sheila's parents. For Leo they hardly existed. But it got her thinking of her own father, and their Sunday morning drives together. The memory, long forgotten, burst in upon her—the way she would get up early, dress, and be ready to go before either her mother or father even climbed out of bed, the sense of adventure that had gripped her as the three of them sat around the breakfast table—she already having had her bowl of Froot Loops and having washed her dish and spoon—while she tried to wait patiently for her father to finish his coffee and cigarette. Then he would smile at her and say, "Why don't the two of us mosey on out of here for a while," as if the thought had just entered his head, as if they didn't go for a drive every Sunday morning.

They almost always went to a part of the city he had never taken her to before. And week by week, piece by piece, the city began to take shape for her. One particular morning they reached the top of a bridge. There were dozens of railroad tracks underneath but it wasn't her dad's railroad. He worked for the other guys and she knew that, and was quietly proud that she knew it, and that her dad worked for a big, important company that spanned the country from coast to coast. But that was not what he wanted her to see. On that particular morning as they reached the top of the bridge, he pointed straight ahead and said, "Look, sweetheart." She squirmed in her seat and lifted her head. And there it was, green for as far as she could see. She was looking at the tops of the trees spreading north around Salter Street. From down there, she never would've guessed it could possibly look like this, and it filled her with wonder.

But at that moment when they started down the other side of the bridge and the forest turned back into individual trees, at that moment when she felt so much love for her father, it crossed her mind that one day this would end, and in her happiness she sensed a new kind of sadness she had never felt before.

She was eight years old, and her memory may have been tinted with the knowledge of a future which on that day she knew nothing about. She had no way of knowing, for instance, that that was their last Sunday together, she had no way of knowing that a few days later her father would fall under the wheels of a freight car he was switching, and that ten days after that he would be dead.

She remembered going to the hospital every day with her mother and watching him fade away. Sometimes he would be asleep and they would simply sit by his side, sometimes he was awake, but that was almost worse than when he was asleep because there would be pain and fear in his eyes, and for a long time even after he died, she thought the man in the hospital wasn't her father—he didn't even look like her father—and that the man who had shown her the forest in the city from the top of a bridge would come walking through the front door and pick her up in his arms like he used to do when she was really little and when her mother smiled all the time and her breath was sweet and her skin smelled of perfumes and lotions.

Leo set the tea on the table and then sat down across from Sheila. She leaned forward to take a sip. Sheila looked up and their eyes met across the rim of Leo's cup but neither of them said anything.

Leo sat back, holding the cup in her hands, and let the warmth soak into her fingers. The temptation to snuggle down was almost too great. She forced herself to sit up. "If I fall asleep," she said, "wake me."

Sheila just looked at her.

They sat like this, grim, their lanterns pegged, drifting towards morning.

Leo didn't hear the telephone ringing until Sheila leaned across the table and nudged her. "Leo," she whispered, "telephone."

"What?"

"Answer it."

She thought of asking who had fixed it and when, but the question seemed beside the point. The phone was ringing. "Yeah, sure," she said. The telephone was in the living room. She couldn't find the light switch, but the phone was over there on the wall. Even in the dark she could make it out. It was the old-fashioned kind with the handle you have to crank and the earpiece that hangs on a hook. She didn't remember them having a phone like that, but then maybe whoever had fixed it didn't have a proper one in the truck. She turned around to ask Sheila what she should say but Sheila was rinsing out their cups in the sink and had her back to her. Wing it, Leo thought, and turned around to find her mother holding out the earpiece to her. At this point Leo wasn't sure if the phone was ringing or not. "It's for you," her mother said.

"Ma? What are you doing here?" She wondered if Eddie had pulled a dirty deal on Mike, screwed him around with the car maybe, and now he and her mother were down here looking for him. She thought of telling her that Eddie wasn't around, but her mother was still holding out the earpiece for her to take.

"It's for you," she said again. As Leo came up to the phone, her mother stepped in front of it and put her hand over the mouthpiece. She was her mother as she was now, her face pinched with worry, her eyes filled with bitterness and regret. "It's your father," she said.

The phone seemed a lot higher up the wall than it did from across the room. Leo pointed the mouthpiece down and stood on her tiptoes. "Hi, Dad." It didn't seem at all strange for her to be talking to him. "What's up?" At first all she heard was a faraway roar as if the phone line were connected to another telephone halfway around the world. She began to feel scared but she didn't know why. Her father would never hurt her. There was a voice in all the noise. She could hear it now. She recognized it. It was her dad all right, but she couldn't make out what he was saying. He kept fading in and out, kept getting lost in all the noise on the line. "I can't hear you, Dad."

Then he said, "The bears."

Her head came up. It was morning. She glanced at the wall clock. It was ten after six. She stood up. Sheila had washed their cups and left them upside down on the drying rack. "Sheila?"

She turned, then turned back again, and spotted the key ring on the table. There was something about it that seemed different but she could not put her finger on it. It was probably nothing. Anyway, it was there. Sheila hadn't driven off. She could see the black grip of the Volkswagen key with the VW logo on it.

"The bears," her father had said. She was still groggy from the dream, still half in and half out of it. A part of her wanted to go back, wanted to talk some more, but she had the feeling he had said all he was going to say. And all he had said was, "The bears."

She couldn't figure it out. But standing in the kitchen wasn't helping her find Sheila. Maybe she had finally gone to bed. Leo went to check but Sheila wasn't there. She hung onto the door frame trying to think. She checked the bathroom. Not there. She looked briefly around the living room, and there was no old-fashioned phone on the wall. She made sure.

She got dressed and went outside, down past the picnic table to the water, and then up to the cottage again and out the back door. The car was there, exactly where they had parked it yesterday.

She went inside. She didn't know what to think. She paced for a few minutes and then sat down at the kitchen table. Maybe Sheila had gone for a walk.

She pushed Sheila's keys around. She picked them up and let them dangle from the end of her little finger.

Then it hit her.

There was a key missing. It had a plastic orange edge fitted along the grip—so you could pick it out quickly. Sheila had shown it to her half jokingly when Eugene had talked to them about the bears. It was the key to the Ackers' cottage, and it was gone. But for how long? When had she taken it off the ring? And why?

A bolt, both hot and cold, shot through Leo's body, and she stood up, knocking over the chair. "Oh my God." She didn't even get out of the kitchen before she heard the gunshot.

It sprang out of the morning silence, a brief bark, then drifted over the lake for a moment, and was gone.

The bears. . . .

She stood frozen in the doorway. The birds soon started singing again, and if she had woken up at that moment she would not have guessed that anything was wrong. But everything was wrong. Sheila had taken the key to the cottage next door, where they kept a rifle and a box of shells ready in case there was a bear that couldn't be scared away.

She ran up to the fork in the dirt road as hard as she could and started down to the Ackers'. Their place was nestled among the trees and looked out over the lake as Sheila's did, and they too used the back door for coming and going.

She stopped dead about ten feet away from it.

The screen door had sprung shut, but she could see the inside door, and it was open.

Otherwise the place was locked up as tight as it was when she had checked it out the other day.

"Sheila," she screamed, and throwing herself forward, she clawed at the door handle, yanked it open, and stood stock still, shaking with fear and hope and disbelief as the screen door slammed shut behind her.

EDDIE

ONE

Fuck me if this isn't a kick in the head:

I meet this girl. Right? Sandy. In the bar. Strawberry blonde. Hubba hubba. Sitting a couple tables over. And then it turns out ... You're NOT gonna believe this.

But let us start at the beginning.

I was there to see this guy—to deal—on a car—but he doesn't show, and I'm thinking this is the way my luck's been lately—all bad. It's one more thing on top of everything else. Like, they're running me ragged at Abel's. We've had our first snow and everybody figures maybe they should get their car winterized. At the same time you get your first rash of fender-benders because half the guys out there forget the streets get slippery when it snows—what a surprise—and go sliding through intersections bouncing off cars and lampposts and whatever else they can find. So every body shop and every garage and every backyard mechanic we deal with, and lots we don't, get on the blower for their parts, and then phone back an hour later asking where's their stuff, and wondering out loud if'n they oughta not go to Big Bill's Auto Parts where they can get everything they want and more—and more, no less, whatever the fuck that is—and at half the price. You wanna go to Big Bill's? Then go to Big Bill's. Leave me alone.

So I'm sitting in the bar waiting for my no-show car deal guy after putting up with eight hours of that kind of crap, and I'm thinking to myself that this has not been a good day . . . when I look up and see this gorgeous girl and her friend sit down, like two tables away.

My dick rolls over. It's been a while. And I'm thinking, yeah, okay. Maybe my luck's changed, just like that.

I order another beer so's I've got something to do with my hands, and have something to leave behind if I want to show I'm pissed off.

I look at her—Sandy, although I don't know her name yet. I sip on my beer, look again. Refill my glass slowly. You don't want them to see you're nervous or anything. Trying too hard, you might as well not try at all. Anxious doesn't cut it, man. Slow is cool, slow is good. And a steady hand. You start shaking they're gonna think like you're a cokehead or you've got AIDS or something—a small dick, a no-boner. So pouring a slow steady beer is important.

I suck off the foam and look again. This time I catch them looking at me. I nod, but I keep my eye on Sandy. You want to be straight up in a situation like this. You don't want to send out the wrong message—raise false hopes.

And they do that weird chick thing. It's like they go into conference. Head to head. Whisper, whisper. Giggle. Oh my gawd. Their cheeks get red, their eyes sparkle.

Then they sit back—conference over. They've already figured out it's Sandy I'm interested in because her friend just looks around. Sandy waits to catch my eye, then looks around.

I'm about to move—okay?—when her friend leans over and says something and they both start giggling. What gives? I got boogers hanging out my nose or what? It's time to reflect. Caution is perhaps called for here. I've been slapped around enough times to know I'm no God's gift to women, boogers or no boogers, so before I go waltzing over there like some smiling Mr. Happy Face just to get torpedoed, I drop a quarter on the floor. I pick it up and quickly look behind me to see if maybe they're playing eyeball with some dude types behind me. But no, there's nobody there, just some empty tables and the wall.

Okay, I decide, I'm gonna give it a shot. I take my beer and saunter over, and they do that other weird chick thing, which is to look the other way.

They make me wait. It's a test. How cool are you really, mister? But I stand there and I wait, and I watch Sandy—the way she pretends I'm not there, the way she's working so hard to keep a straight face, to not look. Her friend glances up at me a couple of times but I don't move a muscle. I can see her out the corner of my eye—chewing gum—and I can feel her starting to get fidgety. Any other day I'd've been happy to hit on her little bod. But Sandy's special. You know? Sometimes you just get that feeling.

Finally, Sandy tilts her head back and her eyes roll up to check me out at close range. It's about now that I start to feel the tension. The rest of the night—and maybe a whole lot more—hangs on the next few seconds. If she decides she's made a mistake she'll turn cold and bitchy, say something like "Do I know you?" or "Can I help you?" Things like that in a go-away voice that I've heard enough times to do me for a lifetime, thank you very much. After one of those it's hard to get it up even for an in-your-face table dancer.

But she smiles and says "Hi," and runs her hand through her hair—like for something to do—because now it's my turn to decide if I'm gonna walk away or not. Of course I don't, of course I sit down.

We introduce ourselves.

Ten minutes later her friend says she's gotta go. Her friend, it seems, has the car, and she asks Sandy a couple of times if she'll be okay.

"Yeah," she says. "Sure. I'll be fine."

"You sure?"

"She's sure. Okay?" I guess I sound a little pissed off. What am I? Jack the fuckin' Ripper?

After she's gone Sandy says, "She's just looking out for me." Then she laughs.

"Tell her I'm sorry. Okay? The next time you see her. Tell her I didn't mean nothing." The band's coming on again. In a couple of secs the only talking we'll be able to do is by yelling into each other's ear. Some people don't mind sitting there doing nothing, and sometimes neither do I. But there's a momentum building here and I don't want to lose it. "You wanna get out of here? You wanna go somewhere?"

"What d'you have in mind?"

"D'you ever go huntin'?"

"No."

"D'you wanna?"

"I don't think so, Eddie."

"It's not what you think."

"What is it then?"

"Come on. I'll show you. You'll like it."

"Is it dangerous?"

"A little."

"How little's a little?"

"A little. You know."

She thinks for a minute. "Okay."

I snap out a crisp new ten-dollar bill and hand it to her. "I'll pick you up by the vendor. Grab a six. Whatever you like."

I get the car, and just as I pull up she walks out, her coat hanging open like she doesn't care and with the case of beer hanging from the ends of her fingers the same way—not tucked under her arm like she's afraid the bottom's gonna fall out.

I like this girl.

She puts the change in my jacket pocket, stuffs it down until she's sure it's all at the bottom, then stuffs it down one more time. Her face is real close. I say, "Crack us open a brew, will ya?" She's stashed the case on the floor behind my seat. She puts one hand on the steering wheel and, dipping her shoulder between the seats, pries the case open. All the time she's pressed up against me, and I'm wondering if maybe we shouldn't oughta go back to my place like right now. But I don't think so. Trust your instincts, and my instincts say not yet, don't rush, take your time, let her get to know you. In a couple hours—maybe. But not yet. Be cool. Besides, I want to

take her huntin' first. It always warms them up—not that I
think Sandy needs a lot of warming up—but there's nothing
like it to make a girl want to go really hard.

She comes up with a beer and falls back into her seat.
Tosses her hair. Her face is flushed. She's sort of bouncing. She
pulls her shirt out at the waist and uses it to pad the bottle cap
as she twists it off. She puts her lips around the mouth of the
bottle and takes a pull.

"Hey, where's mine?" I laugh. Not that I really care.

She gets up on her knees, leans over me, grabs a handful
of hair, and pulls my head back. She sewers up the mouth of
the bottle pretty good, then sticks it between my lips and tilts
it so the beer comes out just fast enough to keep me swallow-
ing but not fast enough so as I start choking. I suck down half
a bottle like this, thinking that beer never tasted so good.

She sits back down, holds up the bottle to see how much
is left, and takes a pull. "Share," she says.

And so we do. And another bottle once we get out of the
parking lot and onto the road, and then another.

I'm not so much surprised as amazed. Just when I'm
thinking the only luck I got is bad luck, I meet this broad who
is as crazy and as fucked up as me. In less than two hours I've
gone from being your regular girlfriendless kind of guy staring
with pleading, weepy eyes at anything that doesn't swing a
dick . . . to the guy I used to be when things were okay with Leo
and me, when I didn't have to worry about getting laid.

"You got a girlfriend, Eddie?"

"Broke up."

"Life's a bitch."

"You got a boyfriend?"

"Broke up."

"A girlfriend?"

"What's that s'pose to mean?"

"Just asking. I had some problems in that department
before."

"No shit." She looks at me.

"No shit."

"Too many fuckin' queers around if you ask me."

"Ain't that the truth."

"You hear about it happening all the time. Some gorgeous guy takes you out. You even do it with him a couple of times. And then he turns around and says he's gay. Well, fuck that noise. It's too fuckin' complicated. I can't figure it out."

"Ditto that. Amen."

"I'm old-fashioned. I'm sorry, it's the way I am. I like it straight ahead. Don't give me this bent shit. I mean, it's getting so you can't trust anybody anymore. Every time you turn around somebody's coming out of the closet—whatever that's s'pose to mean. Closets are where you hang your clothes. Aren't they? I always thought. I mean, give me a break."

I run a red, not by much but by enough. I could've stopped but why bother? There's a guy coming off the side street. He hits the binders, gives me the horn, the usual stuff. "Up yours," I shout, not that he can hear me, and give him the finger too but he probably doesn't see that either, too busy checking his shorts. Sandy sits there cool as a cucumber, looking at me with this little smile on her face.

She hands me the bottle and I finish it off. I get a little carried away and throw it over my shoulder. I don't angle it right and it takes a wild bounce off the roof of the car, hits the backrest up around my head, and pretty near takes out the back window before it falls to the floor. "Fuck," I say.

"Yeah," she says, and reaches into the back for another beer. "So who's your ex? Maybe I know her."

"I doubt it."

"What's her name?"

"I don't want to talk about it."

"She bummed you out pretty good, huh?"

"Something like that."

"She dump you?"

"It wasn't that simple."

"So you dumped her."

"I don't want to talk about it. Okay?"

"Relax. I'm just curious." She hands me the beer. I take a

pull. "You wanna know about my ex?" She turns in the seat getting ready to tell me. I guess I'm gonna hear about it. I'm not totally uninterested. There's a part of me that, yeah, wants to know. I give her back the beer. She downs a mouthful. "Dumped me for a slut. I mean a real slut. Goddam fuckin' schoolteacher. With a house and everything. Shit. Said he wanted to marry her."

"Did he?"

"I don't know. Bought her a ring. He showed it to me, the bastard. A diamond ring. Like for their engagement. I haven't seen him since. Don't want to neither."

"Sounds like a real jerk-off."

"Major league."

"He's got to be nuts. I mean, to let you go?"

"D'you think?"

"Without a doubt."

"But you don't hardly know me. I mean, not really. Not yet anyways."

"That's where you're wrong. I got a sense. I can tell about people. I'm a businessman. It's what I do, and I can tell about people right off. And I can tell about you. You're okay. Hell, more than just okay. You're a princess. Damn right."

"Don't bullshit me, Eddie."

"I wouldn't bullshit you. You're too smart for that."

"Yeah?"

"Absolutely."

She sucks back some more of the beer. She's starting to shine. "What's this huntin' thing you were talking about?"

I put both hands on the wheel and pretend to drive like an old man. "It's the best thing, ever."

"Yeah, but what is it? What d'you hunt?"

"Trust me?"

"Maybe. But I ain't never even been fishin'. What d'you hunt in the city? And where?"

"Are you gonna trust me or not?"

"Sure. Okay."

"You either do or you don't."

"I said okay, didn't I?" She takes a swallow and hands me

the bottle. I take a pull and give her it back. "I trust you," she says. She looks around for a sec. "Where'd we have to go?"

"Not far."

She laughs. "You must be crazier than I thought."

"I'm crazier than that."

She finishes the beer. "You want another?"

"No. Better keep a clear head. You're gonna need it."

She doesn't say anything for the next couple of blocks, and then there's this silence all of a sudden. It's like somebody turned off the music. She's been talking almost non-stop since we left the bar. I'm thinking maybe she's a little pissed at me for keeping her in the dark. I'm about to fill her in on the basics of huntin'. Maybe it's better she knows what we're gonna be up to. It might save some time later, and maybe our ass too. You never know. But before I even open my mouth, she turns to me and says, "So what happened—with your ex? You never said. Don't get mad. I just want to know. I mean, if we're gonna be . . . friends. I'd like to know. I think it's important. I told you about my old boyfriend. Can't you tell me about your girlfriend? Is she, like, with somebody else?"

"Yeah."

"Somebody you know?"

"Sort of."

"Not your best friend kind of thing, I hope." The way she bites down on this I'm thinking it's exactly what she hopes. Scandal, stabbed in the back, who can you trust.

"Remember what I said before?"

"About what?"

"Queers."

"Yeah."

"Well?"

"She's the lesbo? The one you broke up with?"

"You got it."

"And you fucked her?"

"I didn't know."

"That's sick. When you found out. I mean, cheepers."

"It gets worse."

"How?"

"They got married."

"You're shittin' me."

"In a church, no less. Found some faggot minister and bang they're married. Not that there were a lot of people there. Her husband."

"Her husband?"

"And their two kids and this guy, Eugene."

"You know 'em?"

"And one person from the bookstore."

"What bookstore?"

"She owns it."

"Your girlfriend owns a bookstore?"

"No, the other one. She moved in with 'em."

"Who?"

"My girlfriend."

"Your ex."

"Yeah."

"The lesbo."

"Yeah."

"Moved in with the woman from the bookstore and her husband?"

"And their two kids."

"Wow."

"Something happened."

"You're not kidding."

"That's not what I mean."

"What then?"

"Something happened. I don't know exactly. She didn't want to talk about it."

"Who?"

"My girlfriend."

"Your ex-girlfriend."

"Right."

"You still see her?"

"I run into her every once in a while. She works in the bookstore there. It's just around the corner from me."

"I thought she owned it."

"That's the other one."

"Well, whatever. What'd she say?"

"Nothing much. I'd heard rumours. People tell you stuff."

"What stuff?"

Right then I realize I don't want to tell her. It goes too deep. I feel the fear, I can taste it, like Sheila must've been tasting the barrel of the rifle before she pulled the trigger. Actually it was kind of nice seeing Leo again, even if it was only to stop for a minute to chat. If we'd've had longer I might never have asked her the question. When you got a whole evening ahead of you, you sometimes keep putting off what you really want to know because the question's a hard one and you think you'll ask it later, after the next beer maybe or after the next set of traffic lights, and before you know it the person's gone and you never did ask the question. She looked great, Leo did, and it's gonna sound dumb coming from me, but standing there with her on the street I felt happy for her. She had something, a little piece of it anyways, at least for a little while. Not everybody can say that. Not everybody gets it and knows they've got it. So I asked her quickly about Sheila, and so she'd know what I was talking about I said somebody'd told me the rifle didn't go off. Her eyes filled with tears, and I thought, oh shit, I didn't want this, but she sucked them right back and said, "It went off all right. Put a hole right through the roof of the Ackers' place." "So what happened?" Leo shrugged. "She changed her mind. At the last second. I guess she figured there was more to live for than to die for. I don't know. What do you think?" Then she did something she'd never done the whole time we'd been going around together. She reached up, put her arms around my neck, and gave me a hug. Just a hug. Just like that.

Sandy says, "What were people saying?"

"Huh?" It takes me a second to refocus. "Oh, the usual. You know. Bad stuff."

"Was it true?"

"No."

She seems disappointed. "When does this huntin' thing start anyways?"

"We're almost there."

Ten minutes later we're parked between two street lights and she's climbing in behind the wheel while I get the pellet gun out of the trunk. It's colder outside than it was even an hour ago.

While we were driving the last few blocks, I filled her in on what huntin' is, who does what, things to watch out for, warning signs. At first, as what I'm talking about starts to sink in, she gets a real glow on. But as we get closer to where I figure we should start, she doesn't seem quite so enthusiastic. I put it down to rookie nerves. Once we get started the old instincts'll take over—and I know she's got 'em, the instincts—and she'll be humming like a well-oiled hot machine.

"Down here," I tell her. It's the same lane where Leo and I almost got caught. It's where the bad luck started. Now I want to blow it away as much, if not more, than I want to blow away the car windows. We're gonna roll through this, like commandos, and get away clean. I want the good luck again. I want it back.

"Here?" she says. "Why here?" Her voice sounds funny. I can't figure if she sounds angry or just a little panicky, but I'm too busy getting ready for my first shot. I'm still putting the edge in her voice down to nerves.

Boy, was I in for a big surprise.

Let me tell you something. You meet a girl. Right? Wha'd'you do? You get a phone number. The next thing you do is find out where she lives. Did I make a mistake? Maybe. But there's a time and a place for everything. You need to use a little finesse. And I was gonna drive her home anyways. Right?

The thing I didn't know was that I already had.

"What are you doing?" she says. My window's down. The inside of the car is starting to lose its heat and I can see her breath.

I've already told her what we're gonna do. A little bell goes off in my head. It's called doubt. I think, uh oh. But I'm not sure why yet. We've been easing our way past garages and fences, and the first parking pad has just opened up in front of me. And there it is, a Pontiac Supreme nosed in towards a five-foot-high board fence. The back end is almost square to me. I sight the rear window and begin to track it. Sandy has us going at exactly the right speed. I can see the wires of the rear window defroster.

"This is a joke. Right?" she says. "You're not serious."

Part of me wants to laugh, part of me is starting to get pissed off, and another part is listening to this bell ringing in my head. But I'm concentrating too hard to worry about all that now. I'm just gonna have enough time to squeeze off the shot. Slowly I swivel the barrel, waiting for my aim to come dead centre. Almost there, almost there, al— Hey. "What the fuck are you doing?" I try not to sound as pissed off as I really am.

She's pulled the car hard to the left so all I've got is a clear shot down the length of the back lane. "You're the guy," she says. "You're the creepazoid."

"The what?" I start to feel real nervous, not a good kind of nervous either, but a bad kind. "Hey, Sandy, come on, what gives?"

"You little shit."

"Wha'd I do?"

"That's my dad's car."

"That?" I turn around and look at it. "It's a nice car. A real nice car." I nod and turn back to her. "Hey, you didn't think . . ." I lifted the rifle. "With this? Naaaaw. I was just . . . I . . ."

"Bullshit." She leans on the horn.

"Cut it out." I try to grab her arm. "You're gonna get every last Tonto and Kee-mo-sabby on the whole goddam block out here."

She takes the ignition key and scrambles out of the car. She leaves the lights on in case everybody can't see us clearly enough, and starts shouting for the whole neighbourhood to come out and see the guy who's been busting out their car windows.

Needless to say we attract a crowd. As the first few guys gather around, I'm hoping somebody called the cops.

But I don't think so, not this time.

Try explaining that to Autopac.

"You say fifty people surrounded you?" The adjustor looks puzzled.

"Yeah."

"They pulled you out of the car."

"I've been through this with the cops. You know?"

"They tied you to a telephone pole. Mr. Valentine?"

"What're you gonna give me for the car?"

"I'm afraid we've had to write it off."

"How much?"

Not very is the long and the short of it.

They gave me a hundred and fifty bucks. What can you do with a hundred and fifty bucks? Put a down payment on a steering wheel maybe. I mean, the tires're worth more than that.

Two months later I'm still taking the bus to work. Every so often I go with Manny and those guys to the bars, hoping I might spot Sandy. I know it's crazy, but I still got this thing for her. You know? Like she's gonna bring me good luck. The u-drive deal isn't dead. It would fly tomorrow if I could scare up some cash. I can see Sandy working at the counter, you know, leaning over to reveal just enough so the guy thinks maybe he oughta sign up for the extra insurance after all.

What more can I say?